Everybody Hurts
Sometimes

Everybody Hurts Sometimes

Ted Darling Crime Series

'heart-wrenching, compelling crime drama'

L M Krier

LIVRES
LEMAS

Published by LIVRES LEMAS
www.teddarlingcrimeseries.uk

Cover photo
Neil Smith

Contents

Author's Note

Thank you for reading the Ted Darling Crime Series. The books are set in Stockport, and Greater Manchester in general, and the characters use local dialect and sayings.

Seemingly incorrect grammar within quotes reflects common speech patterns. For example, 'I'll do it if I get chance', without an article, or determiner, is common parlance, as is 'should of' instead of 'should have'.

Ted and Trev also have an in joke between them - 'billirant' - which is a deliberate 'typo'.

If you have any queries about words or phrases used, do please feel free to get in touch, using the contact details in the book. I always try to reply promptly to any emails or Facebook messages.

Thank you.

L M Krier

To Neil

Thank you for all the fabulous photos

Chapter One

Something was seriously wrong. Detective Chief Inspector Ted Darling could feel it in every fibre of his being.

The big problem was that he had absolutely no idea what to do with the knowledge.

Ted was sitting in the back of an unmarked German police car, two officers in plain clothes in the front seats. He was meant to be being driven back to the airport at Frankfurt where he had a hotel room booked for the night, before his early morning return flight to Manchester Airport the following day.

They'd turned off the main marked route for the airport long ago. Ulrich, the officer who spoke English, had explained that because of a road accident, there was a snarl-up on the main approach road and they were simply taking a longer route to get round the obstruction.

That could be true. It was plausible enough. Ted had had the same problem himself recently enough, driving back to the police station in Stockport after a meeting at the headquarters building in Central Park.

But there was another factor which was bothering Ted. It might simply have been a coincidence. He didn't like those. They put him on edge. It was the fact that since they'd turned off the main roads, he could find no signal at all for his mobile phone, and he badly wanted to at least send a quick text to his partner, Trev, to let him know he was all right and on course to be back home as planned the following day.

They were in a rural area, with little sign of houses about, but it was still a long time to be unable to find any sort of mobile phone network. Ted half wondered if there was a jammer in effect, then mentally chided himself for verging on the paranoid. And of course, Germany was a much bigger country than England so it was not unusual if its detours took longer than he was used to. Out here with little but forest, it could well be a comms black spot.

At the end of the day, there wasn't much he could do about his situation. He'd asked why the detour, and been told, so he would have to content himself with that for now.

At least he knew the rear passenger door was not locked. As soon as he'd heard the clunk of the lock engaging, he'd asked Ulrich if it could be released. Ted had made light of it, explaining he was a control freak who always liked to have an escape route. He'd been somewhat reassured when the officer had complied immediately and without comment.

But Ted was still not comfortable. He'd been watching the sky all the time, noting the direction of planes both coming in to land, and taking off, and there was no denying it. They were getting further and further away from their destination with every passing kilometre.

Then, still several hundred metres away in front of them, he spotted something which caused his anxiety levels to ratchet up another few notches. A car, parked at the side of the road next to some particularly dense forestry, its bonnet open and two men standing next to it. They were alternately glancing at the engine then looking at the road in the direction of the oncoming car.

Ulrich glanced back at Ted and said in a conversational tone, as the driver started to slow down, 'We'll have to stop here, sir, to check what's going on. We have a civic responsibility, not just a police one, to render aid if someone might be in danger. Hopefully it won't delay us too long, and we'll soon have you safely at your hotel.'

Ted's already raised alert levels went through the roof at his words, and at what he was seeing. A practised eye took in the two men with the car and didn't like what they saw. Hard men. Trained. Simply from the way they held themselves Ted could tell they could present a real danger.

Instead of a simple breakdown of a vehicle with genuine people, it was starting to smell of a pre-arranged ambush. Of which he, for some reason which eluded him for now, could potentially be the target, as the only passenger in the car. And by the lack of any concern, nor of any signs of wariness or risk assessment by the two officers in the front, it was looking increasingly as if they knew exactly what was going on and were in on it.

Ted had a split second in which to make a decision. If he was wrong in his reading of the situation, he was going to look like a total pillock.

If he was right, his actions could potentially save his life.

As soon as he judged the car had slowed down sufficiently, Ted jerked the handle and shouldered the door open in one swift movement.

He launched himself out sideways into space and heard a sickening crack, felt a sharp pain in his hip, as he hit the ground. Ignoring everything but his instincts, driving him on, he rolled and scrambled to the edge of the road then carried on sliding and slithering down the steep bank before plunging into the dense undergrowth at the edge of the forest.

He could hear angry shouts above him but he ignored

everything other than the need to find somewhere to hide and to stay there. Both police officers would be armed. If the other two men had really been there to get him, they would doubtless be so, too. And the anger in the tone of the shouts convinced him more and more that his instincts were right. He was the intended target of some sort of a snatch.

But Ted had one secret weapon in his own arsenal. The gruelling Escape and Evasion training he'd done several times with his special skills instructor, Mr Green.

Green's litany, drummed endlessly into the participants, had been that the best way of tracking anyone was first to understand how and where they would hide.

Ted had been good at it. He'd even foiled Green himself on one memorable occasion. He always referred to himself as a short skinny runt, and his slight build had given him an advantage. He could wriggle himself into the smallest spaces and once there, he had the patience of a hunting feline. He could stay there, still and silent, for as long as it took his seekers to give up the hunt.

Those skills could well be all which now stood between him and the four hard and armed men who were determinedly searching for him.

If for some reason they called in trained dogs to track him, he was done for. His fervent hope was that such an action would raise questions the two officers might not want to answer.

Ted's only hope was to stay in whatever safe place he could find to hide in until his trackers gave him up as a bad job.

If they ever did.

* * *

DI Oscar Smith, on secondment in Stockport from the Metropolitan Police, was still reeling from so many surprises about his current senior officer, DCI Ted Darling.

First and not least that he was gay. Secondly, that Smith was finding himself with his arms round the sobbing young man, dressed in motorcycle leathers, who had turned up at the nick to report Darling missing, lost somewhere in or near Frankfurt and out of phone contact.

He couldn't even rationalise to himself why he'd made the gesture. Smith was definitely not the touchy-feely sort. His team wouldn't have recognised him as the same evil bastard they were used to. But something in the raw emotion of the young man – Trevor, he was apparently called – had touched something Smith kept buried deep within him.

He suddenly found himself looking into the bluest eyes he'd ever seen, still tear-filled, but now staring at him with such evident trust that he would make everything all right. For some strange reason, it actually made him want to be the one to find the boss and bring him back safe.

He'd have to be careful. There was clearly something in the water up here that was turning him soft. That or the hotpot he'd developed an appetite for from the local pub, The Grapes.

That reminded him. He'd been on his way round there to order one and to sample some more of the decent schnapps the landlord kept, when he'd seen what was happening in the reception area and been hailed by the bloke behind the desk. Bill, he'd heard him called. He'd heard, too, that he was a former copper himself, decorated for bravery, so he should be able to filter out what was real or not. And he seemed worried by the way this Trevor had been acting. Perhaps there was something to it, after all.

'We can sort this,' Oscar said, trying to sound assured. 'There'll be a logical explanation for it. Let's go and borrow Ted's office so I can make a few phone calls. I'm sure we can sort it.'

A few of the team were still at their desks as Smith led the way through the main office heading for the DCI's. Several of them greeted Trevor, obviously knowing him well. He replied politely to each, maintaining good manners although clearly distracted by his worry.

Smith sat himself down in Ted's chair, suddenly businesslike and in work mode. He indicated to Trevor to take a seat but he was too agitated, striding up and down in the close confines of the room.

'What happens when you call Ted's mobile?'

'It goes straight to voicemail. I've left dozens of messages but never had a reply.'

'Right, we'll start there, see if we can get a trace on it. Last known whereabouts Frankfurt, did you say?'

As Trevor nodded, Smith was already making a phone call. He was logical, efficient, and so far showing none of the undesirable qualities Ted had mentioned about him.

'This is Detective Inspector Smith from the Metropolitan Police, on secondment to Greater Manchester, at Stockport. I need an urgent trace on a phone in connection with a missing officer. I'll give you the number. I'm also going to give you a number to call me back so you can check I'm *bona fide*. Call back as soon as possible, if not sooner, and ask to be put through to me in Detective Chief Inspector Darling's office. Got that? And I can't stress how urgent this is. Don't keep me waiting too long.'

As he hung up he turned his attention back to Trevor.

'Right, what else can you tell me about this trip? He flew to Frankfurt, and you heard he'd arrived, but he didn't get his booked flight home. Any idea what he went there for?'

'Ted's always very guarded with what he tells me when he goes off to do things a bit out of the ordinary. All he said was that he was going to meet a copper he knew through Mr Green's courses and they were going to some meeting somewhere which would help to solve a major case, but he didn't say which one.'

'Mr Green?' Smith queried.

'Ted's special skills instructor. Ex-SAS. He's known him since his days in Firearms. He's a bit of a mysterious character and Ted doesn't talk about him much. Any time he does get involved with him, it's usually something risky so he does it all on a need-to-know basis, and he prefers me not to know.'

'And was this off the books, do you know, or did he run it past anyone senior first?'

'Ted's usually on the level. He mentioned in passing that he'd run it past the Ice Queen.'

Smith frowned as he asked, 'The Ice Queen?'

'Superintendent Caldwell. Debra.'

Oscar hadn't heard the nickname. Didn't integrate enough with any of the team to have come across it. He'd seen the formidable Superintendent Caldwell in passing, but not spoken to her other than in greeting so had not yet formed an opinion as to whether or not the name was merited.

The desk phone rang before Smith had chance to respond. He listened in silence, then said, 'I see. Keep trying, any way you can, and keep me posted if you discover anything else.'

No please or thank you. Not even a goodbye before he hung up.

He told Trevor, 'His phone is currently not active so there's no way of getting a location trace from it or anything else.

'How did Ted get to the airport? Did he take a car and is it still there?'

'He took his car, but I've not been to check if it's still there. Do you think he flew back and has been in an accident somewhere? But surely I'd have been informed, as his next of kin?'

'Let's not jump the gun. I'm just considering possible explanations. If his car is still at the airport, we need to go and collect it, to save him from a big parking bill, if nothing else. But first I need to go and ask the Super if she knows anything more which might help us.'

He picked up the desk phone again and made a call. It was answered on the first ring. Smith had been about to slope off early when he'd encountered Trevor in reception. The superintendent was clearly not one for finishing early herself.

'Ma'am, DI Smith here. I'm with DCI Darling's partner, Trevor. Apparently the DCI hasn't returned from his mysterious visit to Frankfurt. Trevor tells me you might know something about it. Do you have five minutes to give me?'

There was a pause, then the cold, clipped voice told him, 'I have. Come down now.'

'I've been summoned,' Smith told Trevor. 'Make yourself at home. There's some of that green tea muck Ted drinks, I think. Put the kettle on. I shouldn't be long and I might have some news.'

* * *

Ted was damp and cold. Chilled to the marrow. He'd been lying motionless in his hiding place for hour after endless hour. There was no sound at all from his pursuers but he wasn't stupid enough to think that signalled they'd given up and gone away. They could simply be waiting, with the same endless patience as him, knowing that sooner or later, he was going to have to show himself.

He'd wriggled himself into some sort of tunnel in a bank, not far from a stream. The constant running water was a problem in itself. He was having to tune it out because of the effect it was having on his bladder.

He'd gone down feet first. Not knowing if the hole was some sort of animal lair, he preferred the thought of having his booted feet nibbled on rather than his face, and especially his eyes.

He carefully used handfuls of damp earth to smear his face and hair to stop their light colour showing up to those looking for him. He was keeping his eyes almost closed, peering through narrow slits. Only too well aware of how eyes could betray a hider's location if caught in the beam of a powerful torch.

As he lay there he was mentally checking his resources. His holdall was still on the back seat of the police car he'd dived out of, but it held little other than his wash kit and a change of shirt and underwear. His passport, warrant card, cash and air tickets were safely stored in a body belt under his shirt.

He was glad he'd checked dress code with Jock before

flying out. He'd been told he could wear whatever he liked as he wasn't there officially. When he'd met up with Jock, he'd found they were both dressed in a similar way and could easily have gone straight from the meeting to walking in the mountains as they'd done so many times before. His outdoor gear would be much more suitable for hiding out in a forest than his suit and good shoes would have been.

Inch by careful inch, he'd felt in the pockets of his walking trousers, trying to make no sound. His fingertips told him what he had suspected. The screen of his mobile phone was smashed to pieces, leaving it unresponsive to any touch. At least it wasn't his hip that was damaged, although a cautious exploration with one hand revealed it to be tender, with a slight bleed.

Another pocket was more encouraging and he couldn't prevent a smile at the thought of how Trev liked to tease him about his 'Be Prepared' obsession. The unused foil space blanket would be a godsend when it was safe for him to move enough to put it on. And the few squares of Kendal Mint Cake would keep him going for a bit.

At least he was alive and relatively uninjured. All he could do for now was wait. And hope.

Chapter Two

If her nickname was indicative, Smith decided to play it strictly formal from the start when he entered the Super's office in response to her summons to his knock.

He marched in and presented at attention in front of her, though without the crashing of his foot he would have added when making the gesture ironically.

It was clearly the right move as there was no invitation to take a seat. This was obviously going to be by the book throughout. Smith could do that, if he had to, and in the circumstances, he had more to think about than any petty point-scoring.

'Ma'am, as I said I've just been talking to DCI Darling's…'

He hesitated for a moment, still unsure of what Trevor's status was and for once, not wanting to start off by using the wrong term in front of her.

'… his partner, Trevor. He reports that the DCI failed to return home this morning from his trip to Frankfurt and has not been in touch at all, which is unusual.

'Ma'am, I had a check run on the DCI's phone and it's out of service. Meaning that at the present time, we have no idea where he is. Trevor is understandably anxious, as he says it's totally out of the DCI's character.

'He mentioned that the DCI ran the idea past you before going to Germany, so I'm wondering if you might be able to give me any clue at all as to what the trip was all about or where, precisely, he was going. As you probably know, I'm ex-Military Police. Born in Germany, dual nationality, German is my first language and I still have useful contacts in the German police. I might be able to help.

'Trevor and I are about to go to the airport next to recover the DCI's car, if it's still there, and see if we get any further leads from that. I'll also get someone there to check for his name on the system to see if he was on any flight anywhere.'

He could see the colour draining from her face the whole time he was speaking. If she really had sanctioned Darling's actions off the book, all her pigeons were now coming home to roost and she could find herself in serious trouble. It could even cost her her job, if the DCI wasn't found and brought back safely and soon.

To his own surprise, Smith found himself feeling sorry for her. Damn the water up here. It was definitely turning him soft.

'If it helps, ma'am, I could fly out to Frankfurt and see if I can pick up his trail there, if it comes to that. I could make an educated guess as to where he was heading, in that area, so that would be as good a place to start as any.'

The superintendent was making an effort to recover her composure and remain in charge of the situation. Her voice was cold and steady as she responded.

'As I understand it, DI Smith, now that the case you were sent here to liaise on has been brought to a satisfactory ending, barring you completing all your paperwork, there is nothing to justify extending your time here with us.'

Smith risked an ironic smile as he replied, 'Believe me, ma'am, my Det Sup, Murray Aird, would consider any excuse to have me out from under his feet for longer than he'd expected to be a gift from above.'

She looked at him for a moment longer then said, 'In which case, DI Smith, sit down. I'll give you as much information as I have, which isn't much. The DCI and I kept it on a strictly need-to-know basis as the whole idea was, to put it mildly, irregular.

'I'll also give you a telephone number for someone who might also be able to help you. He was mentioned in context. I should warn you, though, that he is not known for being cooperative, but there is an outside chance he might react more favourably to an ex-military person, being one himself. Mr Green is his name.

'Everything about him is a little, shall we say, irregular. You have to phone his answering service, leave brief and concise details about what you need and he may call you back. Or not.

'In the meantime, I will phone Superintendent Aird and clear the extension for your secondment. I'll attend briefing tomorrow morning, if there's still no news, to put all the team in the picture before rumours start. It's probably better coming from me.

'Thank you, DI Smith. That will be all.'

As soon as Smith left her office, the superintendent made two phone calls. One was to request an urgent appointment at Headquarters, Central Park, the following day, allowing time to brief the Serious Crime team first. The second was to book a car and driver to take her there.

* * *

Even when full darkness fell, Ted was not ready to leave the sanctuary of his burrow. He hadn't heard a sound from his pursuers for quite some time, but he was still not prepared to take any unnecessary risks.

If he was right in his guess that the plan had been to kidnap him to use as a bargaining chip in a trade for suspected multiple rapist-turned-killer, Joel Hammond, he didn't think they would risk killing him. But that wasn't to say they'd stop short of putting a strategic bullet in him to prevent him getting away, then dressing it up as some sort of unfortunate incident.

His feeling was that the two police officers wouldn't hang around. They couldn't afford to be off the radar for long, no doubt, and could be recalled for other duties at any moment. They'd probably head back with a convincing story of having dropped him off near to the airport, at his own request, so he could walk to his hotel. No doubt his holdall would be disposed of somewhere it may never be found.

The other two men were total unknowns. If they were in the pay of Joel Hammond, or someone close to him, they were unlikely to give up until they got their hands on Ted. And even if they were constrained to deliver him alive, it might not be totally unharmed.

One reassuring sign to Ted was that he could hear sounds of birds and animals in the forest where he lay hiding. Foxes barking. Owls calling. Quite close to him at times. He knew they would not be doing that if they sensed any human presence out there in the darkness.

He'd also heard animal noise from much lower down in the tunnel where he was lying. Snufflings, grunting, and what sounded like growling. He was hoping it was badgers, grumbling at not being able to come and go freely. With luck they may not go on the attack unless directly threatened, because he'd heard they had powerful jaws and could deliver a nasty bite if cornered.

He hoped his increasingly pressing need to relieve himself, to which he'd had to surrender, would help to deter them. At least keep them down in the depths of wherever this tunnel led before Ted felt it safe enough to leave them to it. Another good lesson learned from Mr Green's training. How to pee in confined spaces without getting your clothing wet. Ted would have smiled at the memory had his predicament not been so serious.

At some point soon he knew he was going to have to risk a look up at the night sky outside to check the stars for positional purposes. With the phone broken, he couldn't use its compass app, and he was worried the backlight on the military-style watch which Trev had given him as a present, which had all types of gadgets on it, would risk showing up far more than putting his now dirty face close to the entrance.

With nothing else at all to while away the time, Ted was trying to work out what was going on, why he was being hunted, and what he could do about it.

For the 'why', he couldn't think of anything more probable than a clumsy attempt at a hostage exchange for a wanted person. That would never work, and he knew it. Too dangerous a precedent to set.

Time to employ another of Mr Green's tactics. Think the way your enemy would and do the exact opposite of what they would expect you to do.

The police officers knew Ted spoke no German so would be vulnerable. They knew he had a hotel room booked near Frankfurt Airport so he could catch an early morning flight. One which would be leaving before much longer with not a hope in hell of Ted being on board.

They'd almost certainly expect him to try to make his

way back to the airport he was already familiar with. They might even have played it clever and dropped his holdall off at the hotel the evening before, saying that the owner was on his way but had decided to stretch his legs for the last kilometre or so, having spent the day sitting through meetings. That should help to concentrate any future search efforts in the area around the hotel itself, not anywhere out here in the sticks.

He'd put money on there being no cameras of any sort, not even speed cameras, on any of the route of the diversion they'd made, away from the direction of the airport.

The last place Ted wanted to try to head for was the airport. He had no idea where the next nearest one was, nor how to get to it. Even as he'd been fleeing his pursuers, he'd logged into his memory what direction it was in, so once he could see the stars to get his bearings, he could set off in another direction entirely, hoping to find someone, somewhere, who could help him.

There was water not far away to deal with his thirst, and his Kendal Mint Cake would at least give him a bit of energy to add to the adrenalin which was currently all that would keep him going. His first priority was to find somewhere he could use a telephone to let Trev know he was alive and well, hopefully eat something, and then speak to Oscar.

If anyone would know a way to extricate him from his current dire situation, an ex-Military Police officer who knew Germany and spoke the language fluently, definitely would. Ted had simply never visualised any situation where his life was potentially in the hands of Oscar Smith.

* * *

Trevor was still striding round the confines of the office when Smith got back there, occasionally picking up something belonging to Ted, like a pen, as if it could bring him some sort of comfort. Smith noticed that he hadn't made himself a drink. He didn't blame him. He didn't fancy any of that green shite the boss drank, so could quite understand if Trevor didn't either.

'Right, the Ice Queen has given me someone to contact to see if they can throw any light on what took Ted to Frankfurt. If I can pin down his reasons, I might be able to find the right person to speak to. I'll go over there myself if necessary, to get answers. She's talking to my Super to extend my time here. He'll no doubt be glad to see the back of me for even longer.'

'I could go with you. I speak good German. I lived there for two years. I could help,' Trevor told him, lapsing into the language to make his point.

Smith looked at him and sighed.

'Trevor. Mate. An accent like that would be all right for a cocktail party at the British Embassy in Berlin. The kind of places I need to go and the sort of people I'll want to talk to would never agree to saying anything to you, hearing you talk like that.

'Besides, don't you have a houseful of pussy cats to look after while the boss is away? He told me about them. What's the little one called? Adam, is it?'

Trevor looked at him in surprise. He knew Ted so seldom spoke about his private life to anyone at work, yet he'd clearly told Smith about the cats, at least. Perhaps Ted had seen something in the man which Trev was yet to discover.

'So this contact I have to phone. Mr Green. Special skills you said. Do you know anything else about him which might be helpful for me to know before I speak to him?'

Trevor expression changed in an instant. He looked suspicious. Hostile, even.

'Mr Green? Is he involved in all of this somehow? Not just putting Ted in touch with someone?'

'You do know him, then? Can you give me a heads-up before I talk to him?'

'Not know him, exactly, no. All I know is that whenever Ted goes off on one of his training exercises with him, it seldom goes well. Come to think of it, Ted and I had one of our very rare fallings out because of Mr Green one time. He took Ted on a training march up on the Brecon Beacons but confiscated his phone and kept him longer than Ted had thought. I was going frantic with no news from him, imagining the worst.'

Smith frowned at that.

'So is it possible that something like that has happened again, since his name's been thrown up, I wonder? But I did get the feeling that this was more actual police business, to do with an outstanding case or a warrant or something, rather than training.

'Apparently I have to phone and leave a message, then Green might condescend to call me back. I'll do that from my mobile then leave that clear in case we do get a response from him.

'Meanwhile, did Ted happen to mention the name of the hotel he was meant to be staying at?'

Smith was calling the number the Ice Queen had given him for Green. The recorded message kicked in almost immediately. He held up a hand to stop Trevor saying anything which would be picked up.

'Mr Green? DI Oscar Smith. I've been given your details by Superintendent Caldwell, Greater Manchester Police. We're trying to trace DCI Ted Darling who went to Frankfurt yesterday to attend some sort of meeting and hasn't been heard from since. The super seems to think you might have some knowledge which could be useful to us. A name, perhaps. Grateful for any help.'

Then he added a 'sir', not knowing who he was speaking to and what rank they might hold.

'Right, which hotel was Ted meant to be staying at?' he asked Trevor.

Trevor gave him the name and was looking it up on his own phone for the number when Smith's rang.

Smith picked up the call and responded with his name and rank.

An unfamiliar voice with a thick, clipped accent spoke briefly in his ear.

'Green here. Bloke you need to speak to is Jock McClintock. Here's his number. Keep me posted.'

Then the call ended abruptly, before Smith could say anything in response.

Chapter Three

Inch by cautious inch, Ted slowly eased his cold and now barely responsive body out of the sanctuary of the tight hole he'd been lying in all night.

As soon as he got unsteadily to his feet the pins and needles started, painfully. It was the only sensation he could feel in his lower extremities. Until his circulation started to return to normal, he was going to be clumsy, unsteady. An easier target for anyone tracking him who was waiting nearby.

He'd dearly love to unfold the space blanket and wrap it round himself, but he was still conscious of making as little noise as possible. And of not providing an easy target in the shape of covering himself in shiny foil.

He kept still for a moment, using the dense trees as cover, waiting for blood to reach his lower limbs before he set off walking. He'd managed a glance up at the stars during the night, without hearing or seeing anything of his trackers. He would like to think they'd given him up as a bad job, but suspected that would be over-optimistic to hope for.

He started to move carefully on the spot, from one foot to the other, all the time looking around to see what he could learn about his surroundings which might be of use to him. He was in a belt of fir trees, rather than broadleaf. That was hopeful. Conifers might suggest a managed forest, a cash crop. In which case there could well be roads and tracks running through for access. Possibly even forestry workers.

But first he needed to find water clean enough to drink, and to eat a couple of squares of his iron rations. He'd also need to clean himself up a bit before he could approach anyone he might come across. Looking like he no doubt did, and with hardly a single word of German, he was unlikely to get a good reception from anyone he might see. If indeed he ever reached civilisation and found someone he could trust and with whom he could communicate.

* * *

'Right, before I phone this bloke Green told me about, I'd better phone the hotel. Just on the off- chance that Ted is there and might simply be ill or otherwise unable to contact anyone,' Smith told Trevor, although he didn't believe it as a possibility. Not for a moment. And he could see from his face that Trevor thought the idea was too far-fetched to consider.

Trevor could follow everything Smith said when talking to someone on reception at the hotel. Smith was certainly persistent in his questioning, leaving nothing to chance. Once he'd ended the call, he updated Trevor on the replies he'd received.

'It was a call that needed making, but that's one line we can rule out, at least. Ted definitely didn't arrive at the hotel. Failed to check in, but his luggage is still there. Apparently a police officer came in to say Ted was on his way but wanted to walk because he'd been sitting in a meeting all day. But he'd asked the officer to drop his bag off for him to save him carrying it.'

Trevor was frowning and shaking his head before Smith

31

had even finished what he was saying.

'That's not right,' he said emphatically. 'Ted only took his small holdall with him, with hardly anything in it. There's no way he'd use a police officer like a lackey to go and deliver it to his hotel. He'd have carried it himself. It has a shoulder strap.

'Ted's stronger and fitter than he looks. He still keeps up his training. He's done the Fan Dance with Mr Green, for one thing. He can carry a heavy, full Bergen up a mountain. Not to mention all the martial arts he does whenever he gets time.'

Smith was trying to hide his surprise but aware that his eyebrows were betraying him by rapidly disappearing up under his hairline. He'd discovered to his cost that the DCI could outrun him, when they'd been chasing the same criminal and Darling had got there first. But to find out he'd completed the gruelling twenty-four-kilometre SAS selection march, over the highest point of the Brecon Beacons, had astonished him. And all this talk of martial arts? He couldn't reconcile that with the short, slight, quiet man he'd been working alongside for a while.

'All right, fair enough. But perhaps he'd injured himself, and didn't want to carry it?'

Even as Smith said that, he realised how lame it sounded. He was trying to stop Trevor's evident anxiety, but then realised what would help him more was for Smith to start coming up with something much more likely by way of an explanation.

'Absolutely not. Ted's not the sort of senior officer who would expect someone to run his errands for him. He really isn't. He's too much of a Socialist to do the whole pulling rank thing like that, and certainly not in a different country.'

'If you say so. You know him a lot better than I do. So if that's not likely, the next most probable explanation is that whoever the officer was who took the bag into the hotel was trying to set up something of a plausible explanation for his disappearance, either for themselves or for someone else. Or they knew exactly what had happened to him and they wanted to concentrate all subsequent attempts to find him to the area around the hotel and the airport.

'In that case, what I need to do next is to talk to this bloke Jock McClintock. The one Green told me about. If he's the one who got Ted to go out to Frankfurt, for whatever reason the meeting was being held, then it's likely he would know how Ted was getting to and from the venue. Which, of course, opens up the possibility that he knows even more about what's happened to him, and where he might be now.'

* * *

It wasn't all that long until Ted came in sight of what he'd been hoping for. A well-used track running through the forest. Wide enough to take large vehicles. Unsurfaced, just compacted earth and stone, but in good condition and clearly in regular use. That was a hopeful sign.

The road wasn't going in exactly the direction he'd been hoping for, but it was definitely a 'beggars can't be choosers' situation, as far as he was concerned.

Logically one end, if not both, should connect with a road somewhere. A road might mean houses, and at some point, he should come across somewhere he could find help from someone.

He wasn't about to step out onto the surface of the track and put himself in full view. Mr Green had trained him too well for that. He'd stay in the comparative cover of the trees, trying to keep in sight of the track without showing himself.

He could at least now risk wrapping the foil blanket round himself to try to thaw out. He'd found running water from which to slake his thirst and clean up, and had eaten some of his precious energy source. It wasn't much but it would have to do for now.

There were a lot of trees down in the section where he was now walking. The damage looked recent. Some were simply snapped off and left hanging, making it harder to walk in some places. Wind damage, Ted guessed, although for an imaginative moment, he could almost picture a bad-tempered giant striding along, breaking them off in a fit of pique. He shook his head to clear his thoughts. Much too soon to start fantasising, no matter how cold or hungry he was. Keep it real. Stay in the here and now.

He could at least use his watch in the daylight, when its glow was unlikely to give him away. He walked for some time, stopping for the occasional drink when he could, always keeping the track in sight, until he came to a fork in the trail. From there he could hear the unmistakeable sound of traffic, still some distance away. It was coming from the branch in the track, which was going slightly downhill.

It was the most promising sign he'd had so far. There may well be houses where there was traffic. Worst case scenario, he could possibly thumb a lift to the nearest town and at least find a phone. Whatever he did would present him with some level of risk, but he had to do something. He was wary of going to a police station, having no way of knowing if he'd been posted as wanted for some alleged crime or another. That was the tactic he would certainly have used himself, had he been in the shoes of his attempted abductors.

He took a gamble on the downhill fork and it wasn't long before he could smell woodsmoke, then see the roof of a tall, old, half-timbered building. A farmhouse, to judge by the barn and other outbuildings close to it.

The road carried on past the house, still heading in the direction of the traffic noise, louder now, but with nothing yet in sight, except the buildings he was looking at. He was picturing himself inside, thawing out by the fire, drinking something hot – although they might not have tea to offer him. Eating some hot food, too, hopefully. His stomach was rumbling in anticipation.

But he couldn't forget the extensive training from Mr Green. Never walk in anywhere without doing a thorough recce. Not unless you didn't care if you could ever walk out again.

He shrank further back into cover as a dog came out of one of the outbuildings and paused, stiff-legged, glancing in his direction. A man came out behind it. Thickset, probably in his late sixties. He said something to the dog and rubbed it behind the ear, then led the way back into the house with it now calmly trotting at his heels.

It was a cosy little snapshot of a domestic scene. Ted's stomach was increasing its sounds of protest just thinking about what treats might lie ready in that house for man and dog. But before he could even think of going near, he had to be absolutely sure his previous pursuers were not still on his trail, and that there was no one or nothing else to be wary of.

Ted had difficulty thinking like a bent copper, so it was hard to second guess what they might do. In their shoes, he was pretty sure he would alert anyone in the area that there was a dangerous wanted man on the loose who should not be approached and who didn't speak German. Anyone sighting him should instead call the police immediately, at a specific number they would give them, and stay well out of the way.

Ted needed to wait and to watch for any signs that the people in this house were on high alert for someone coming to the house to ask for help. A stranger, who would not be able to make themselves understood.

If that meant another cold night sleeping out in the open, then so be it. It was better than the alternative.

* * *

'Jock McClintock? This is DI Smith, from the Met, currently with Greater Manchester. Mr Green gave me your contacts. I believe you were in a meeting with DCI Darling yesterday?'

Smith could sense the suspicion in the silence which followed his opening statement over the phone, so went on, before the person at the other edge could speak, 'You need to check me out, of course. Call this number, ask to be put through to DCI Darling's office to speak to me. And don't take too long about it. The DCI's missing. Failed to return from Frankfurt, and you're the last person I know of who had contact with him.'

'You've said enough already for me to believe you are who you say you are, sir. Especially if Mr Green gave you my number. He'd only do that in an emergency. When was the last contact from Ted?'

Smith noticed the familiarity. They clearly knew one another well. He didn't know if that knowledge extended to knowing Ted's domestic circumstances, and again he found himself unsure of the correct terminology. He didn't want to say the wrong thing, especially with Trevor still looking at him like he was the answer to everything.

'He contacted his partner yesterday morning just after he landed at Frankfurt, but he's not been heard from since. He failed to get his booked flight back to Manchester and there's been no further contact.

'I phoned the hotel where he was meant to be staying but he never checked in. They told me there that a police officer had called in to leave Ted's bag but said he'd got out of the car to walk the last couple of Ks to stretch his legs.'

He could sense the other man's frown as he replied, 'That makes no sense at all. I found the officers myself, picked one who speaks good English as I know Ted doesn't speak German. Their brief was to drive him to the hotel. He only had a light holdall with him, so why on earth didn't he carry it, if he wanted to walk? I've trained with Ted under Mr Green. I know the size of Bergen he can carry, and it's not like him at all to treat police officers as his personal gophers.'

'What was the meeting about? Any clue as to why it might be followed by the DCI disappearing?'

McClintock hesitated.

'Sir, you must surely know it's not something I can discuss over the phone with someone I don't know. You clearly do know the DCI, and you've had contact with Mr Green, but I really can't talk about a confidential case over the phone with someone I've never met.'

'Go to visual!' Smith snapped, doing the same.

McClintock did so and found himself staring at Smith's warrant card, shoved right up against the phone.

'This is my fucking warrant card. A DI. So unless you outrank me, it's me who tells you what to do. And while you're pissing about worrying over correct procedure and playing it by the book, the DCI is missing somewhere, in a foreign country, his mobile phone is out of service and we need to find him. So start talking.'

Smith cut visual and put the phone back to his ear before McClintock said anything. He didn't want Trevor hearing anything confidential. He certainly didn't want him hearing anything which might only serve to worry him even further.

At least McClintock, who'd now identified himself as a DS, seemed switched on. He filled Smith in on the chance Ted had had to pitch for the extradition of Joel Hammond on the murder charge, which out-trumped all those present with only rape charges against him.

'So your best guess, sergeant, is …?

'Probably the same as yours, sir. Someone's snatched Ted in the hope of using him as a bargaining chip to block the extradition of Hammond back to UK on the murder charge. Probably thinking that he can ride out the rape allegations much more easily.

'But you and I both know that any such plan would never work, sir. If someone's holding Ted, it's not going to stop Hammond's extradition. No matter how many bits of his anatomy they might decide to cut off and post back to Manchester to show they mean business.'

Chapter Four

The entire Serious Crime team leapt to their feet in unison, even DI Oscar Smith, when the door to the main office opened and Superintendent Caldwell marched in, her expression impossible to read.

It was the usual time for morning briefing but there was no sign of their boss, DCI Darling. They'd been expecting him back the previous day but he hadn't been seen and there was no word from him. DI Jo Rodriguez had received a late evening phone call from an enigmatic Ice Queen, telling him very little other than that his presence in Stockport would be required for longer than anticipated.

She seldom betrayed any emotion, always appearing detached and somewhat cold. Hence the long-standing nickname, which had followed her throughout her career.

'Thank you, everyone, please sit down,' she began, standing in front of them all as they did so.

She paused for a moment before speaking. There was total silence, not so much as a shuffle of feet, a fiddle with a pen. All those present were half-dreading what she might be about to tell them.

'As you will all know by now, DCI Darling was due back yesterday morning from a meeting he attended in Germany involving an ongoing case. He failed to return on his booked flight and at this moment, we do not know where he is or what has prevented him from returning as planned.'

A murmur and a movement went through the room at the news. Shocked faces. DC Gina Shaw, whose own older sister had disappeared without trace years ago, went white at the words.

'For the moment, I've asked DI Rodriguez to remain here in post rather than return to Ashton, until we have further news. Meanwhile DI Smith, whom most of you know is ex-Military Police, a fluent German speaker and with good knowledge of the country, has been trying various contacts to see what he can find out. DI Smith.'

'Ma'am, the DCI's partner Trevor came in late yesterday to report him as missing. I made various phone calls and now know where he was and what case it involved. I also phoned the hotel where he was supposed to be staying. He never turned up there, but police officers delivered his hand luggage and said he'd got out of the car to stretch his legs by walking the rest of the way to his hotel.'

It was, inevitably, DC Jezza Vine who broke in at that point, with one of her characteristic snorts.

'Sorry, ma'am, but that's just bo … nonsense. We all know the boss wouldn't do something like that. He'd carry his own bag, not use officers as his personal porters.'

The superintendent gave her one of her frosty looks, although her tone was rather more indulgent as she said, 'Quite so, DC Vine. That would indeed be out of character for the chief inspector.

'Please continue, DI Smith.'

'More as a belt and braces than anything, the DCI's partner and I went out to the airport yesterday to check on his car. It was still where he left it. Trevor drove it back here to save it running up a big bill. So if you see it in the car park, don't get your hopes up. The DCI didn't put it there.

'So to sum up, the DCI was last seen at a meeting in Frankfurt on Tuesday, then leaving in a police car, supposedly to go to his hotel, where he never arrived, and there's been no word from him since.

'Superintendent Caldwell has been in contact with my senior officer, Det Sup Aird, so with their agreement, I am flying out to Frankfurt later today to talk to people in the flesh, lean on anyone who needs it, and hopefully find where the boss is, with a view to bringing him back.

'I've been involved in various exfiltration exercises in my army days and I still have contacts in Germany, so I'm remaining optimistic of a positive outcome.'

There was silence for a moment while those present digested his words. Then the superintendent, still brusque and businesslike went on, 'I have to be at a meeting in Central Park shortly and I don't as yet know how long I will be out of my office. In the meantime DI Rodriguez is in charge.

'This shouldn't need saying, but I will stress it. All matters discussed in briefings are confidential, not to be discussed outside this building. In this current case, that applies more so than ever. If so much as one word leaks out from here, I will hear about it and there will be consequences.

'So, DI Rodriguez, what cases do you have on the books at the moment?'

'Ma'am, we're tying up the child kidnap case, but that's almost done. And something new came in this morning. A referral from SCIU.'

Ears pricked up at that news. It was unusual for Serious Crime to have something passed on to them from the Serious Collision Investigation Unit. It sounded like something out of the ordinary, and most of them would welcome the chance of a challenging case to get their teeth into to distract from the worry of what had happened to the boss.

'It's a hit and run. A nasty one and, according to several seemingly reliable eye witnesses, a deliberate targeting.

'A big black vehicle, of the kind very much favoured by drug dealers in particular, as well as others from the criminal fraternity, mounted a pavement to hit a young man, walking home from sports training. There's no chance it was accidental according to current available intel. They hit him, hard, and at speed, and he's gone through a shop window. They made off in the chaos of it all. A sharp onlooker got the reg number, but the plates are false, unsurprisingly.

'It has all the hallmarks of a punishment crime. Witness accounts, plus evidence from the scene, indicate that the driver could have killed the victim outright if they'd wanted to, but chose to leave them alive – just – possibly as some sort of a warning that they were not to be messed with.

'The victim is a seventeen-year-old black teenager …'

Normally placid and good-natured DC Dennis 'Virgil' Tibbs rumbled into life at that moment.

'Just because he's a black teenager doesn't necessarily mean he's a drugs runner.'

'Not what I said, Virgil, nor even implied,' Jo told him mildly. 'In fact I was going to say the opposite. He's a good student and a very good athlete. He's had a trial for a league football club, and he coaches juniors in football and other sports at the various clubs he belongs to.

'At least he did do all those things. He's currently in intensive care, fighting for his life, although the guarded prognosis is that he should survive, but with life-changing injuries. He's certainly unlikely to be playing football again and he may have some brain damage which could well affect his speech.

'SCIU passed it to us as a probable attempted murder, with a big question mark over why a young lad like that, with all he had going for him, had had any contact at all with drugs dealers. Enough for them to know and to target him. Plus the big question of what on earth he might have done to annoy them so much they've wanted to make an example to others of what happens to anyone who crosses them.'

'Certainly one for this team initially,' the superintendent said once Jo had finished. 'Now I must leave for a meeting at Central Park. I'll be out of contact for some time but please at least send me a text if you have any news at all of the DCI.

'Good luck in your efforts, DI Smith. It goes without saying that all of us here hope you achieve a successful outcome.'

* * *

Ted was up and watching early, not surprised to see that the same man as the day before was already bringing cattle in to one of the outbuildings, helped by his dog, which was weaving to and fro behind the beasts as they wandered placidly into the place, clearly knowing the routine well.

Only about a dozen of them, so the place appeared to be more of a smallholding than a commercial farm. The animals all looked in good condition. The work was taking the dog's attention, so it didn't so much as glance in Ted's direction, although it would probably have got a scent of him on the light breeze.

Ted stayed hidden until the man let his cows back out,

presumably after milking them, and was walking back from the field he'd driven them into. This time the dog, running in front of him, stopped and started barking ominously as Ted emerged from cover and stood stock still, wary of getting himself bitten. He was always nervous around unknown dogs.

He'd taken his warrant card out of his body belt and was holding it in front of him like some magic 'open sesame', which he hoped it would turn out to be.

He'd seen the German word for police written down and heard it spoken, so attempted what he hoped was the right pronunciation.

'*Polizei*. British. English.'

Then he had a go at a phrase he'd heard so often in the old black and white war films Trev loved to watch, hoping he wasn't massacring the pronunciation beyond recognition.

'Spracken see Inglish?' he tried.

Both man and dog were looking at him more in bewilderment than any sign of aggression. At least the man didn't appear to have been warned about a dangerous fugitive posing as a British police officer. Ted's biggest fear had been that his details may have already appeared on local TV or radio, putting the man on his guard.

'*Englisch? Nein,*' the man responded, shaking his head.

Ted swore under his breath. Why was he so stupid at languages? He relied far too much on Trev.

'I need to telephone,' he made the universal sign with thumb and little finger, at the same time as fishing out his mobile phone, holding it up to show the cracked and shattered screen. 'My telephone is *kaputt*.'

He was fairly sure that, at least, was the right word. The man shook his head and said something which Ted took to mean he didn't have a mobile phone. He looked hopefully towards the house, seeing the unmistakable telephone wires appearing alongside the track leading towards the traffic noise.

'Is there a telephone in the house, please?'

He made the gesture again, at the same time as pointing towards the house.

The man smiled kindly enough and beckoned, striding away down the track, following the wires.

'Kommen Sie mit, bitte.'

Ted couldn't imagine why the phone would be elsewhere other than in the house, but neither the man nor his dog was showing any sign of aggression, so he went after them. Not far.

They'd only walked perhaps a hundred metres when Ted saw what the man had been trying to tell him. The bad-tempered tree-snapping giant had been at work here, too. Two telegraph poles had been snapped off and now lay on the ground, nothing but a tangled and broken muddle of cables between them, down which no phone signal could possibly pass.

The man gave him a sympathetic smile, still showing no signs of being concerned or hostile towards this strange Englishman who'd walked out of the wood. He was instead eyeing him up carefully, assessing him.

Then he asked him: *'Möchten Sie essen?'* and mimed knife and fork movements with his hands.

Ted could first have cried at the prospect of no phone at all, then hugged the man at his clear and generous offer of food to a complete stranger.

He nodded his head enthusiastically and said, with more confidence than before, *'Ja, bitte.'*

Even if it might not had been quite grammatically correct, the man smiled at him again and led the way back to the house.

The dog totally ignored the strange visitor and went to curl up in its basket just inside the front porch. The man led the way to a dark kitchen/living room where an ancient-looking range was burning away, filling the place with blissful warmth. He paused in the doorway to take off his boots, still carrying traces of the shippon. Then he patted his chest as he said, '*Ernst. Mein Name ist Ernst.*'

Then he pointed towards a woman of similar age who was busily making coffee at the range and said, '*Meine Frau, Luise.*'

Ted paused in taking off his own muddy boots and pointed to himself.

'Ted. I'm Ted.'

Ernst launched into an explanation, by the sound of it, of which the only words Ted caught were '*Telefon*' and '*kaputt*'.

Luise smiled at Ted in a sympathetic way, motioning him to take a seat at the table, the one nearest the range, as she could see how cold he looked. She put a cup of coffee in front of him which looked strong enough to trot a mouse across. Not Ted's usual beverage of choice but he was chilled enough to drink anything hot, so he smiled his gratitude and said '*Danke,*' which he hoped was correct.

She started to speak then, some kind of an explanation for something about telephones, but Ted simply looked bewildered and spread his hands in apology.

Luise went to take a framed photograph from the wall, then put it on the table in front of Ted. A family group, clearly three generations of the family. She pointed to figures in turn as she spoke.

'Ernst. Luise. *Unser Sohn, Josef. Seine Frau, Julia. Ihr Sohn, Emil. Unser Enkel.*'

She pointed to herself and her husband once more then at the last figure, a teenage boy, perhaps sixteen or seventeen. There was no mistaking her pride in him. Their grandson, Ted thought. Pleased he could at least understand something.

Luise was talking again, something about the boy, Emil. Pointing to him, then to the kitchen, then miming someone speaking on a telephone. Ted figured it out. They couldn't be going to call him, with their phone out of order, so she must be saying he was coming to see them and he had a telephone.

Another ray of hope, to go with the fact that Ted had not seen or heard either a television or a radio in the house, so if there were any police bulletins about him being wanted and dangerous, it was likely that Ernst and Luise hadn't heard them and might not until the visit of the grandson, with or without his parents, at some time.

Food appeared in front of both Ted and Ernst at the same time. Fried potatoes and possibly the biggest sausage Ted had ever seen. He tried a '*Gut, gut,*' in what he hoped was enough of a German accent. Another word dredged from his memory banks of the old films. He'd have eaten anything by that point, but his first mouthfuls told him it was delicious and well cooked. Even the much stronger than he would ever normally drink coffee was just what he needed by now.

The good food and the warmth of the kitchen was doing a great deal to restore his morale, but he was desperate to know when this Emil was coming with his telephone. He could do absolutely nothing until he could make contact with the outside world.

Once he'd finished his food and drink, he tried a bit of

pantomiming of his own, using the photo and the wristwatch.

'When is Emil coming? What time?'

Ernst simply looked bewildered but Luise was good at this, for some reason. She tapped at a number on the face of Ted's twenty-four-hour watch. Sixteen hundred. Four o'clock.

'Today?' Ted asked her hopefully.

This time she frowned, clearly not recognising the word. Then she smiled and went to take a calendar down from the wall. Something from some sort of farm equipment supplier, to judge by the photos.

She pointed to a square. *Donnerstag*. Thursday. Today.

Ted offered up a prayer to every deity he could think of, despite not believing in any of them. In a little over seven hours, if all went according to plan, he should have his hands on a mobile phone from which to call Trev to tell him he was all right, then get in touch with Oscar Smith for a plan of how he was going to get himself back home in one piece.

Chapter Five

It was the turn of Superintendent Debra Caldwell to present herself, stiffly at attention, in front of the desk of a senior officer. In her case, that of Assistant Chief Constable (Crime) Russell Evans.

'No need for formality, Debra, while it's just the two of us. And I'm sorry it's me and not the Chief, as you requested. He had a fall during his squash tournament at the weekend and has dislocated his shoulder. Quite badly, by all accounts, and they can't put it back until some of the inflammation has gone down a bit.

'So it's probably just as well you aren't seeing him, to be honest. He didn't sound in the best of humour when I spoke with him on the phone. Now, what can I do for you in his place?'

'Sir, I have come to tender my resignation, with the earliest possible effect. I made a serious error of judgement and as a result I have potentially put the life of DCI Darling in serious danger.'

Russell Evans sat back in his chair and looked up at her, trying to maintain a neutral expression to hide his astonishment.

From anyone else, he would have suspected a leg-pull. A joke in bad taste. But he knew of no one more straight-laced than the Ice Queen. Like every other officer in the service, he was well aware of her nickname, and her reputation. He'd seen nothing, in his time of knowing her, to suggest it was unjustified.

He stifled a sigh and picked up his desk phone.

'Vanessa? Could you please push back my next appointment by half an hour? And if you could do a couple of coffees for us, that would be wonderful. Thank you.'

Then he looked again at his visitor with a wave of sympathy. He'd never seen her show so much emotion. He had a horrible feeling she was close to tears and had a moment's panic when he realised he would have no idea how to handle an Ice Queen showing signs of being human.

'Sit down, Debra. Please. Tell me what it is you've done, and how it affects Ted. I'm sure whatever it is can't be bad enough to warrant your immediate resignation. Or even at any time in the future.'

Vanessa slipped into the office with the coffees, discreet and silent as a shadow, then withdrew. She said not a word but her glance to the ACC spoke volumes as she read the scenario.

'*Here if you need me*'.

Debra Caldwell did sit, although she remained poker-stiff, on the edge of her seat, looking anything but comfortable.

Russell Evans took a sip of his coffee, as much to marshal his thoughts as any immediate need for it, especially as it was uncomfortably hot still. His visitor showed no inclination to touch hers.

She began talking, presenting the situation in her usual clear and concise fashion. As he listened, Russell Evans couldn't prevent a no doubt selfish thought about wishing this had happened when the Chief had been at his desk, instead of languishing at home, mainlining on strong painkillers.

He let her finish, then paused to assemble his thoughts before saying anything.

'Having listened to what you've said, I'm struggling to see in what way I would have done things any differently to how you handled it,' he began.

'We both know that Ted can be a stubborn little sod. He'd probably stop short of disobeying a direct order, but it's my guess he would have pushed boundaries to the limit to make sure he had a seat in that meeting. I'd have done the same myself, in the circumstances.

'Without the insider tip-off from the McClintock bloke, we'd never have got a sniff of our rapist/killer, and if we could have got our hands on him, that would have been a big tick for us at a time when our reputation, together with that of too many others, is not exactly bright and sparkling.

'And speaking of reputations, Debra, are you really going to hand the press and media the misogyny card? You'll say you resigned. They'll claim you, as a female senior officer, were the sacrificial lamb the male executive officers were hiding behind. They love a discrimination story. Believe me, I know a thing or two about that sort of thing, as the grandson of a Windrush immigrant.

'Don't do this to us. Please. Or at least take time to think it over and promise me you won't do anything hasty. At least not until the Chief is back at his desk and you can talk it over with him. I know he'd say the same as me. You're a bloody good role model and, forgive the cliché, we need strong female role models like you in the service.

'You know you have, and always have had, my backing, and I'm sure the Chief would say the same thing. That's why I asked you to keep a watching brief over Serious Crime, if ever Ted needed a nod and a wink quickly from someone senior and couldn't immediately run it past me.

'I'd say take a bit of leave to at least think about it before making any rash decisions, but you know how things stand. We've just lost Sammy as Head of Serious Crime, on medical grounds. Our Deputy is now, you tell me, lost somewhere in Germany, and off the radar. We simply can't afford to be without your guiding hand on the Stockport tiller at the same time.'

Russell Evans was shamelessly prepared to use every metaphor in his arsenal if it meant he could persuade Debs to stay on, at least until the Chief was back in charge.

'Drink your coffee, then promise me you'll hang fire and think about it for a bit longer.'

Once she'd done so and left his office, the ACC couldn't resist leaning right back in his chair and letting out a long, self-satisfied breath towards the ceiling. Had buck-passing been an Olympic sport, that would have been a certain gold medal winner, he thought, mentally patting himself on the back.

The Ice Queen's driver, a former Roads Patrol Officer, Hector, universally known as 'Eck for his habit of using 'oh 'eck' in place of swearwords when driving senior officers, was waiting outside when the Ice Queen strode out of Central Park, her head held high, as always.

She didn't fool 'Eck. Not for one moment. He jumped out smartly to hold the door to the rear seat open for her and, taking in her pallor and the tightness around her mouth, he risked, 'Ma'am, permission to take you to the nearest pub and buy you a coffee, if not a small brandy?'

She looked at him, hard, for a moment. Then to his astonishment, she replied, 'Permission granted, Hector.'

* * *

Ted was feeling decidedly more human and considerably warmer. After the hearty breakfast, Luise, who was showing great ingenuity in trying to communicate with him, and clearly enjoying the challenge, had managed to make him understand her suggestion he should wash himself and borrow some of Ernst's clothes while she washed his.

There was no shower in the tiny bathroom, only a well-used tub. Sliding himself into water as hot as he could bear it was the height of luxury and made Ted feel much more like himself. Ernst's clothes almost went twice round his slight frame, but they were at least clean, and the hand-knitted thick socks were wonderful for feet only just thawing out.

He was mortified to find Luise hand-washing his things at a deep old-fashioned sink. He'd assumed she would put them in the machine under the work surface nearby. With mime and facial expressions, he managed to convey his surprise that she wasn't using it.

She laughed, pointing to it in turn and said '*Kaputt. Heute ist alles kaputt.*'

Ted smiled in turn. He'd got the gist of that. He wished he knew more of the language so he could thank the couple for everything they had done for him. When the grandson arrived later, he had so much he needed him to translate to express his thanks. Most importantly, he hoped he really did speak enough English to help, and that he didn't choose today to come without his mobile phone. He thought that unlikely, though. He couldn't remember the last time he'd seen any teenager without one seemingly glued to their hand.

After the copious breakfast, he wasn't sure he could face eating at midday. But when another well-filled plate appeared in front of him, he felt it would be rude to refuse. Ted had always been a good trencherman and had learned from experience, and especially at the hands of Mr Green, that it was always best to fuel up when possible, to have a better chance of surviving when meals might be few and far between.

He insisted on washing and drying up afterwards, to show in actions, if not words, how grateful he was to the couple who had taken him in unquestioningly and were looking after him so well. He only hoped they were as on the level as they seemed and hadn't somehow signalled his presence to the police or to anyone else.

Afterwards, he went out for a walk about, as much to have a watchful eye on his surroundings as any need for exercise. All seemed quiet, apart from the ever-present distant traffic noise, and the sound of chainsaws working somewhere deep in the forest.

Certainly no signs of circling police helicopters, which would indicate a full-scale manhunt, with him as the intended target.

He was back in the kitchen, helping Luise to sweep and tidy up, when he heard the sound of an approaching moped. Luise's face lit up immediately. The face of a proud grandmother as she told him, 'Emil. *Unser*

Enkel. Er ist hier.'

She rushed to the door, still beaming. For a moment, it reminded Ted of visits to his own grandmother, long ago, before his mother had left his father and he'd had no more contact with them. Not until his mother had come back into his life to report the sudden, violent death of his grandmother.

Luise chattered away to the grandson nineteen to the dozen, indicating Ted, who caught his name mentioned, but understood nothing else of what was said, except for catching that word again, *'kaputt',* with a few mentions of telephones.

The young man smiled at Ted a little shyly, then spoke in an English heavily influenced by American. The internet had a lot to answer for.

'Hello, I am Emil. I speak a little English. How can I help you?'

'I'm so pleased to see you, Emil. I don't speak any German and my phone is broken. I'm a police officer and I really need to contact someone to tell them where I am. Can I please use your phone? I'll pay for the call, of course.'

Ted already had his wallet out, looking for a note, but the young man smiled and said, 'No problems, my dad pays and he's just topped up my credit for me. Here. Please.'

Ted pounced on the phone like a drowning man grabbing at a lifebelt. He knew Trev's mobile number off by heart and punched it in. It was answered almost on the first ring. Ted couldn't begin to imagine how worried Trev had been, with no news for nearly forty-eight hours now and, knowing him, panicking and fearing the worst.

'Hello, it's me.'

'Ted!! Oh my god, Ted, you're alive! I've been imagining all sorts of things, none of them good. Where are you? What happened? When are you coming back?'

'I'm sorry, I didn't mean to worry you. I had …' he paused, trying to think of a sanitised version of his adventures. 'A bit of a problem over transport, and my phone got broken. I'm fine, but currently stuck in Germany so I urgently need to talk to Oscar to help me sort things.'

'I can translate for you, Ted, you know that. Let me help.'

Ted was thinking fast on his feet. He couldn't say too much without giving away how precarious his situation was and worrying Trev even more than he had been already.

'I know, and that's kind of you. But this is with some police stuff that's a bit delicate. Restricted circulation sort of thing. Can you get hold of his number for me and phone me back on this number? It's a borrowed phone, but I think I can use it for a bit.'

He was looking questioningly at Emil as he spoke. The youth nodded agreement and said, 'Yes, I will be here for some hours. I've come to eat with my grandparents.'

'I have Oscar's number already,' Trev told him. 'I went to the station when you didn't come home and met him. He's been so kind. He's so much nicer than I was expecting. I was worried sick and Oscar gave me a big hug and has been helping so much with trying to find where you were. Where are you, come to that?'

'Still in Frankfurt,' Ted told him, with no real clue as to where he actually was. He was reeling from the mental image of Oscar Smith, of all people, displaying a soft side and coming to Trev's rescue. 'I'll try to phone him now and I really am fine. Don't worry if you don't hear from me for a bit. Like I said, this is a borrowed mobile and the landline to where I'm staying is down at the moment. I'll be home as soon as I can, promise.'

He would have liked to say so much more, but even though young Emil was tactfully trying not to listen, his English was clearly not bad and Ted was feeling self-conscious enough about his predicament. He'd have some serious making up to do when he got to see Trev again – and not for the first time.

* * *

Rumour had it that one copper could always recognise another, even in a crowd. Certainly Oscar Smith already had the stocky, slaphead bloke waiting in Arrivals at Frankfurt Airport pegged as one of the firm, even without seeing the piece of card with SMITH written on it, which the man was holding.

He'd not seen enough of him on his phone screen when talking to him briefly to be able to identify him accurately as the man he could now see. But everything about the way he stood and held himself marked him out for what he was if not who.

'DS McClintock? DI Smith.'

Jock McClintock was doing some rapid assessment himself of the big, brash Met officer, wanting to know from the off how best to deal with him. Formally, his instincts told him. No handshake. Call him 'sir' at all times. Play it totally by the book. He could tell from a shrewd glance that this man was as far-removed from Ted Darling as it was possible to be.

'Sir. I have a car outside. Do you want to go to your hotel first, or to talk to the police officers who are investigating the DCI's disappearance?'

'What I want, sergeant, is to talk to the two bastards you sent to drive him back to the hotel from the meeting. I want to talk to them one at a time. Alone. In a quiet place, with no one watching. I guarantee that if either of them knows anything at all, I'll get it out of them.'

Jock McClintock was busy trying to work out how he could prevent a potentially major international incident if Smith was intent on assaulting German police officers on their home soil when they were interrupted by Smith's mobile phone, as they walked out of the terminal towards the waiting car.

Smith glanced at the screen, saw the incoming call had a Germany country code, so answered in his native tongue.

'Oscar, it's Ted. I really need your help.'

Chapter Six

Hector, the driver, knew just about every watering hole in the Force area. Especially the ones where he could take people for a quiet drink, without interruption or being stared at.

He left the motorway and headed off deep into the Cheshire countryside, an area the Ice Queen didn't recognise. He pulled up outside a country pub. The absence of many cars parked outside suggested a peaceful place for a lunchtime drink.

'We'll be fine here, ma'am,' he told her, once again holding open the rear passenger door for her while she got out. 'I know the landlord well. There's a small snug at the back I often use when I'm with someone who wants a bit of privacy. The food is decent, too, if you get hungry. But first let's get those coffees, and what about that brandy? I'm in the chair.'

Debra Caldwell was a private person. She found it hard to confide in anyone, especially about work-related matters. She'd fought hard to get where she was and was plagued always by the thought that she needed to do more than any male counterpart to prove her worth.

She found it particularly hard not always having anyone she felt she could talk to about work. The last thing two married coppers tended to want to do once they were off duty was to talk shop. Her husband, an inspector, was in Roads.

She knew that Hector probably knew more about the various senior officers he drove than anyone else. Probably more than their own families, in some areas.

Despite also knowing that it was a disastrous financial situation which had brought him back as a driver – his police pension commutation lump sum invested in something shady which promptly went bust, leaving him with a big financial hole to plug – she also knew he was as straight as it was possible to be. No gossip, no blackmail, nothing. The perfect father confessor.

Whether it was the silent and steady presence of Hector, the warmth from the log fire, or the indulgent brandy she had allowed herself, she wasn't sure. But she found herself relaxing and telling him rather more about the difficult morning she'd had than she had expected to. She surprised herself even more by how good it felt to talk about it with someone like Hector.

He listened in silence until she'd finished, which coincided nicely with the landlord bringing their food order. They'd decided to have something, at least. It felt rather like playing truant to Debra Caldwell. Not that she had ever done that. She'd always played by the rules, all her life. Which was why she was beating herself up so much over the one time she'd gone out on a limb having ended so disastrously.

Hector had proved to be the perfect listener, not interrupting her by word or gesture. When she'd finished, her cheeks were flushed, whether from the brandy or the unexpected circumstances she found herself in. It was the most human and vulnerable her driver had ever seen her.

When he spoke next, he dropped the 'ma'am', but that was as informal as he dared risk with the frosty Ice Queen. He couldn't begin to imagine the effort it had taken her to confide in anyone.

'For what it's worth, I agree with the ACC. I think the last thing you should do is resign. You and I both know Ted is a stubborn little so-and-so. He doesn't often go out on a limb or break the rules, but I'd say in this case it's a racing certainty his mind was made up. If you'd said no, he'd have found a way to go anyway, then dealt with the consequences when he got back.

'And the ACC is right about needing women like you in senior posts. Misogyny was bad enough back in the day when I first joined up, heaven knows. We didn't lose the W for Woman in ranks like WPC until the nineties, for goodness' sake.

'It should be getting better, in the twenty-first century. But you and I both know the entry process isn't as tight as it was. We're not doing a good enough job of policing who we let into the ranks these days.'

He paused for some more of his coffee, the second cup he'd ordered. Definitely no drinking on duty for a driver as conscientious as Hector.

'Before I could even join the Cadets, back in the day, someone came round to talk to my mam and dad, and they did a thorough background check on me. There's much less of that nowadays.

'So no, don't go. Don't give the misogynists that satisfaction. Show them you're more than capable of dealing with all of this, and more. Don't worry about Ted. They don't call him Teflon Ted for nothing. It's well known that whatever shit is flying about, pardon my French, none of it sticks to him. Whatever has happened, he'll find his own way out of it.'

Superintendent Caldwell smiled at his words, to her own

surprise.

'Do they really call him Teflon Ted? I hadn't heard that.'

'They do, ma'am, and it's well merited.'

Hector reverted to the formal now they were finishing the cosy chat and getting back to on duty mode.

Then he risked a sly wink as he said, 'But you didn't hear that from me.'

She gave him a rare smile as she replied, 'My lips are sealed. As I know yours will be about this conversation which we categorically never had.'

* * *

'I've just this minute landed in Frankfurt …' Smith started to reply, but Ted dived in to stop him short.

'Unless you're alone, say nothing. And seriously, trust no one. No one at all. Ring me back on this number, as soon as you're somewhere by yourself. It's urgent.'

At least Smith was quick on the uptake, as Ted hoped he would be. His tone was testy as he replied, 'I've told you before, he won't eat salmon with carrots in it.'

Ted heard Smith's aside to whoever he was with, 'Bloody cattery. I had to leave my moggy with them to travel and despite full written instructions, they still keep fucking up.'

Then he spoke again to Ted.

'I have somewhere to be now, but I'll call you back as soon as I can.'

'I know it's wrong to judge but I would never have had you down as a cat lover, from first impressions, sir,' Jock McClintock told him, leading the way out of the airport to where his car was parked.

'Always risky to go off appearances, sergeant,' Smith

told him, something of a warning edge to his tone as he said it. 'Coppers should bear that in mind at all times. But I do need to sort my cat's basic needs, before I can concentrate on other pressing matters in hand.

'Wait here by the car while I go and find a quiet corner. I won't be long.'

Smith opened the rear door to toss in the small backpack which was all the luggage he had with him. Then he strode away far enough to be out of earshot of anyone, before redialling the number which had just called him.

'Guv, where the hell are you? Your Trevor has been going frantic. That's why I've come over to Frankfurt, to try to pick up your trail.'

'It's a long story, but it involves bent coppers. Ones provided by Jock McClintock, supposedly to drive me to the airport, but who drove me straight into what looked like an ambush. That's why I said trust no one. Not even Jock, and I thought I could trust him.'

'So where are you now?'

'I don't know, to be honest. At a farm in the middle of a forest. Kind people, who've helped me, but I don't speak the language. I need you to come and get me, on your own, then we can start to work out what it's all about. I'm with a young man who speaks English, thankfully. I'm using his phone because I broke mine jumping out of a moving police car. I'll pass you to him for directions.'

'I don't have a hire car yet, but I can soon sort that. Ditching McClintock might be harder, though. He's bound to be suspicious. Are you sure he's involved?'

'I'm not sure of anything or anyone at the moment. Hence having to trust even you, Oscar,' Ted made light of it, an attempt at humour, but Smith could still pick up the concern in his voice. 'Right, I'll pass you over to Emil now and hopefully see you as soon as you can get here without a tail.'

* * *

DI Jo Rodriguez had the unenviable task of trying to rally the team back to the job in hand after the devastating news that their well-loved boss was currently missing in Germany, possibly in some sort of danger.

But they also had a young man whose dreams had been shattered by criminals, who might never walk again, nor be able to speak as before, and that case needed to be dealt with at the same time. Their remit was serious crime, and it didn't get more serious than such a cynical attempt on a young life.

'Our victim is Martin Jackson, seventeen. Seriously into sports, with the intention of going on to study Sports Science, hopefully at either Loughborough or Birmingham, although all that is, of course, now out of the window, barring a medical miracle.

'An excellent student, no trouble at all. No truancy, nothing. No known association with any kind of gangs or violence in any form, although SCIU are saying this has all the hallmarks of a gang-related punishment attack. It's apparently not the first they've come across, though none identical to ours.

'It's one which is going to need tactful handling all along. As Virgil has already pointed out,' Jo nodded in his direction as he spoke, 'we risk coming up against an assumption that because Martin is black he must be involved in gangs and trying to deny it to avoid blame.

'Luckily, there are plenty of witnesses. Unsurprisingly,

some of them are staying tight-lipped and unwilling to say more than the basics, so it's going to take time and patience to get anything out of them.

'Gina, I wondered if you might speak to Martin Jackson, and to his family? You're the only one of us to have direct experience in Drugs, so you might perhaps be able to frame your questions accordingly. As long as you're happy with that. It's not going to be easy, certainly, and you'll need to liaise with his family, and his medical team, as to how best to approach it.'

'More than happy to try. If it's all right, I could liaise with my old team to see if any of the eyewitness accounts trigger any bells with them. Carefully and discreetly, of course.'

Jo nodded agreement then said, 'Mike and I will sort out actions for the rest of you, to cover what's needed, but let's throw everything we have at this one. It's a big tick on our books if we can solve it, not to mention bringing justice to a young man for his life and his dreams being shattered.

'Just don't forget to turn in any and all paperwork from the kidnap case first. We want a watertight file on that for CPS, so there's no chance of any of them getting off.'

'Jo, what can any of us do to help with locating the boss?' Jezza Vine asked him.

Jo tried his best to sound as stern as the boss could do in similar circumstances, although it was not his usual style.

'What you can do, DC Vine, is to get on with any actions you're given on this case. Unless, that is, you want to explain to the boss on his return that you let things slide on that front because you were too busy worrying about him.'

* * *

Now that Ted knew help was finally on its way, the time seemed to pass more slowly than ever. His hosts couldn't have been kinder nor more welcoming, and at least, with Emil now there to translate for him, he could properly express his thanks. But once Ted had got a sniff of the fact that bent coppers were behind his attempted abduction, he wanted to be out there, finding them and seeing they were dealt with.

He was in something of a quandary about Jock McClintock. He knew full well that many of the participants in Mr Green's courses often operated in the shadowy zone at the edge of legal procedure. That went with the territory and the training. Some of the tactics he'd been taught himself were hardly in any standard police training manual.

All his instincts had suggested that Jock was one of the good guys. Someone he could trust. Which is why he'd flown out to Germany in the first place at his request. But then there had been the little niggling query at the back of his mind. The one which had made him call Green for his advice and to ask whether or not he should trust him.

And now Green's words were coming back to haunt him in a big way: 'If you even have to ask me that, then you don't trust him and you should go with your instincts.'

He hadn't done so and now here he was, stuck in the middle of a German forest, totally dependent on Oscar Smith, of all people, to come and rescue him.

At least he had his own clothes back on, after Luise had carefully dried them in front of the range, then insisted on running a cool iron over them for him – hi-spec walking gear that not even Trevor ever ironed – whilst Ernst had scrubbed his walking boots clean outside.

What was concerning Ted most was that the day was getting on, still with no sign of Oscar appearing. Clearly young Emil would be wanting to get back home at some point and when he left, he would be taking with him Ted's only current form of communication with the outside world.

He was tempted to ask to use the phone again to chase up Oscar, but even as the thought came to him, he heard a vehicle engine, coming slowly down the track, towards the farmhouse.

That immediately put all of Ted's senses on full alert. With luck, it was Smith, as promised. But Ted was not about to show himself until he'd made certain.

He told Emil, 'Please ask your grandparents not to open the door before I check to see who this is.'

He went to the window, keeping himself well out of sight, as Emil translated his instructions.

If the vehicle outside in the yard was a police car, it was an unmarked one, and not the same make as the one Ted had been travelling in before he escaped.

It was parked so that the driver's side was away from the house which meant that for the moment Ted couldn't see the driver clearly, except enough to see it was a man. He seemed to be twisted round in his seat, getting something from the back seat.

That movement alone was increasing Ted's concern until he could see who the person was, and what he was reaching for.

Then the car door was opening and Oscar Smith was unfolding his big and bulky frame out of the front seat and striding towards the door of the farmhouse, a carrier bag in his hand, and Ted was nodding to Emil that there was no danger. The visitor was someone he knew.

Ted was astonished by the good manners Oscar displayed as he was invited inside, first approaching the older couple, then Emil in turn with a handshake each and what was clearly a polite greeting in German. When he reached Ted he was grinning broadly.

'I'll spare you the embarrassment of a man hug, guv, but I thought I'd better pick up a few things for you, knowing you'd been separated from your holdall. Some shreddies and socks, toothbrush and paste, that sort of stuff. Oh, and I even found you some green tea, because I didn't want to be dealing with you suffering from withdrawal symptoms.

'So, now I'm here, what's the plan of action?'

Chapter Seven

Gina Shaw decided to start by speaking to the parents of the hit-and-run victim, Martin Jackson, before she even thought about asking to see the young man himself. The whole case was going to be delicate and she needed them on side right from the start.

When she phoned the father, she wasn't surprised to hear that both he and his wife were currently spending most of their time at the hospital, seeing Martin whenever they could. Sometimes he was responsive but quickly became distressed and agitated at his inability to communicate with them as he clearly wanted to.

His prognosis was now guardedly optimistic in that his doctors were more confident that he wouldn't die from his injuries. They were, however, remaining tight-lipped about how much of a recovery he would make, both physically and mentally.

The parents agreed to meet Gina in the family room which was becoming as familiar to them as their own home, at the time when Martin would be receiving some of the essential care he now needed daily to give him the best chance of any sort of a recovery.

Unsurprisingly, both parents looked shocked to the core by what had happened to their eldest son. Gina knew there were two younger sisters at home, twins, and that Mrs Jackson's sister had moved in temporarily to take care of them, and to provide both practical and moral support for her sister and brother-in-law.

'Thank you for sparing the time to talk to me, Mr and Mrs Jackson,' Gina began. 'I'm so sorry for what has happened to your son. Please be assured that my colleagues and I will do everything we can to see that the people who did this to him are found and brought to justice.'

'My son was not involved in drugs,' the father, Walter, began emphatically, his tone verging on belligerent. 'Not in any way, and never would be. I know that's what people are assuming, and even saying. Martin is a sportsman, and a good one. He wouldn't destroy his body with any of that filth. Besides, there's random drugs testing for some of the teams he plays with, and we support that fully. He has never, ever either failed or refused a drugs test.'

'I understand that, sir, and I assure you, I'm not here to make any assumptions. I'm from the Serious Crime team, and we are taking this incident very seriously. There's no question of any victim blaming. The case is being treated as an attempted murder.'

Jackson looked slightly mollified at her words, but still on the defensive.

Gina's attention was drawn to his wife, trying to read the fleeting expression she had seen in her eyes. Her intuition told her that all was not quite as it seemed on the surface here. She needed to find a tactful way of speaking to the parents separately at some point. It could make a critical difference to how she took her questioning of the victim forward. Whenever she was able to talk to him at all, or get any answers from him.

She couldn't even use the excuse of asking the husband to go and find them some hot drinks, because there were the makings of a brew in the room they were in. She'd need to leave that topic for now; mentally log it for further attention.

'What about witnesses?' the father asked, his tone still verging on aggressive. 'I suppose they're like the three wise monkeys. A black boy, getting run down by a drugs gang car. That's what the media are saying about it. So he must have been involved. That's what people will be thinking, no doubt. County lines. Running their filth for them then not paying over his dues. Is that about it?'

'Everyone who saw anything is being questioned by other officers, Mr Jackson. We really are keeping an open mind and trying to find those responsible. Has Martin been able to tell you anything at all that might be helpful to us?'

Again, Gina saw that elusive something in the mother's expression, before the father replied, his voice breaking with emotion at the words he uttered.

'He can barely say his own name. My wonderful, brilliant son, with his whole life in front of him, can barely string two words together without struggling and stuttering and stammering. That's what those bastards have done to him. Serious brain damage, they say. They can't even tell us if or when he might improve.'

His wife reached out a hand to touch him on the arm. A small and simple gesture which spoke volumes.

'Don't upset yourself, love. The news is better today than yesterday. At least the doctors are more confident that he'll survive. And we know our Martin's a fighter. As long as he keeps on improving every day, there's always hope.

'Look, why don't you go and find someone to ask when we can take this young lady in to see him? I'll wait here with her while you go.'

It was such a blatant attempt to get rid of him that Gina

was surprised he didn't seem to catch on. Instead he went off meekly to do as she had asked.

Thelma Jackson turned quickly to Gina, looking furtive.

'I didn't want to say anything with my husband here. He's so fragile at the moment. But Martin has always confided in me more than his dad. He's been being pestered recently by someone from some drugs gang, wanting him to become part of it. To pass on drugs to some of the young people he works and trains with at the sporting clubs. To get them hooked so they'll keep coming back for more.

'Martin wasn't having any of it. He kept refusing, telling this person to get lost and leave him alone; he wasn't interested in any of their dirty stuff.

'I don't think he realised how serious it was, to stand up to people like that. I tried to get him to go to the police, but he said that would be too dangerous. He thought that if he kept saying no to them, eventually they'd give up and leave him alone.'

Tears were flowing down her face now as she went on, 'If only I'd insisted. Taken him to the police station myself to get help, then none of this would have happened.'

'Please don't blame yourself, Mrs Jackson. These people are persistent and dangerous, but you couldn't possibly have foreseen anything like this happening.

'Did Martin say anything about the person who was pestering him? Anything at all which might help us to trace them, and through them, to find the people who made this attempt on his life.'

The woman shook her head, reaching for a handkerchief to try to stem the flow of tears before her husband came back.

'He didn't really say very much about it. He was quite

dismissive about it all. He told me because he tells his mum everything. He's such a good boy like that. Never in any trouble, never given me a moment's worry. Before this.

'The only thing I can remember of what he said was that the person who was pestering him most often was called JJ. I don't know if that was initials or perhaps the name Jay, but twice, for some reason. That's honestly all I can remember of what he said.'

She clammed up instantly as the door opened and her husband came back into the room.

'They've nearly finished with his therapy. They said we can see him briefly in about ten minutes. They warned he's very tired, so perhaps I'll wait here while you and the officer go in to see him, love. As long as I can have a couple of minutes afterwards, just to tell him how much I love him.'

* * *

Ted had suggested he and Oscar should take a stroll round outside to speak further. Knowing there was someone present who could speak any English at all had him on edge. He got Oscar to explain to his hosts that he felt in need of a walk after all the kind hospitality they had shown him. They were pressing both men to stay for an evening meal before going on their way. Luise was already preparing enough food for a squad of hungry soldiers.

They were clearly quite taken with Oscar Smith. Ted suspected it was helped by him having taken a call from his grandmother, who lived in Germany, soon after he had arrived. The patient and respectful way in which Smith had spoken to the old lady had clearly impressed them.

'To put your mind at rest, as soon as I heard what had

happened, I phoned a contact and had Joel Hammond moved to a safe, secure location, known to few, and certainly not to your Jock McClintock, or the coppers he picked to transport you,' Smith began by telling Ted once they were out of earshot.

'So if wanting you out of the way was an attempt to do a hostage exchange – you for Hammond – the bad guys are going to be stuffed because they won't now know where Hammond is now. Nor where you are, with a bit of luck.'

'Do you think we should stay here any longer, or move off somewhere straight away?' Ted asked him, always anxious to put his Escape and Evasion training into practice by keeping on the move, unless he was fully confident of where he was and of those around him.

Smith turned to him with an expression of outrage.

'Have you seen what she's cooking? I'm German. I grew up on meals like that, mostly made by my Oma, my grandmother. I've not eaten much today, chasing round trying to find you. The only way you're going to get me to leave here without eating first is by arresting me and dragging me out in handcuffs.

'It's my guess we're as safe here as anywhere for now, and we should only risk moving on under cover of darkness. These are good people. Honest. I'd stake my pension on it. And the dog will certainly warn us if there's anyone about. That way we can at least set off with full stomachs.'

'Move on to where? Have you made plans about that?'

'I went on the assumption that you'd want to stick around to find out who set you up, so I booked a hotel for us both tonight. Not the one you'd booked, in case anyone was keeping an eye on that one. Something a bit further out.

'I told McClintock I wanted to speak to the two lying

bastard coppers who said they'd dropped you off on the way then taken your kit bag to the hotel. He didn't seem keen on the idea of me doing that, to say the least. How much do you trust him?'

'I've trained with him, but never served with him. I thought he was on the level, but I didn't check him out and I should have done.'

'I'll give him a quick call to say I've run into someone I know and will see him in the morning. That should stall him, for the time being, at least.'

They'd walked slowly as far as the fallen telegraph poles, still lying uselessly at the side of the track. They did an about turn and headed back the other way before Ted spoke again.

'But someone was out to remove me from the scene and so few people knew where I was going to be. And there was so little time to set anything up. It was all very last minute, and all kept on a strictly need-to-know basis.

'What opinion did you form of him? Of Jock, I mean?'

'I barely had time to form one. Not reliably, anyway. He was edgy when he met me, but then I do tend to have that effect on people, although I can't imagine why. He wasn't keen for me to talk to the coppers who drove you, but that might be because he somehow thought I might present a danger to them, which couldn't be further from the truth,' he winked as he said it.

He posed a question of his own.

'What did you make of those coppers? Did they seem legit?'

'I thought so, to begin with. I heard the locks go on when I got in the back. That would be standard in a police vehicle for transporting a suspect, of course, so they couldn't jump out at the first red traffic light. I don't like it, though. Total control freak.

'I asked for them to be undone and the English speaker, Ulrich, did it straight away, without batting an eyelid. I rather let that lull me into a false sense of security, and I shouldn't have done. That was the second serious error of judgement I made on this trip.

'As soon as I saw their reaction, or rather lack of one, to a potential kidnap situation – the two blokes standing with a supposedly broken down vehicle – I knew I was in trouble. The locks should have gone back on immediately at that point, to protect me from any potential danger. But they didn't. That would make me a sitting duck in the back seat. That's when I shoved the door open and jumped out before they'd even pulled up. And that's also when I smashed my phone.'

'Ah, speaking of phones, guv,' Smith reached into the inside pocket of his jacket and took out a small mobile, which he handed to Ted.

'I always carry a spare burner or three about my person, in case of dire need. Ones I've acquired in the course of things. This one's clean, with a couple of calls' worth of credit on the card at least, so you can phone your Trev or someone and get them to call you back.

'Phone your mother, perhaps. Trevor said he speaks to her every day and would try to stop her from worrying about you until he had any news.'

Ted hid his surprise about how much Trev had told Smith. He must have been at a low ebb because he knew how much Ted disliked anyone knowing anything about his private life. He could hardly complain, though. If Smith hadn't flown out to the rescue, he had no idea of how he would have got himself out of his present predicament, although he'd have had a good try.

'I also got you a beanie; it's in the bag with the other stuff. We can't do much about changing your size and shape but all that light-coloured hair of yours is a bit distinctive. I didn't know if I could persuade you to shave it off in disguise, so I thought a hat was the best compromise solution.

'Because if we really do want to know who arranged for your disappearance and why, we need to go back to the beginning. Back to places like the airport, and wherever you went for the meeting. And we can't risk anyone recognising you too easily while we do that.'

'That's what we're going to do, is it? Two of us alone in a foreign country, up against goodness knows who is out to get me, and probably now, by association, to get both of us? Isn't that all a bit Batman and Robin? So which one am I?'

Smith turned to him with a grin.

'With respect, guv, I'm too tall to be Robin.'

Chapter Eight

Gina Shaw followed Martin Jackson's mother into the hospital room where he was lying, attached to so many life-saving devices it was hard to see much of him. A nurse was just changing a drip and greeted them both with a warm smile.

'Hello again, Mrs Jackson. I'll just finish this, then I'll be out of your way. He's doing a bit better today, aren't you, Martin?'

Only a flicker of his eyelids showed that the youth was even aware of their presence in the room.

Mrs Jackson went to the bedside and bent over to plant a kiss on her son's face.

'Hello, darling. How are you today? Dad will be in later. This lady with me is a police officer. A detective. She needs to talk to you, if you can manage it.'

The nurse was finishing up as she said, 'He is a bit tired this morning, aren't you, Martin? But I'm sure you'll know when he's had enough. I'll pop back in a little while, to see how he's doing. If you need someone, just press the button there.'

Thelma Jackson motioned Gina forward, closer into Martin's limited field of vision, then told him, 'The lady's name is Detective Shaw. She just needs a few words.'

'Gina, Martin. My name's Gina. I know you're finding it a bit hard to speak, so if it's all right with you, can I ask you a few questions that just need a yes or a no? Make a gesture if it's easier for you, whatever you can comfortably manage.'

Both the young man's arms were in plaster, one of them to above the elbow. Slowly he twitched the thumb on the other hand in an attempt at an affirmative gesture.

'That's great, well done. Let me know if it gets too painful to do that, or if you get tired and want me to stop.

'So, was there anything about the car or anyone in it which you recognised?'

This time the thumb dropped. Not by much, but a clear sign in the negative.

'Thank you. Did you recognise the make or model of the car at all?'

Another drop of the thumb.

His mother put in, by way of explanation, 'Martin's never been all that interested in cars.'

'That's fine, Martin, don't worry. We have plenty of eyewitness testimony. I just wanted to know what you could remember.'

Martin was trying hard to make another movement. Keeping his thumb as still as he could, he managed to raise four trembling fingers, let them fall, them lifted them again, wincing at the pain and the effort it took.

Gina saw and understood immediately.

'It was a 4x4? That's great, Martin, thank you. And were you able to see anything of the occupants of the vehicle?'

Martin's heart monitor gave a beep at that point. His hand was now making almost convulsive movements to signal thumbs down, his head was attempting to move from side to side and his mouth was struggling to form a word.

'N-n-n-no,' he finally managed to force out.

The monitor was going wild now.

Martin's mother jumped to her feet and hurried to push the button as instructed, then went back to the bed, trying to reassure her son, speaking gently to him, stroking his hair.

The same nurse reappeared quickly, weighed up the situation at a glance, then said, 'I think that's enough for now, Mrs Jackson. Martin's looking a bit distressed. Why don't you go and have a cup of tea with your husband while I settle him down?

'I promise to come and find you when he's had a little rest and is up to seeing you again. But that's definitely enough questioning for today.'

Martin's mother made to leave the room, turning frequently to look back at him. Gina guided her gently out into the corridor heading towards the family room, not far away. She wanted to ask her a question, though, before they returned to the room to rejoin her husband.

'Mrs Jackson, clearly you know your son better than anyone. What did you make of his reaction when I asked if he'd recognised anyone?'

'He looked terrified,' the woman replied promptly. 'Scared to death, I would have said. Do you think he did see someone he knew? This JJ, or whatever their name is?'

'I don't know, but I think, based on his reaction – unless that was something purely medical – that it's a strong possibility.

'I can't promise anything, Mrs Jackson, and I don't want to get your hopes up, but I'm going back to the station now to speak to my inspector to see if it's at all possible to put an officer onto watching Martin's room. And also to try to see that there's no press speculation about what, if anything, he's been able to say to the police. Preferably even to suggest he can't currently tell us anything, for his own protection.'

The woman's hand flew up to her face in alarm.

'You think he might be in more danger? They might try to get at him in hospital to finish what they tried to do?'

'That's what I'm hoping to sort out with my inspector. Something to avoid any such risk. Try not to worry, Mrs Jackson. I promise I'm going to do everything I can to make sure Martin is properly protected.'

* * *

Ted had half hoped that the darkness might make Oscar Smith drive a bit more slowly and less erratically than his usual style. Especially as he insisted on not putting on the headlights, saying he didn't want to draw unwanted attention to their departure.

It added nothing to Ted's state of nervousness that Smith had had two large glasses of wine with his meal, insisting that would still leave him well under the legal limit, and in full possession of all of his faculties. Ted didn't know enough about the drink-drive laws in Germany to know if he was right.

Ted had told Smith before they drove off that he wanted to pay his hosts for their hospitality, so as not to leave them out of pocket, but he had cut him short.

'Don't do that, guv, you'll insult them. Rural folk are like that in any decent country. They always help anyone in need, no questions asked. They never think twice before doing so. And I did tell them how grateful you were, which they brushed off.'

'Well, I was more than grateful for their food and hospitality after one night down a badger sett and another one out in the damp forest.'

Before they'd eaten, Ted had borrowed Oscar's phone to call Superintendent Caldwell, to report to her in person. He was touched by the obvious relief in her voice at hearing him. He had no way of knowing she had tried to resign over his disappearance, for which she still blamed herself in no small measure. Knowing he was at least alive and seemingly well must have reassured her enormously.

'I am relieved to find you alive and unharmed, chief inspector,' she told him, setting the tone as formal, as ever. 'I look forward to your return soon and to hearing your full report on everything which has happened. I have recalled Inspector Rodriguez to cover in your absence, but he has his own team to lead.'

'I'll be back as soon as possible, ma'am. Clearly I first need to ensure that our suspect, Joel Hammond, is safely out of harm's way in case of any further attempts to secure his release. I will also need to give statements in connection with what I firmly believe was an attempt to kidnap me to use as a bargaining tool against Hammond. I'll keep you posted at all times, of course, ma'am.'

'See that you do, chief inspector.'

As Ted ended the call and handed back the phone, Oscar laughed.

'DCI Darling, that sounded suspiciously like a whopper you told your boss there about Hammond and his whereabouts, when you know full well I've already seen to that. Surely not?'

Ted's grin in response was sheepish.

'I think you must have misheard me, Oscar. As if I'd do any such thing.'

'Your secret's safe with me, guv.'

Oscar was concentrating on his driving now, before he

spoke again, swinging the car out onto the road at the far end of the track up to the farmhouse. He did at least put on the headlights once they were on a proper road. The last thing he wanted to risk was getting pulled over by local police for a traffic violation when neither he nor Ted felt inclined to trust any of them, given their experiences to date.

'As I said, I've booked us a hotel room for tonight. One room, two beds. In the circumstances, I thought it might be better that way then one of us can be awake at all times, in case anyone is on the lookout for either of us with the idea of paying us a little night-time visit.

'I've booked it in my name. My German name. There's plenty of Schmidts about, so that shouldn't raise any alarm. I've told McClintock we'll both see him for breakfast tomorrow and given him a neutral location to meet up. We'll need to get there early to see if it's safe or being staked out.

'I don't know the bloke but I have to say he's either a first class actor or he was genuinely relieved to hear that I'd located you and you were safe when I filled him in. Obviously I didn't mention where we were currently, nor where we would be staying tonight. And I still want some time to talk to those two scrotes who escorted you, before we even think of heading back to Blighty.'

'Oh, I fully intend to ask them some searching questions myself. You'll need to get in the queue, DI Smith.'

* * *

'You see the trouble is, bonny lad, that I don't actually believe a word you're telling me.'

Detective Constable Maurice Brown was interviewing one of the witnesses to the attack on Martin Jackson. Or trying to.

Sixteen-year-old Ian Hedges shifted about in his seat, clearly uncomfortable at his words.

Maurice's tone stayed pleasant enough, nothing overbearing or threatening. He needed this witness onside if he was to get anything useful from him. And he needed everything he could get on this one. Soft Daddy Hen was, as ever, deeply touched by the news of the attack on Martin Jackson, and how serious his injuries were.

Someone must have seen something of use to them, but it would take patient questioning and understanding, rather than anything heavy, to get it out of witnesses who would be understandably afraid of the consequences to themselves of talking to the police.

'I weren't there,' Hedges repeated stubbornly, for at least the fourth time since Maurice had started talking patiently to him.

Maurice and Gina Shaw had gone round to the teenager's house at a pre-arranged time. At least the youth had been there and they hadn't had to go looking for him.

They'd decided between them that Maurice should do the questioning. He was usually the one who could get something out of even the most reluctant of witnesses.

Maurice was talking to Ian in the presence of his mother. For all the use she was as a chaperone. She had the television on, the volume only down a notch or two so still clearly audible, and with her glued to some daytime soap or another.

'Yet two of your mates, who seem to know you, both claim that you were there during the attack, but that you ran off as soon as the first of the emergency service vehicles started to arrive.'

'I weren't there,' the youth said again.

'So where were you at the time? Do you have someone who can provide a reliable alibi for you?'

'I were here, all that night. Me mam can tell you that.'

The mother barely glanced in their direction as she said, ''S'right. He were here all night.'

'Which night was that, Mrs Hedges?' Maurice asked her. 'And how do either of you know the incident happened at night? I didn't mention the time of day. Nor what day we're talking about.'

The woman looked sufficiently disconcerted to shuffle in her seat and look towards the two of them.

'He did, didn't he, Ian?' she asked her son.

''S'right,' the son said in his turn. 'He did.'

'Trouble is, you see,' Maurice told them, pleasantly enough, 'I'm recording what you say, Ian. I did ask if that was all right and neither of you objected. I can play the recording back to you if you like, so you can check both things. I simply asked if you'd been present during the attack on Martin Jackson because I know you know him through sports.'

'It's been on telly, ain't it?' the mother put in, trying to dig them out of a self-inflicted hole.

'Fair enough, then,' Maurice told them, not believing a word of it but anxious not to waste time. 'So, Ian, your mam says you were home with her yet your two mates both say you were there and you saw the whole thing. Which is it? Because I know you know Martin, so I'm hoping you want to see justice for him.'

'So will we get witness protection, if our Ian tells you owt?' his mother asked, her mind clearly already running to thoughts of white sandy beaches under warm southern skies, far away from currently cold and wet Stockport.

'That's not up to me, Mrs Hedges. If you're thought to be in real danger you'd be put somewhere safe, though.'

He didn't tell her what the standard safe house looked like. He needed their cooperation and that would put them off, for sure.

He turned again to the son. He needed something, anything, to help take them forward.

'Come on, Ian. You know Martin's a good lad. He doesn't deserve any of this. And what he does deserve now, more than anything, is justice. There must be something you can tell me. Anything.'

Ian Hedges sat silent for a moment, looking from Maurice to his mother to the telly and back.

He couldn't be a bad lad, Maurice knew. He had no criminal record. He'd checked before visiting. A bit of truancy from school, but nothing much, and he was highly thought of at the sports clubs to which he belonged, though not quite at Martin's previous level. And he'd got himself a good placement as an apprentice electrician when he left school.

Eventually he sighed and said, 'I did see someone I recognised. JJ were there.'

* * *

Oscar Smith insisted on being at the appointed meeting place with Jock McClintock at least half an hour before the man was due to arrive. Ted was happy with that. Both of them wanted to make sure the coffee bar Smith had picked was not under observation, with a reception committee waiting to greet them and potentially whisk one or both of them away.

Ted had his woolly hat on, pulled down low, and Smith had lent him a fleece jacket. Way too big, but with the collar turned up, he would be barely recognisable from a distance. The early morning was chilly enough for him not to stand out dressed like that.

Smith was about to go and order coffees but Ted stopped him.

'Don't get me one yet. I don't want to be a sitting duck until I know for sure that Jock is coming on his own and everything seems to be on the level. Get your own and forget about me. I'll come and join you both if and when I think it's safe enough to do so.'

Then he melted soundlessly away.

Jock McClintock was early, as both men had suspected he would be. He was alone, and there was no sign of anyone else coming into the place at the same time who could be connected with him. No telltale vehicles lurking outside, either.

He greeted Smith politely enough and waited to be invited to sit down.

'It's a relief to hear you've found Ted safe and sound. Where is he?'

'He's behind you,' a voice said in his right ear, causing the man to nearly jump out of his skin.

'Jesus God, Ted, you always were the best on Mr Green's stealth courses and you've clearly not lost the touch. What on earth happened to you?'

Ted took a seat and motioned to McClintock to do the same.

'That's what we need to find out, Jock. Starting with you telling us exactly what you know about all of this.'

Chapter Nine

Once again the entire Serious Crime team leapt to their feet when Superintendent Debra Caldwell strode in, this time at the end of the day. Her face seldom gave anything away, but there was a noticeable lightness to her stride which raised hopes that there might possibly be some better news.

'Thank you everyone. Please be seated. First of all, the very good news. I have now spoken to DCI Darling who is well and unharmed but currently still stuck in Germany where he went to attend a case conference.'

A collective sound of relief went through the team members. Ted Darling was a popular boss. Definitely classified as firm, but fair.

'He was apparently the victim of an attempted kidnap, which he managed to foil, but he's had to keep a low profile until he was certain there was no further risk. In getting away from danger, he unfortunately broke his mobile phone, hence being out of contact.

'He is now safe in the company of DI Smith who went out to recover him, having finally had contact with him. As I mentioned before, DI Smith is a fluent German speaker, with contacts in the police over there. The two of them need some time to carry out enquiries about exactly what happened and why. They are also making arrangements to have our suspect from the rape and murder cases, Joel Hammond, who is currently being held in custody in

Germany, removed to a secure location to avoid him being snatched, so the DCI will not be returning immediately. But we at least know he is safe, and in the meantime DI Rodriguez will remain with us here to oversee things.

'Now, what progress on our ongoing cases? Are the files on the baby kidnap case fully up to date yet? And what news of this terrible hit and run? We need some progress on that to report to the press and media, not to mention to start to get some justice for the victim. DI Rodriguez?'

'Ma'am, too early to talk of a breakthrough, but we do now have two separate mentions of someone known as JJ, in connection with the attack.

'DC Shaw went to the hospital today to see what, if anything, she could get from Martin. Gina?'

'Ma'am, Martin was not able to give me much at all, although he did indicate that the vehicle which hit him was a 4x4, which fits with other witness evidence. When I asked him if he'd seen anyone in the vehicle he might have recognised, he became very distressed, his heart monitor was all over the place, and I had to discontinue questioning him and leave the room.

'His mother did then speak to me in confidence, away from the father. She told me Martin confides in her more than his dad. He'd mentioned someone he only knows as JJ who'd been harassing him, wanting him to run drugs, to sell to youngsters in the sports clubs he belongs to. He kept telling them to get lost, he wasn't interested.

'I'm going to see one of my old teammates in Drugs to see if the name, or perhaps the initials, JJ, mean anything. We might possibly get somewhere with that, although it's a long shot. The name doesn't immediately ring any bells with me from my time in Drugs but there are always new names popping up. Plus it sounds like a possible nickname, so I might have known the person by a full name, not that.'

'And ma'am, we went to talk to an eyewitness to the hit and run today,' Maurice Brown put in. 'He started off denying having been there at all, but finally admitted that he was, and he also mentioned this JJ person. He either didn't know, or wouldn't say if they're male or female, and couldn't or wouldn't give a description. That was about as much as I could get from him for one session, ma'am. I think if I spent a bit more time talking to him, he might just say more. His mam is already asking about witness protection and stuff.'

'Speaking of protection, ma'am,' Gina went on, 'both Mrs Jackson and myself were certain that Martin was terrified at the mere idea of trying to name anyone involved. For that reason, I wonder if we should have twenty-four-hour armed protection for him whilst he's in hospital. After all, it's been on the news that he's in hospital and it wouldn't take a genius to work out where he's been taken.

'In addition, perhaps we should at least consider putting out a statement to the effect he's not currently able to speak to us. That's essentially true, after all. He can't speak much at all, although he did try to communicate using the digits on one hand. Any attempt at actual speech sees him stammering with the effort.'

Jezza was sitting near enough to Gina Shaw to see some emotion she couldn't immediately identify pass across her face. She made a note to take her for a drink at some point to find out what might be troubling her.

'A very good point, DC Shaw. DI Rodriguez, please liaise with Firearms to provide an AFO watch on him round the clock until further notice.

'What else were either of you able to find out about this JJ which might help us? Ethnicity, distinctive marks? Anything at all.'

Gina and Maurice both shook their heads.

'Whoever the person is, ma'am, it seems clear that it's someone to be feared,' Maurice told her. 'Ian Hedges was bricking himself when he talked about JJ, and that seemed to be why he'd legged it from the scene, and why he lied about being there in the first place.'

DS Mike Hallam spoke up next, sensing that the Super was about to wind things up and leave.

'Ma'am, in connection with the baby Evie kidnap case. There's a potential spanner in the works, to put it mildly. I took a call earlier from Tony Taylor, DI Smith's DS from the Met. He tells me they have a warrant for our two suspects in custody, Georges and Beverley Williams. Their warrant is for suspected murder, so it trumps ours for accessories to the kidnap. DS Taylor was wanting to make arrangements for their transfer.

'I have to say, ma'am, he didn't sound all that happy about it.'

'I see,' she replied, in a tone which dripped with frost, in keeping with her nickname. 'Well, I have to talk to Superintendent Aird about the continued loan of DI Smith, which is clearly crucial in the current circumstances, so I will certainly bring this matter up with him.

'Thank you everyone. Good work today, and please keep me posted on any and all developments.'

* * *

'Sit down,' Smith told Jock McClintock, making it clear it

was an order not a request. 'And start by telling us why you sent the DCI off with dodgy cops with a remit to take him out, for whatever reason.'

'I didn't,' McClintock replied immediately, then he looked towards Ted as he went on, 'Ted, you know me better than that. I would never have set you up like that. Why would I?'

'For the money,' Smith put in, leaving Ted no time to say anything. 'Who else could it have been, other than you? From what Ted's told me, everything was on a strict need-to-know basis, so who else could have known he was going to be at that meeting, then needing a lift back to the airport?'

'That wasn't supposed to be the arrangement. Ted, you know that. I told you I'd personally collect you and take you back. It was just when the meeting ran on longer than anticipated that I needed to sort someone else out to drive you. How would I have had the time to set anything dodgy up, for one thing? I was in the meeting with you all day and it overran considerably.'

Smith was still on the offensive but Ted held up a hand to stop him. Strangely enough, it worked.

'How did you pick the officers you chose to transport me?' he asked him.

'I didn't, as such, it was pure chance. I know you don't speak German so I asked a mate of mine if he could find an officer who spoke English. Ulrich was walking past at the time, as we were talking. It was as random as that. Ulrich Meyer. Speaks excellent English, if accented, but that's because he's married to an American.

'I didn't have the time to fix up anything dodgy. You know that. I wasn't out of the meeting long enough, for one thing. And why would I? I thought we were mates, Ted. Old muckers, for sure, if nothing else.'

'I did wonder why you suddenly got in touch, after all this time, to bring me out here.'

'Ted, seriously?' McClintock asked him. 'Because I owe you one. A big one. I've never forgotten the time you half-carried me down from the top of the Beacons when I'd slipped and dislocated my knee. You certainly saved me from exposure, not to mention a massive bollocking from old Green. And you ruined your own overall score on the course to do it. I saw a way to repay that debt, at least in part, so I took it.'

Smith was looking at Ted in undisguised astonishment. The more he heard about him, the less he could reconcile it with the short, quiet man sitting next to him.

'All right, fair enough. So what do you know about this Ulrich Meyer? And what about the other officer in the car with him? If it wasn't you, then it must have been one or other of them. Or whoever you spoke to, to set up a driver.'

McClintock shook his head at the suggestion.

'He's someone I know almost as well as I know you, Ted. The one I spoke to to try to set something up. I can't imagine for a moment he's bent and on the take.'

Smith was clearly getting restless and frustrated. He'd have handled McClintock a lot harder if Ted hadn't been sitting there. He'd have hauled him halfway across the table by his throat by now.

Or perhaps not, come to think of it, he thought to himself. He was discovering that both the men he was sitting with were clearly made of much sterner stuff than he'd first thought. All this talk of SAS-type exercises in the mountains was leaving him uncertain as to what the two of them were capable of.

Then there was this mysterious bloke Green they both talked about, with an edge to their voices which spoke of more than a degree of respect for him, and probably a measure of fear. He'd hardly said enough words to him on the phone for Oscar to get any idea of the measure of the man. He remembered suddenly, with something of a jolt, that Green had told him to keep him posted about Ted, which he had not yet done. He'd get round to leaving a message on his answering service when he found the time.

Smith's phone rang even as he was thinking about phone calls. A masked number. He picked it up, in case it was either relevant or urgent. Uppermost in his mind with unexpected calls was always the one he dreaded most – the worst possible news of his Oma.

He nearly jumped out of his chair when a decidedly testy voice barked into his ear, 'Green. Sitrep. You were supposed to keep me posted. I don't like to be kept waiting.'

Smith surprised even himself by mumbling and stammering out a, 'Sorry, sir, I'm with him now, I'll put him on.'

He handed the phone to the DCI, mouthing as he did so, 'Green'.

He wasn't at all surprised to see both men straighten up slightly in their seats. Oscar determined to find out more about the mysterious man at the other end of the line. A lot more. And soon.

For himself, Ted was not remotely surprised at the sudden call. Green always had had the ability to display an uncanny way of knowing when he was being talked about, anywhere.

'Mr Green,' he began, his tone respectful.

'I gather you totally ignored me telling you to trust your first instincts and managed to walk yourself right into a trap.

Sloppy, Gayboy, very sloppy. You need more training, clearly. I'll check my diary and get back to you.'

Ted had time for no more than a meek, 'Yes, Mr Green,' before the line went dead. He handed the phone back to Oscar.

McClintock grinned at him across the table.

'Black mark from Green? Well, hopefully now you're remembering what we went through together at his hands, you'll accept I'm not the bad guy in all of this. So shall we all go together to see if we can talk to Ulrich Meyer and the other officer, to find out what they have to say for themselves? Do you want me to drive, or shall we go in your car, sir?' he asked Smith.

Ted cut in quickly before Oscar could reply.

'Yours, please, Jock, if you can get us back here to pick up the hire car afterwards.'

'I'll bring you both back myself. I'm not taking any chances of losing you again, Ted.'

* * *

It was definitely the right idea to get Jock to drive them, Ted decided. Although still on the fast side, at least his driving was far less aggressive than Smith's, so Ted wasn't constantly worried about arriving in one piece.

They started the journey in a charged silence. Ted wasn't sure if Oscar was sulking because things weren't going the way he would clearly have preferred them to, and he was not in charge of the situation. He hoped it might purely be that he was mulling over what he had learned to date, to see if it would advance them at all.

Jock McClintock used his phone hands-free to set up an

interview with the two officers who had been in charge of transporting Ted. Although he couldn't understand Jock's words, Ted got the gist of what was being said when he heard the name Ulrich Meyer being mentioned a couple of times.

He was assuming that Jock would not be trying to send an indication to whoever he was speaking to that he was not alone. To send some sort of warning in advance, but then ruled that out as pure paranoia. Despite his earlier doubts, despite the dressing down from Mr Green for carelessness, Ted still believed he could trust Jock. They'd been through too much together for anything other than that to be a possibility.

He smiled to himself, remembering all too well the effort of half-carrying the much heavier man down the mountain, against the odds. He still couldn't believe he'd done it, but they were a team, the two of them. It was a team-building exercise, in part, and times would only be counted if both men crossed the line together.

They'd had the slowest time of anyone, but Ted had at least had a nod of acknowledgement from Green for his superhuman efforts in finishing at all. A gesture as rare as hens' teeth.

Oscar Smith was clearly itching to find out about the obviously strong bond between the two men in the car with him. He'd done similar training to what Mr Green's seemed to involve during his military days, but it sounded as if they'd taken it to extremes he'd never needed to learn and had never felt inclined to volunteer for.

Eventually he asked, 'So who exactly is the mysterious Mr Green, if that's not classified info?'

Ted and Jock chuckled in unison. It was Ted who asked him, 'How's your Gilbert and Sullivan, Oscar? Mr Green has a lot of nicknames, and probably knows them all. Not much gets past him, at all. Probably the most fitting one is the Lord High Executioner, which should tell you all you need to know.'

Chapter Ten

As the team members were packing up at the end of the day, Jezza walked across to Gina's desk and told her, 'My detective skills tell me you're someone who's putting a brave face on a shit day. Fancy coming round to The Grapes and getting completely off our tits together?'

The way she phrased it was of itself enough to make Gina laugh out loud. It was so typically Jezza. She wouldn't have dared say it had the boss been anywhere around, though. He had incredible hearing and didn't approve of any such language in the workplace.

Jezza and Gina were not exactly close friends, but enough to show solidarity and to empathise after a difficult shift.

'Well, I've never had such an appealing invitation. It certainly beats going back to an empty flat and having a glass of wine or two and a ready meal in front of the telly, which was the best I was aspiring to.

'But what about you? Don't you have a nice man to go home to? Not to mention a younger brother who doesn't seem to like his routine changed, from what you've said.'

'Oh, I have my menfolk well trained,' Jezza assured her. 'If you're up for it, watch this.'

She called up a saved number on her mobile and when it was answered, fairly swiftly, she said, with a wink at Gina, 'Nat, sweetie, it's me. Sorry, working late again tonight. No idea how late, at the moment. There's plenty of food in the fridge. Will you be all right feeding yourself and Tommy until I get home?'

There was a pause as she listened, then said, 'I honestly don't know, it depends how things pan out, but it might be a late one, and we might go for a drink afterwards. I know it's a pain, but we might be on the brink of a breakthrough. Are you sure that's okay with both of you? And is Tom-Tom all right? Not being too obnoxious?

'Fabulous! Thanks so much. I promise to make it up to you when I get back.'

She listened again then gave a throaty laugh as she said, 'That too, if you're lucky.'

As she rang off, she grinned at Gina as she said, '*Voilà*! And just like that, it's sorted. I have a free pass for as long as necessary. The old drama training never lets me down.'

Gina was shaking her head in disbelief. She borrowed the boss's stock phrase when trying to call Jezza to order.

'DC Vine …'

'Right, let's leave our cars here, like sensible grown-ups avoiding a breath test, then go and get absolutely bladdered. I'm sure Dave will happily lend us the back room. After all, we might be damaging to his reputation in public, once we get going.'

'Oh, I do hope so,' Gina told her fervently. 'If we don't, we've not tried hard enough.'

It wasn't until after the third tequila slammer that Gina started to relax enough to talk. Dave, the landlord, had been more than happy to let them use the small room away from the public bar. He had a good working relationship with the local police. They were excellent customers and always behaved themselves. If the two DCs needed to let their hair down, away from the public eye, that was fine by him.

As a precaution, he'd got his wife Susan to make them some sandwiches, on the house. Something, at least, to soak up the worst of the alcohol. He looked on it as an investment, and suspected he wouldn't finish the evening out of pocket. He knew Jezza could outdrink many of her male colleagues once she got started and she had the look of someone determined to make a night of it.

'It was listening to Martin, stuttering while he was trying to speak to me. You know I had an older sister, Jenny, who disappeared when she was fifteen. She developed a stammer once she hit her teens and it got steadily worse. I don't remember it when we were much younger, but you know how awkward it can be, once we start to grow up a bit and our body does things we're not always as prepared for as we think. She was very self-conscious about stuttering, so she became more and more withdrawn and much less talkative.

'She was always so pretty, so clever, when she was growing up. Full of self-confidence. She was going to take on the world. She wanted to go into medical research when she was older, and she could have done it, too. She was certainly intelligent enough. She chose that because she had a best friend, growing up, with a genetic condition which was life-limiting, and she was determined to find the cure for it.

'Then everything changed, almost overnight. All the confidence went. She hardly spoke and when she did, she struggled to say anything without stammering. Her schoolwork suffered, too.

'Our parents tried taking her to see various experts, but Jenny hated that. She wouldn't cooperate so it was all a bit pointless. She barely spoke to anyone, even me, any more, and we used to be close. Then one day, when she was about fifteen, she'd been for her extra coaching sessions as normal, then came back home with my father as she always did. But by the following morning, she'd disappeared without trace. I've never heard from her since. Nor have my parents. Nothing.

'My parents did everything they could to find her. Press appeals, posters, all the things you would expect.'

Dave appeared, without being summoned, with another round for them. He was keeping a tally on their bar bill. He knew they'd tell him when to stop bringing refills.

Jezza knocked back her latest shot in one. It barely touched the sides. Her voice became serious as she spoke again.

'You realise, don't you, that what you're describing is a typical pattern of behaviour for a sexual abuse victim. Especially a victim of incest.'

It was Gina's turn to toss her drink back, but hers made her shudder and then sneeze.

'I did wonder about that. Not at the time, of course. I was too young to know what it was all about. But later. Certainly since I joined the police. I never did pluck up the courage, even as an adult, to ask either my mother or my father if that could have been a possibility. Especially my father. I thought the world of him. How could I ask him if he'd raped his own daughter?

'My parents kept saying they were sure Jenny had "got in with the wrong crowd" – their words – and it was all to do with drugs. That's why I went into Drugs in the first place. To try to find her, or at least uncover what was behind her disappearance. But I never have.'

Jezza took a bite of the nearest sandwich and finished

chewing it before she spoke again. Her tone was matter-of-fact, almost casual. Stating a fact, nothing more nuanced than that.

'My father raped me.'

Gina reached out a hand and took hold of one of Jezza's, tears springing to her eyes.

'Oh, god, Jezza, I am so, so sorry. I didn't mean to dredge up any bad memories. I had no idea.'

Jezza squeezed her hand back as she said, 'It's fine. You had no way of knowing. I don't exactly broadcast it. My early sex life is not really much of a glowing success story. The next man, after my father, was a knife-wielding maniac serial rapist.'

At that Gina abandoned all thought of food and drink, leaned forward and enveloped Jezza in a big hug, her own tears mixing with the ones which Jezza, caught for once with her guard right down, shed herself.

They stayed that way in silence for a couple of minutes before Gina spoke again.

'I really had no idea, and I can't imagine how you pulled yourself back from that.'

With her face still buried against Gina's neck, Jezza said, 'I did it by sleeping with Maurice.'

Gina pushed her gently away to arms' length so she could see her face as she replied.

'Maurice? Shut up! You didn't. Did you?'

Jezza's tears were turning to laughter now as she said, 'I did, and it was the best thing ever. He's my very best friend and he was so sweet and kind. He restored my faith in men.'

The next time Dave appeared to check on drinks levels, he found the two women, laughing hysterically, arms wrapped round one another, as they danced away to Katy

Perry's 'I kissed a girl and I liked it' blaring at high volume from Jezza's mobile.

Dave withdrew discreetly. He was used to coppers letting their hair down and as long as they didn't break anything, he was fine with that. And he wasn't about to say a word to anyone about whatever he might see or hear from off-duty officers. He remembered 'no names, no pack drill' from his military days and stuck to it religiously.

* * *

Jock met up first with the person he'd been talking to at the police building to which he'd driven them. Introductions were made, hands shaken all round. The man was in plain clothes and was introduced as a *Kommissar*, by the name of Hoffmann, which Ted took to be around Inspector equivalent.

Jock, whose German seemed to be almost as good as Oscar's, from what Ted could judge, told him that initially the interviews with Ulrich Meyer, and the driver of the vehicle, carried out separately, would be informal, as a means of information gathering. He also stressed that the three of them were there as a courtesy, to try to clear up any misunderstanding. They had no authority of any kind.

Ted was the only person present who didn't speak German. He was there as a guest so it wasn't up to him to set the rules. He was happy to accept the suggestion of holding the meeting in German, with Oscar translating for him.

They headed for an interview room where there was recording equipment, but not set up for use. Ulrich Meyer was sitting, seemingly totally relaxed, in a chair at the side of the table furthest from the door. He snapped smartly up to attention and greeted the *Kommissar* deferentially before turning to Ted with a disarming smile. He spoke to him in English.

'Hello, again, sir. I'm relieved to see you're fine. I was worried when I heard you hadn't returned to your hotel from your walk in the woods.'

Oscar Smith translated the words for the *Kommissar* then said something in German to Meyer in a sharp tone, which left Ted in no doubt that the man's card had been marked for him, and he'd been brought to heel.

They took their places. The layout was informal, to match the tone of the meeting. Smith made a point of sitting directly opposite Meyer so he had direct eyes on him all the time. Jock McClintock sat next to the officer, Ted and the *Kommissar* took a side seat each.

Meyer was asked to give his account about what had happened to Ted. Oscar translated simultaneously for Ted, who hoped he could trust him not to be too liberal in his interpretation. He felt confident that Jock would jump in quickly enough if he strayed too far from what was actually being said.

'He says that they had to take a detour to the airport because of a reported RTA, which will be easy enough to check out. They stopped on the way when they saw a car, apparently broken down. They explained to you that they were obliged to check for immediate danger, which they got out to do, leaving you in the car, the rear doors of which were unlocked, at your request.

'When they returned to the car, they found you had gone but had left your bag behind. They tried to find you by walking into the forest and calling your name, but they couldn't see or hear you anywhere. They decided you must have gone for a walk, but they didn't have time to wait any longer, so they took your bag to the airport hotel for you, which wasn't far away, to save you carrying it.'

The *Kommissar* posed a question of his own at that point, which Oscar translated for Ted.

'He's asking why the officers didn't follow up later to make sure you did actually make it to the hotel safely, by phoning there, or leaving a message for you to phone them on your return. Which is a reasonable question, after all.'

Even without understanding a word of what he was saying, Ted had the feeling that Meyer's answer was glib and convincing none of those present.

'He says they got another shout to go somewhere else, which is again easy enough to check, and by the time they got back from that, they were going off duty and didn't think any more about it.'

At that point Oscar spoke himself, addressing the *Kommissar* in a respectful tone which surprised Ted. Then he told Ted, 'I mentioned to him that where I picked you up from was nowhere near the airport hotel, certainly not within easy walking distance, even allowing for the distance you'd walked to get to the farm. So I queried how they thought you were going to get yourself there, on foot, in a country where you don't speak the language.'

Ulrich Meyer spoke rapidly at that point, clearly replying to what Oscar had said.

'He says it wasn't all that far and you could have easily walked it, across country. But then he is clearly a lying bastard who wouldn't know the truth if it bit him on the arse.'

The volume of Oscar's voice went up considerably as he said the last part. Ted's eyes were locked onto Meyer's face, watching for his reaction. It was clear the words had hit a nerve. It seemed as if he'd been hoping to wing it in the interview. He was doubtful that he'd expected to encounter the throw-the-rule-book-out-of-the-window interview techniques of the Met officer.

Oscar had risen half out of his seat as he addressed Meyer, hands on the table between them, leaning forward on his arms, latent menace in his posture.

Even the *Kommissar* reacted, in a way which suggested he might possibly understand at least enough English to get the gist of what had been said. Although the tone and the posturing had probably told him much of what he needed to know.

He also got to his feet, snapping out something to Smith which he didn't bother to translate. Oscar was too busy trying to out-glare Meyer.

Ted still didn't entirely know what, if any, authority he had, but someone needed to take control of Oscar before he thumped Meyer, or anyone who tried to stop him doing so.

He stayed seated, keeping his voice even quieter than usual as he said, 'I think it would be best if everyone sat down, calmed down, and stuck to facts. DI Smith? Sit down, please. Personal attacks are not helpful in this instance.'

For a moment, he thought Smith was going to ignore him and carry on in the same manner. Ted had no idea of what he would do if he did. He wasn't sure he had any authority over the Met officer here, especially as the man was a German citizen.

Another thing which was clear to him was that Meyer was not going to deviate from the yarn he was spinning them, whatever threats he faced. They might as well stop, put Meyer where he couldn't talk to or even contact anyone else, and let him stew for a while, until they had talked to the driver and heard his version of events.

No doubt he was going to spin them exactly the same story, so Ted had a feeling they were going to get nowhere with the whole thing, for lack of concrete proof. His complete lack of understanding in German could possibly have been the cause of a major misunderstanding, although he didn't believe that for a minute. Harmless enough of itself. Besides, he needed to get back home, for so many reasons. It was getting time to draw a line under things.

As long as Joel Hammond was in a secure new location, known to as few people as possible, that would have to do, until Ted heard whether or not his poker hand had sufficed to get their suspect extradited back to Britain. Although clearly that was not going to happen overnight, and there would be a forest worth of paperwork before it could happen at all.

Another valuable lesson Ted had learned at the hands of Mr Green. Pick your battles, and don't waste time or effort on ones doomed to failure. Even if it went totally against the grain to give a bent copper a free pass.

Chapter Eleven

Despite a banging head and a mouth as dry as sandpaper, Gina Shaw somehow managed to be at her desk early, having taken a taxi, arriving before anyone else was in. She'd lost count of how much she'd had to drink the night before but was sure she'd still blow positive.

She hadn't had chance before heading to The Grapes to phone any of her former colleagues from Drugs to ask about JJ as she'd intended. Jezza had seen to that. But the evening had turned out to be a great idea. Just what they both needed. Now Gina wanted to get the task done early on so she might at least have a lead to offer up at morning briefing.

'Where have you come across JJ?' was the first response to her initial question. 'Because we keep hearing them mentioned but we're buggered if we can find out anything much about them.'

'Them?'

Even the hangover from hell didn't stop Gina from picking up on the ambiguous pronoun and pouncing on it.

'Does that mean you don't know if the person who goes by that name is male or female?'

Her question raised a chuckle.

'Still sharp on detail, I see. Despite sounding as if you've been out on the piss half the night, even by this time in the morning.'

Gina groaned, then rather wished she hadn't.

'God, is it as obvious as that? I feel like death warmed up and I swear my tongue is bigger than it used to be. I don't know what possessed me. I was led astray.'

More laughter from the other end of the conversation, forcing Gina to hold her phone further away from her ear to spare her pounding head.

'Okay, quick round up of what we do know about JJ. Bugger all, in effect. Androgynous. Is that the word? Bit early in the morning for me and big words. No one seems to know for sure if it's a male or a female. Shaved head, piercings, tatts. Skinny as a rake so no one's sure if they have tits or not. Hardly ever speaks. But seems to put the fear of god up anyone who encounters them.

'Well in with the drugs crowd, but we're not yet sure to what extent. A foot soldier rather than top of the hierarchy, we think. Certainly always where the action is, especially the dirty stuff, but vanishes in a puff of smoke every time we get close. We've certainly never nicked them and can't find any record on anyone who fits the profile, so clearly no one else has either.

'They don't seem to dirty their own hands with anything physical. Maybe the odd kicking or two. But they seem to be someone who only needs to whistle and the gang's hard men appear in a flash, so they must have some clout. More like a runner, something like that, and a recruiter of other pushers, but clearly an important one.

'Right, I've scratched yours, you scratch mine by telling me what your interest is and what you know. If it's Drugs related, it would help us both to share and pool ideas.'

Gina had made herself some paint-strippingly strong black coffee as soon as she'd arrived in the office, to follow up on what she'd already drunk first thing. She had a couple of swallows of it, winced, then continued.

'You'll have heard of the near-fatal RTC on our patch, and, knowing you lot, will have picked up the hint of a possible drugs connection. The victim, Martin Jackson, is in a bad way. Bad enough for the collision to be treated as attempted murder.

'He's not capable of saying much at the moment, even if he wanted to, and it seems he's terrified to even try. But his mother told me he'd previously confided in her that he was being pestered by someone called JJ to run drugs for some gang or another. And one of our DCs, who could get anyone to tell him anything, got an eyewitness to say that he'd seen someone known as JJ at the site of our RTC. No more details yet, but our man, Maurice, is going round there again today to see what else he can persuade the lad to offer up.

'We're working on the likelihood that the hit and run was a reprisal on Martin for refusing their advances to him, and/or a reminder that he needed to keep quiet about anything he knew, or thought he knew, if he wasn't prepared to play along with them and their dirty tricks.

'The eyewitnesses we have – those who aren't suffering from convenient amnesia – all say the vehicle involved was a black 4x4 …'

There was a loud snort down the phone at that, which produced another low groan from Gina as it ricocheted around her already suffering skull.

'Well, that narrows it down to pretty much any drugs gang in the country! They're the must-have accessory. No make or model? Nothing of any practical use?'

'Nothing, and getting that was like drawing teeth, all the interviewing officers are saying.'

'Just watch yourself, Gina. The lot we know this JJ hangs

111

around with are some of the nastiest. It sounds as if we – or our respective teams, at least – would do well to work together on this one. You can keep your RTC, we're not interested in that, but if we pool resources on the actual drugs angle, it could be in both our interests.

'I'll talk to my boss here, you talk to yours, and let's see about having a liaison meeting between us asap. Two lots of minds are always better than one.

'Meanwhile, get plenty of water down yourself before you try to do any proper work.'

* * *

The interview with the driver of the car which had picked up Ted, supposedly to take him to the airport, was a carbon copy of what Ulrich Meyer had said to them, in almost every respect.

The man seemed relaxed and at ease; sure of himself, although he did wait for permission from *Kommissar* Hoffmann before taking a seat.

The senior German officer began with another reminder that the interviews were informal, of no legal standing, simply done in a spirit of cooperation. Similar standards would, however, be applied as for anything formal. He looked hard at Oscar as he said that, and Ted noticed that he asked Jock to translate his words into English for Ted's benefit. He clearly had the measure of Smith already and didn't trust him not to make light of what he was saying.

The driver's name was Tobias Becker and, even without knowing the language, Ted could tell he was spinning much the same story as Ulrich Meyer had done, looking completely at ease and comfortable with the script he was following.

Oscar was translating again, making a visible effort to stick to the facts. Hoffmann was watching him closely for any sign of intimidation, making Ted wonder again if he spoke at least some English.

Becker also smiled pleasantly at Ted and said how relieved he had been to hear that he was safe after the unfortunate misunderstanding which had occurred.

Hoffmann was clearly a shrewd judge of character, or perhaps he knew the men, or their reputations, because he questioned the driver himself, at some length. Probing, countering every glib reply, constantly wanting to know the whys and wherefores of everything.

Why, when they'd discovered the English officer had left the vehicle and wasn't immediately visible, had they not radioed in with a sitrep? With a missing passenger, why had they not made contact to say they might be delayed whilst they looked for him? Why had they even left the scene, with a visiting British senior officer unaccounted for and possibly lost in a forest?

Becker's body language was becoming increasingly uncomfortable. His antiperspirant was letting him down, too. There was a rank smell starting to emanate from him as the questioning went on and became ever more intense.

Ted waited for the briefest lull in the questioning then addressed Hoffmann in a respectful tone, still unsure of which of them held the senior rank, and what formalities were like with the German police.

'May I please be allowed to ask a question at this point, sir?'

He vaguely recognised the words '*bitte schön*' in reply

from hearing Trev speaking German on holidays together, and certainly the accompanying hand gesture was an unmistakeable invitation to proceed.

'Officer, is the place where you stopped because of the car at the side of the road a known comms black spot? Somewhere there is no mobile phone signal? Because there was none for my phone in the back of the car, certainly. Almost as if something was jamming any signal.'

Before he translated, Oscar turned to Ted and said, 'Well, that's bollocks, as I told you when I picked you up, guv. I came in on that road, the long way round, like I said, because Emil said it was easier to find the way to the farm from that direction. He was right, too. And I didn't lose signal.'

Jock seamlessly took over the translation as Oscar was speaking. Hoffmann's eyes narrowed, hearing what was being said, but he didn't comment.

Becker was stammering out something which, even before it was translated for him, Ted could tell was a load of old rubbish, simply by looking at Hoffmann's reaction.

'He says the reception in that area can be a bit patchy sometimes,' Oscar translated, in a voice dripping in scorn, then went on, 'Which, as I have said, was not my experience at all. But perhaps the patchy reception only affected the inside of the police car you were in.'

Jock obligingly translated his aside for the benefit of Hoffmann.

They were clearly not going to get anything more from Becker, who was sticking resolutely to the same script as Meyer had used. Hoffmann dismissed him curtly, and the driver scuttled out of the room, in obvious relief.

As soon as he'd left the room, Oscar spoke first, in German, to Hoffmann, letting Jock translate his words for Ted.

'I don't believe a word either of them said. Especially as it was too perfectly the same. One of them knows something. My guess is Meyer is the brains. One or other of them clearly knew somehow what, and particularly who, the meeting was about. But Meyer must have known who to contact with his information, and at short notice, which means he had the contacts already in place. My money's on him being the one behind all of this.'

'But you have now had your suspect moved to a safe location?' Hoffmann queried. 'Am I permitted to know where?'

The three men sitting with him exchanged loaded glances. By silent agreement Ted, as the ranking officer, told him, 'With the greatest respect, *Kommissar*, it might perhaps be better to keep that knowledge to the three of us for now. But thank you for your help and cooperation, which is much appreciated.

'Myself and DI Smith should now return to UK as soon as possible, but DS McClintock can liaise on our behalf, I'm sure. Thank you for your cooperation.'

The four men stood up, Hoffmann extending his hand first to Ted then the others as he said in reasonable, though accented, English, 'Excuse me for my officers. They will be disciplined.'

Ted dearly wished he could respond in kind, but the best he could manage was a mumbled, '*Danke schön*'.

As the three men walked out of the building, Jock turned to Ted to ask, 'So you don't think it was me any more? The one who fitted you up?'

'After listening to those two, I'm satisfied they had more than a little to do with it,' Ted told him.

Jock laughed at that.

'Wasn't your degree in Politics? That's a politician's answer, if ever I heard one.'

Jock turned to Oscar as he said, 'What about you, sir? Do you still think I'm behind it?'

'My jury's still out,' Smith told him. 'So it's probably just as well Ted and I need to get the next available flight back.'

* * *

'Bloody hell, bonny lass, don't breathe on the poor lad or he'll be too drunk to question,' Maurice Brown told Gina Shaw as she slid into the passenger seat of the car they were using to go back to speak to Ian Hedges once more.

'Sorry, is it as bad as that?' Gina asked him, reaching in her bag for yet another mint to try to disguise the alcohol fumes which had clearly not yet left her to the extent she had hoped.

'I was seriously led astray last night by a certain Jezza Vine and a succession of tequila slammers.'

Maurice chuckled as he pulled the car out of the parking area and onto the road.

'There's no stopping Jezza when she's in that kind of a mood.'

Gina felt suddenly uncomfortable, now she knew the history between them. She did a rapid but hopefully seamless change of subject.

'Do you think we'll get anything useful out of Ian? Anything more than he's already told us?'

'Hard to say. He's edgy, for sure, and by the sound of this drugs lot, I can't say I blame him.'

'My contact in Drugs has said they've heard of JJ but have no idea who it is, and the only word on the street, apart from no one seeming to know if they're male or female, is that they're not to be messed with. They may only be one of the troops, not an actual boss, but they certainly have a high enough ranking in the hierarchy to be able to order up swift and unpleasant retribution on anyone who crosses them. And I'm not talking about a few slaps, from what I've heard.'

Gina had relayed everything she'd been told by her contact at morning briefing, led again by Jo Rodriguez. She'd also raised the suggestion that they should work with Drugs on a possible joint operation, including trying to track down JJ as a priority.

Maurice mentioned again the mother's desire for a cast-iron guarantee of witness protection before the son would tell them anything.

'That would need clearance from higher up,' Jo told them. 'I'll go and talk to Superintendent Caldwell after we've finished here to update her, to see what, if anything, can be worked out for them.

'Gina, if you and Maurice are going straight from here, I'll phone you with an update if there is anything we can offer them. Let's hope they don't set their sights unrealistically high with what they're expecting.

'Meanwhile, we need to find out anything we can about this JJ. Who they are, where they're from, if there's anything at all on the system about them. Steve …'

'On it now, sir,' Steve Ellis replied, already glued to his computer as his fingers flew over the keys.

* * *

'Well, I can see why the mother is hoping for an upgrade to somewhere a bit more salubrious. I'd forgotten quite how grim this place is,' Gina commented, as Maurice pulled up outside the house where the Hedges lived. Mother and son. When Maurice had asked whether there was a Mr Hedges on the scene, the mother had scoffed a response.

'Never married any of 'em, and the one I think was our Ian's dad buggered off as soon as 'e heard there were a sprog on the way. Better off wi'out 'im.'

'So can we come in and talk to Ian again?' Maurice asked her, as she stood in the front doorway, blocking their entrance.

'Not 'ere is 'e? Little bugger got right scared about talking to you lot, once he'd had time to think about it. He knows too much, but he never told me about any of it, so it's not worth asking me. He's took his phone and a few clothes in his backpack so it looks like 'e's fucked off completely.'

Chapter Twelve

Jock McClintock drove Ted and Oscar straight back to the airport after their interviews were finished.

Oscar had managed to secure the last two seats on an evening flight via Amsterdam which would get them into Manchester Airport at ten o'clock. Later than Ted would have liked but it was better than the alternative which was to spend the night in a hotel and fly out first thing the following day.

Ted wanted the chance to talk to Jock alone before he left. He still had a lot of unanswered questions. Oscar was happy enough to go off in search of his favourite brand of schnapps, leaving the two men to talk over hot drinks.

'Sorry about Oscar, Jock. Being with him is like being in a time warp, back to the seventies. I was surprisingly pleased to see him coming to my rescue, though. An unlikely knight in shining armour.'

Jock laughed as he said, 'If either of us saw that character in a book or on telly we'd say he was too far-fetched for the twenty-first century. How long have you got him for?'

'I've honestly no idea. Nor do I know who's picking up the tab for his expenses in riding to my rescue. I'll let his Super and mine fight over that.

'So, Joel Hammond. You've got him somewhere safe now, but what does the future hold? Do you think we will get him sent back to UK, and how long will it take for a decision to be reached? It seems obvious that Meyer and Becker were involved in trying to get me out of the way. I didn't find either of them remotely convincing, even without understanding them and relying on translation.'

Ted paused for a drink of his hot chocolate. He'd felt the need of something warming and sweet.

'What I'm not sure of is what my intended fate was. They must surely have known that killing me would make no difference to the various charges against Joel Hammond, in different countries. And they surely can't be naive enough to imagine they could have traded me against Hammond's release. That sort of rubbish would only occur in a particularly bad book or TV series.'

Jock took a swallow of his black coffee before replying, 'This probably sounds daft, Ted, but are you sure this kidnap attempt, or whatever it was, was connected to the Joel Hammond case? Could that be simply a smokescreen and someone is after you for something else?'

'Oh, come on, Jock. That really is into the realms of the worst crime fiction scenario possible. I make a rare and practically spur of the moment trip to Germany and someone not involved in the case I'm here for finds out about it and tries to take me out?

'Besides, I'm a DCI, in Serious Crime. You know as well as I do that's mostly a management and admin post these days. I have little to no say in any decisions on arrests and prosecutions. Certainly not ones requiring extradition from another country.'

'You're right, of course, I'm clutching at straws here.'

Jock was looking off in the direction Oscar Smith had gone in search of his purchase.

'And Smith. How much do you trust him? I know he

came out to find you, but could he have been involved in the botched kidnap in the first place, and playing a clever game to cover up when it went wrong?'

'Trust him? Not even as far as I could throw this paper serviette. I'd certainly never turn my back on him. But unless he has someone on the inside, he can't have known where I was going or what for. And if it was him, why come and rescue me? I'd given him directions to where I was, after all. Why not send his contacts, whoever they might be, to finish the job they'd started and bungled?

'To be honest, Jock, none of it makes any sense to me.'

'I didn't want to say any of this in front of DI Smith, Ted, because I trust him even less than you do. But now I've got you here safely and you've got a flight, I'm going to go back and pull all the strings in my possession, call in every single favour I'm owed, and get your man Hammond shipped back to UK asap.

'I'm pretty sure, when I've had a word in a few of the right ears, the German authorities are going to want him off their hands in record time. These things usually take forever and a day, but I'd bet good money they'll want to play pass the parcel with him before the ink's dried on the mountain of paperwork it always takes.'

Jock drained his coffee cup and got to his feet, Ted mirroring his action.

'It's been good to see you again, Ted. Really. I'm sorry about what happened to you, and I hope you really do believe I wasn't involved.

'I'm sure you will anyway, but I'd watch out for Smith, if I was you. Not someone I'd want to turn my back on, for sure, for fear of getting a knife in it. Figuratively, if nothing else.'

Ted laughed at that.

'Mr Green already gave me a bollocking for coming over here with not enough of a risk assessment.'

That made Jock chuckle and he said, in a fair imitation of Green's distinctive accent, 'Sloppy, Gayboy, sloppy.'

'He's threatening to summon me for some update training. Be careful he doesn't decide to rope you in too.'

'Oh, bloody hell! You and me back on the Beacons together with him, after all this time. Now that would be something, eh?

'Take care, Ted, and I'll do my best for you with Hammond. Oh, and give my love to DI Smith.'

He said it with a wink as he turned and left the airport terminal.

* * *

Maurice and Gina went straight to find Jo Rodriguez when they got back from their fruitless visit to see Ian Hedges. Jo was in the office he was sharing with DS Mike Hallam, who was out of the building somewhere. Jo had clearly recently made a brew for himself and indicated the still steaming kettle, gesturing to the two of them to sit down. It was a golden rule on Ted's team. No one, not even the DCI himself, was above brewing up for other members.

'We drew a blank with Ian. It seems as if he's legged it, according to his mother,' Maurice told him.

'Let's get him reported as a misper, then, straight away. We need to talk to him, and clearly, alone and on the run, he's made himself even more vulnerable, if any of the gang get wind that the police are looking for him,' Jo replied.

'It's going to be a tricky one,' Maurice told him, adding

a 'ta' as a hot cup of tea appeared in front of him. 'If we make it known we're looking for him, there's a risk someone from the gang, possibly even this JJ him or herself, will guess why and start looking, too.'

'Any word from the Super about a liaison with Drugs on this one?' Gina asked him.

'I've not been able to get time with her at all yet today. She's been in and out of meetings all day but she has said she'll catch up end of play without fail. It's clearly our best way forward on this one, and I can't see her objecting. But I'm only keeping the boss's seat warm. I don't want to make executive decisions in case there are reasons against that I don't know about.'

'Any news of the boss?' she went on. 'When he's likely to be coming back? Not that I think you aren't doing a good job in his absence,' she finished hurriedly.

Jo laughed as he said, 'No worries, Gina, no offence taken. A quick phone call earlier to say he's fine, he's with DI Smith but they're unlikely to be back until late tonight or tomorrow morning, depending on when they can get a flight.

'For now, finish your drinks, talk to Inspector Turner about getting Uniform and especially PCSOs to ask all their contacts in the areas round where Ian lives or hangs out and to report any sightings of him, but keep it as low key as possible. Then get back out there and see if you can find him before JJ or anyone else does.

'Maurice, you're good at talking to people. Someone, somewhere must know something, and you're the sort to convince them it's in the lad's best interest if we find him before the gang does. Before he ends up under the wheels of another black vehicle-turned-weapon.'

Ian Hedges' mother hadn't proved to be of much use

when Maurice had been asking her earlier where she thought her son might have gone. They'd asked for his mobile phone number and that had taken her enough of an effort to find. She hadn't seemed to be deliberately obstructive, simply not all that interested in her son and his whereabouts.

They'd tried the phone several times without success. Gina had asked for a location check on it but it was currently not in use.

The mother had also struggled to find a photo of Ian to help with locating him. The only one in the house seemed to be a school one from at least a couple of years earlier, taken on a sports day when he'd won a prize for a sprint race, his mother told them.

Gina's look towards Maurice at that point spoke volumes. All the team knew Maurice was not much of a sprinter, and Gina knew she herself wasn't on top form currently. If they located him at all, they'd need to use all their persuasion to stop him from doing a runner, which would almost certainly mean them losing him.

Mrs Hedges professed to know little of her son's friends and likely hangouts. She even struggled to give them much information on how he spent his days.

'At Ian's age, he is required to be in some form of education or training, Mrs Hedges,' Gina told her patiently. 'You know he's left school, you told us that, so you must know how he's fulfilling that requirement, which is also your legal responsibility to ensure, as his mother.'

'I know he goes training somewhere,' she responded vaguely. 'Something with 'lectrics, he said. 'Not sure if he said for houses, like, or maybe motors. He likes cars and stuff, does Ian.'

Maurice tried to keep any judgement out of his voice as

he spoke to her, but he was having difficulty understanding any mother taking so little notice of her son's welfare. He took his own responsibility as a father seriously, and always had done, even after the break-up of his marriage.

'We need to find him, Mrs Hedges. He could be in danger. It looks like he may possibly have got in with the wrong crowd. But even if he's gone on the run, they'll probably find him and that could be very serious.'

It crossed Maurice's mind as he spoke that the woman would have shown more of a reaction if he'd pulled the plug on the telly she was yet again glued to as he tried to speak to her. Then he pulled himself up short. He had no idea what had gone on in her life to make her seem so uncaring. He wanted to give her the benefit of the doubt, but a young boy's life – her son's – could well be in serious danger unless they found him, and soon.

She turned her head from the screen to look at him at those words, frowning in concentration.

'Somewhere up Wellington Road, he goes. To do this leccy stuff. I remember that. He might have gone there, I suppose.'

Gina tried not to roll her eyes. Apart from being unprofessional, she knew it would hurt too much to do so in her current state.

'Wellington Road North, or South, Mrs Hedges?'

'Now you're asking. I get the two mixed up.'

She mentioned a pub name and with a sigh of relief, Gina said, 'South. Thank you, Mrs Hedges. We'll go and look for him along there. Here's my number. Be sure to let us know if you hear anything from him. It's really important.'

126

* * *

'Have you got a car here, or will we need a taxi?' Ted asked Oscar as the two men headed for the exit at Manchester airport, shortly after landing, on time. He knew from Oscar that Trevor had driven his car back to the nick to save a big bill or getting it clamped for being in the wrong section, not knowing how long Ted was going to be away.

'Taxi. They wouldn't let me have a service vehicle because I didn't know how long I was likely to be. Or perhaps that was an excuse because they don't trust my driving.

'And you are going to go straight home, aren't you, guv? No sneaking into the office for a catch-up and staying there half the night? I faithfully promised your Trevor I'd see you went straight back.'

'I'm only going there to pick my car up. Can I drop you at your lodgings, while I'm mobile and you're not?'

'You're all right, guv. I need the exercise. You get off back to Trevor and all your pussy cats.'

There was an awkward moment between the two of them when the taxi dropped them off at the police station, before they parted. Ted was acutely aware of how grateful he was to the man, but uncertain of how to express it in a way which would not leave either of them feeling uncomfortable.

Ted stuck his hand out to shake the other man's.

'Thanks, Oscar. I appreciate all you've done for me. Well over and above the call of duty.'

'No worries, Ted. I have a few things to tie up over the weekend, then I suppose I'd better be heading back down south. I'll see you before I go, though. Safe home.'

With that, he melted into the darkness, walking at a good

clip, while Ted got into his car and headed home to Offerton.

Trev had clearly been looking out for Ted's return. He was on the doorstep waiting for him, when he'd driven in through the garage doors, which were open in inviting welcome, then parked up and closed and locked the doors behind him.

He walked into a bone-crushing hug from his partner which nearly knocked him off his feet with its intensity. Curious feline eyes were looking out to see who was about to enter their territory.

'God, Ted I have missed you so much! I was worried sick wondering what had happened to you.

Ted hugged him back wordlessly. It felt good to be back home, at last.

'Are you all right? Really all right? Are you hungry? There's enough food for an army. I wasn't sure if you'd have eaten.'

Trev reverted straight into nurture mode. Now he knew Ted was safe, he wanted to take care of him.

'I've snacked a bit on the way, but I could manage a bit of something.'

Trev was leading the way into the kitchen, the two of them now surrounded by cats weaving in and out of legs, making progress perilous. Ted paused to stroke each one, briefly, then sat down thankfully in his usual chair whilst Trevor busied himself putting things together for a light meal for both of them.

'I've not eaten much myself. I was so relieved to hear you were on your way safely I couldn't settle.'

Full plates appeared as he sat down opposite Ted.

'I honestly can't believe how nice and kind Oscar was to me, after the things you'd said and hinted about him. He couldn't have been nicer or more helpful. I want to invite him round for a meal before he goes back to London, as a thank you for everything he's done for us.'

Ted paused with his fork halfway to his mouth, frowning at that.

'You know I don't like to have anyone from work round. Big Jim sometimes, yes, he's more like family. But I really don't fancy the idea of Oscar invading our personal space and knowing too much about me outside work. I'm more than happy to invite him out somewhere nice for a meal with us. That's the least he deserves. But I'd really prefer not to have him in our home.'

'Ted that's awful! He really does deserve one of my special meals and you know he likes cats.'

'I don't want to argue, not when I've just got home. But no. A meal out, with pleasure, anywhere you fancy. But not in our home. Please.'

Chapter Thirteen

Gina and Maurice were on their third premises visited before they found where Ian Hedges was doing his apprenticeship. Or at least where he should have been doing it, except that his boss, a man by the name of Faulkner, told them he hadn't turned up that day, nor been in touch.

'It's not like Ian. Not at all,' he told them. 'He's a good lad, mostly. Keen as anything. Brighter than I expected, too. Certainly from his school reports. They weren't exactly glowing.'

'But you took him on anyway, despite the reports?' Gina asked him. 'Why was that?'

'I've had no end of young lads coming here wanting to train. A lot of them have dropped out when they realise they have to work hard and study a lot, to keep up to date. Ian came in person to ask about a placement here. I was busy, so I gave him a time to come back the next day. Early doors, because that usually sorts out the serious ones. He was standing outside when I got here to unlock. It was cold and pouring down and he looked wet through and freezing, but he was there, before the time I'd told him, and that impressed me.

'I let him in, just as my other workers were turning up to get going, and put him by the heater to dry out a bit before I interviewed him. One of the vans was being a sod to start. Ian went over and asked if he could have a look. I let him, just in case he might spot something the driver hadn't. I like to give people a chance when they're keen.'

He laughed at the memory as he went on, 'Beggar me if he didn't spot a dodgy wiring connection! Well, I had to give him a chance after that, didn't I? We're electricians here and he spotted a wiring fault we didn't. I asked him how he knew such stuff. I thought maybe he had a dad or a brother in the motor trade.

'He said there was just him and his mam at home and they didn't have a car but he was interested in them so he'd taught himself online. That impressed me, too, so I offered him a position here, and he's never let me down. Not until today.'

'Do you know anything about him outside work? Anything which has ever given you cause to be concerned about him?'

'He's never once been late. Never turned up hungover. No backchat, no slacking, nothing. He's the best trainee I've ever had, to be honest. He's a young lad though, at the end of the day. Of course he goes out with his mates of a night. Sometimes he looks as if he's been on the bevvy a bit, but it's never affected his work, although I've always lectured him about not going near electrics if he's been drinking too much. And certainly not if he's been anywhere near drugs.'

He was looking at them shrewdly, eyes narrowed.

'Is that what this is about? He's in some sort of trouble with the police? Under-age drinking, or drugs, or something? He's a young lad, but a good'un. If he's done summat daft, just the once, I'd still stand by him, and give him a reference, if it comes to that.'

Maurice Brown replied to him.

'At the moment, we can't find Ian and we need to talk to

him. As a witness, not a suspect. His mam doesn't know where he is and we're a bit concerned about him.'

The man made a scornful noise.

'His mother? She's a fat lot of use. I don't know if she's a bit thick or on some sort of medication, maybe even drink, or drugs. I needed her signature to take Ian on, because of his age, and it was like getting blood out of a stone. I gave Ian the forms to take home and get her to sign but it took so long I wondered if perhaps she can't write and didn't like to say so.'

'You mentioned Ian's into motors, Mr Faulkner,' Gina said. 'So it's likely that he would be able to give an accurate description of a vehicle he'd seen, is it? He'd be able to say more than the colour and general category about a car he may have seen. A bit more detail than, say, a red SUV?'

Faulkner's eyes narrowed and his expression was shrewd.

'Is that what this is about? Ian's witnessed something and you think he may be hiding out because he knows too much and he's afraid of reprisals? I'd find that much more likely than him nicking off work, for sure.

'And you said red SUV, so I'm guessing that's about the opposite of the vehicle in question. I know the police are appealing for information on a black 4x4 in connection with that nasty crash, with the young lad so badly injured. Is that what Ian saw? He was a witness to that? Not surprising he's gone on the run in that case.

'Ian could certainly tell you every detail of any vehicle he saw, even at a glance. Passionate about motors, he is. I thought he'd have gone to be a mechanic but he's a smart lad. He said fewer people would be likely to have cars in the future, but they'd still want greener energy, and electricity to charge their cars.

'He'd give you make, model, colour, year, any modifications at all on any vehicle you were asking about. Every detail, right down to any kind of air freshener hanging up inside. It's a knack and he's bloody good at it.'

Faulkner was sharp, for sure. Gina wasn't going to waste time denying what he was saying about the RTC vehicle. Her main priority was to try to find Ian Hedges before he came to any harm.

'Is it possible he may come here, Mr Faulkner, or try to contact you in some way?' she asked him.

'Quite likely, I would say. We're much more of a family to him than his mam seems to be. I like to think I'm more of a dad to him than a boss. I think a lot of young Ian. Even if he does occasionally do daft things like go on the booze of a night, like I said. We've probably all done that as teenagers. I know I did. But as long as he turns up sober and does his work, that's fine.'

'Here's my card,' Gina told him. 'If he should get in touch in any way, please do let me know. We're concerned about his welfare, and his safety really is our primary concern. Please tell him that if you see him, or hear from him.'

* * *

Ted was in work early on Saturday morning, anxious to have a full handover with Jo so he could get back to his own team in Ashton. He'd need to pop out shortly to sort himself a functioning phone, but he wanted to find out what had been going on in his absence.

Jo was in his old office, finishing up paperwork. No one else was in.

Jo looked up as Ted walked in, smiling at the sight of him.

'Good to see you back, boss. You had us worried for a while there. What happened to you?'

'Nothing serious,' Ted made light of it. 'A misunderstanding over transport put me in the wrong place.'

'Must have been one hell of a misunderstanding, if it took Oscar to fly over to sort everything out,' Jo told him shrewdly, but Ted wasn't going to be drawn further, asking instead for an update.

'I'm glad you're back to take over the reins, for sure,' Jo told him.

No point even trying to get any more out of the boss if he wasn't feeling talkative, Jo knew. He'd interviewed hardened criminals who said more than Ted Darling would if he'd made his mind up to stay quiet.

'I need to get back to my team. We've got a serious assault case which could still become a murder, or at least attempted. Two farmers have been knocking lumps off one another and it got well out of hand. One's in hospital, currently in a coma, and his prognosis is guarded. And it was all a row over freemartins.'

'Freemartins?' Ted queried. 'Is that some little-known branch of the Masons? I've never even heard of them.'

'I hadn't either, until I spoke to our rural policing sergeant, so I didn't make a fool of myself, not being a country boy. They're cows. Only they're infertile, so not much use to anyone. That happens in ninety per cent of cases when a female calf has a male twin. And a farmer would always know if there were twin calves, clearly, unless the male dies in early pregnancy.

'Calves have to be registered these days, for sale. All strictly controlled, but if the bull calf dies before twenty-seven days and the farmer quietly disposes of it – maybe gives it to the local hunt kennels for the hounds – then no one's the wiser, and he can sell the female, if he's unscrupulous, without saying anything. And with heifers selling for up to a grand or more, buying one or maybe a few of them, which are infertile so of no earthly use is not likely to go down well with any buyer who suspects the seller knew full well that they would be barren.'

'And here was me thinking it was all quiet and peaceful out there in the countryside,' Ted shook his head in disbelief. 'Well, I'm happy for you to get back to your freemartins, as soon as you've updated me on what's been happening here in my absence.'

'The file on the baby Evie case is all there bar the shouting. I put Virgil on that. Just a little reminder to him how much detail matters, after his slip-up on the Dr Berry case. He's usually better than that, so I thought a little tug on his chain might hammer the message home. He's tying off the last ends of the Berry case too. Definitely an NFA, after he's finished checking and double-checking everything.

'Meanwhile we've been dealing with an RTC serious enough to be treated as a possible attempted murder.'

Jo quickly filled the boss in on all the details they had so far. The serious injuries received by Martin Jackson. The mentions by his mother, and by a possible eyewitness, who was now being treated as a missing person, of a mysterious gang-member so far known only as JJ. He stressed the lack of any proper description, and of the ambiguity over their gender.

'Steve is trawling everywhere for any reference to the JJ person, on anyone's patch, but they're as slippery as an eel, it seems. Not high ranking, so he's finding fewer hits. Just a few fairly vague references to date, nothing to get too excited about, and certainly nothing much to go on. And you know that if there's anything anywhere, Steve will find it.'

'Is Martin able to say anything at all? Would he, even if he could?'

Jo paused for a swallow of coffee. He'd offered one to the boss who'd shaken his head. Jo's coffee was too strong for him. He'd make himself a green tea when he got back to his own office.

'Gina got the distinct impression that he was scared out of his wits, and I can't say I'm surprised, given the extent of his injuries. When I say RTC, a big black 4x4 mounted the pavement and shoved him through a plate glass window, deliberately, going on the evidence at the scene and the lack of braking marks, so they weren't messing about.'

'What's his prognosis? Ted asked him.

'Still guarded, but slightly more optimistic with each passing day. In terms of will he ever be in a state to speak to us, that's looking extremely unlikely, in the short to medium term. Always assuming he would want to, and that's not certain.

'If this is the gang's idea of a warning, which it seems to have been in this case, I dread to think of what they would do to anyone who really crossed them. I don't give much for our chances of getting anyone to even talk about them to us, let alone to testify against them.

'Copies of reports on everything we've been working on in your absence are on your desk, for if and when you want to look them over for more details.

'Are you sure you don't want a drink, boss? I need another, and I promise to water yours down a bit.'

Ted was shrewd. Not much got past him. He asked,

'What have you got to tell me that you think needs me fortified with caffeine first?'

Jo laughed at that.

'No fooling you. There is something I suspect you're not going to like. To finish off on the subject of Martin Jackson first, though. Gina talked to her old Drugs colleagues and they're suggesting a joint meeting to pool ideas and info. They're not interested in our possible attempted murder by motor vehicle, of course, but it's possible they might have something useful to add on the drugs and gang front.'

Jo put mugs down on the table and sat down again.

'Right, don't shoot the messenger boss, but while you were away, Oscar did a bit of playing before he disappeared to collect you.

'Mike took a phone call from his DS, a man called Tony Taylor. He said he sounds like a decent bloke, and, reading between the lines, it seems he's not always thrilled at the dirty work Oscar gets him to do for him. On this occasion, it's a suspected murder warrant for our couple in custody, Georges and Beverley Williams. The two people who had baby Evie in their care when they were raided.

'Clearly the Met's poker hand on that case outweighs what we have, so in theory, they could drag them back to London. I spoke to the Super about it straight away, and she was going to talk to Oscar's boss, but she's been running round in ever decreasing circles this week, so I honestly don't know where we're at with that one at the present moment. But I imagine we could expect a Met vehicle to turn up at any time, with their warrant, and whisk the Williamses out from under our noses, with nothing we could do about it. And maybe Oscar would get a lift back with them, since I imagine his work here is now done.'

Ted went quiet. Ominously quiet. Jo was looking at him anxiously across the desk.

'Say something, boss. At least reassure me you aren't about to start kicking things. You know I'm a pacifist who runs away from any hint of conflict.'

'I knew I was right not to trust him. I should have realised he'd do something underhand and self-serving, the minute he got the chance. It's time I had a word with him. But don't worry, Jo, I'll go back to my own office to do so.'

Ted still had Oscar's burner phone until he got his own repaired or replaced. He suspected it would need to be the latter. He called up Smith's number on it. Unsurprisingly, it went straight to voicemail.

'DI Smith? DCI Darling.'

His tone and formality made it clear this was not a social call.

'Phone me as soon as you get this message. It's important.'

He did at least add a 'please'. Ted's dad had brought him up properly, with good manners. Something he never forgot, nor let slip.

He didn't remotely expect a response. He had a feeling Oscar would avoid him for as long as he could. Probably until the moment he tried to exercise his warrant in a poker game against Ted and his team.

Ted was still seething with silent fury when, much later in the morning, his desk phone rang. He half hoped it might be Oscar, with some sort of an explanation. Not that Ted could think of one he would find acceptable.

Instead it was Trev calling him.

'Hey, you. I didn't know if you had a functioning mobile yet or not. How's it going? Have you asked Oscar about us taking him out to dinner? Because if you still refuse to have him in the house, I should really book somewhere before he goes back, and anywhere decent might already be filling up for the weekend.'

Ted took a moment to control his temper before he replied. The last thing he wanted even to consider was sitting down to a meal opposite Oscar, knowing the underhand trick he'd played. At least the man himself had given him the perfect get out of jail free card.

'I've been trying to get hold of him but he's not currently answering his phone. He did buy himself a rather good bottle of schnapps before we left Frankfurt, so I imagine he's treating himself to some of that on his day off.

'When I hear back from him, I'll let you know. Promise.'

Chapter Fourteen

DS Rob O'Connell was talking to a sergeant from the Serious Collision Investigation Unit, at the scene of the crash which had nearly cost Martin Jackson his life.

This case was going to involve multi-disciplinary cooperation between Serious Crime, SCIU, and Drugs. Rob was taxed with making the arrangements to set up an initial meeting as soon as possible, with all interested parties represented.

SCIU had more or less finished with the site, but Rob had asked to see it for himself, with one of their team, Evan Thomas, to walk him through what had happened. He also wanted to check at close quarters for any other CCTV cameras they hadn't yet had footage from, and that needed eyes on the ground.

So many commercial premises these days had their own cameras, intentionally not always easy to spot. Up to now, the investigators had not found one which directly covered the point where the black vehicle had mounted the pavement in pursuit of Martin.

Rob knew that SCIU had put out appeals for any dash-cam footage which might be useful. He wasn't optimistic. With the details which had so far been released, and knowing how people liked to put two and two together to make five, he was imagining any driver with such footage might well have erased it rapidly. Most people would deduce from the information made public that this had all the hallmarks of a gang attack. The sort of thing almost anyone would want to steer well clear of.

The scene was still closed off and both men slipped on shoe covers before ducking under the tapes, in case the surrounding area had not yet given up all of its secrets. Although that was unlikely, purely a matter of routine.

'You can see straight away that there's no sign of braking. None of the indications you would expect to see for an accident where a driver had simply lost control of their vehicle for some reason and was desperately trying to regain it to prevent a collision,' Evan told Rob.

'Quite the opposite, in fact. Look at the rubber trace there, on the kerb. The driver was actually accelerating at that point. Giving it a bit of welly to be sure of maximum impact.'

Rob was looking up and down the road, on both sides, studying the various shop fronts and commercial premises there.

'Was the driver trying to kill him, do you think?' he asked. 'Or was it intended merely to cause injury, as a serious warning? Risky, if that was the intention. They couldn't have known for certain if he'd survive or not.'

'You'd probably know better than me but surely if there is a drugs gang behind this, they'd have killed him if they'd wanted to. Maybe they didn't care either way, as long as they made their point. Made an example of him as a warning to anyone thinking about double-crossing them, or whatever it was about.'

'That's what we've been thinking, but I needed your expert opinion on that. We've been going on the theory that this attack was as much a warning to others as a punishment to the victim, Martin. A sort of "mess with us and this is what will happen to you next". And I suppose, for that reason, this would be the ideal place on this road to do it. Straight through a plate glass window like that – there's no mistaking that for anything but a serious warning.'

'Float glass,' Evan told him, smiling. 'That's what it's correctly called these days, I'm told. This isn't my first vehicle through a shopfront case, but it is the first which is clearly deliberate.'

'Does that make any difference to the potential for injury or death? The type of glass? Not something I know much about,' Rob confessed.

'I don't know a lot either, to be honest. I was just corrected on the term on the last similar case. Although that one was definitely accidental. Sad, really. The driver got shunted from behind, slammed his foot down without intending to and couldn't regain control in time. This is my first attempted murder with a vehicle as the weapon. You'd need to ask some sort of glass specialist to get a definitive answer.

'Another factor for you to consider, although I'm sure you have, is whether or not this road is a regular route for your victim, or were they tracking him randomly until they found the ideal spot.'

'Martin coached juniors for a few sports clubs, so this might be on his way back from one of the clubs he attends. Attended, I should say, as it's looking so far as if those days are gone. But it's a good point. I'll get that checked. Is there anything more you can tell me about the vehicle? All we've got from eye witnesses so far is that it was a black 4x4, which doesn't narrow it down all that much.'

'Our techie people are working on that now. They'll

analyse things like paint scrapings, and signs of any fragments from the vehicle's lights, if one happened to get damaged on impact. They'll also use all the measurements taken to assess the dimensions of the vehicle, because that should help to narrow things down a bit. That can be done fairly accurately these days. Plus we might get something from that rubber mark to help us.

'There's a lot of crossover in car design and building now. Way back, it was always a safe bet that if it was heavy, built like a tank and designed to withstand anything, including enemy artillery, it was German made. But those days are gone, sadly.

'I'll let you know as soon as we have anything at all to give you a steer, pardon the bad pun, of course. Likewise, if you turn up anything, give me a bell.'

'Thanks, will do.'

Rob turned to go then paused and looked back.

'What d'you even call an expert in glass? I can't think of the word.'

Evan chuckled.

'Not the sort of thing you need every day, is it? A glazier. I only know because of speaking to one on the earlier case. He was a very helpful bloke. I can send you his contacts, for a start, if he's not retired. He was knocking on a bit.

'If he has, you could do worse than talk to a good window cleaner, as well or instead. If you can find a proper one, they could probably tell you a fair bit about the properties of glass. They'd be well placed to know which types were more fragile and needed careful handling for one thing, I would think.

'Good luck, anyway.'

* * *

John Faulkner, the electrician, awarded himself the rest of the day off. He'd allocated tasks for the day and knew he could rely on his team to complete their work to his high standards. He treated his employees well and they repaid him by doing a good job and not cutting any corners.

The earlier visit by the police had rattled him. He was genuinely fond of young Ian Hedges and worried to hear he'd got himself into what sounded like a serious situation.

If he'd had any clue as to where he might be, he'd have been out looking until he found him, then gone with him to the police station to sort things out. Assuming they would accept him as a responsible adult for the lad, to be present whilst he was questioned.

Certainly a lot more responsible than that useless mother of his. At least he genuinely cared for his young apprentice. Could see the potential in him and tried to help him to cultivate it. From the little he knew of the mother, he didn't get the feeling she did more than the basic minimum for her son. Sometimes not even that.

He wasn't even sure how she supported herself and Ian. From the odd remark the lad had made to him in an unguarded moment, it sounded as if she might have been on the game. It made him sad. His own family life was great. Seeing how well young Ian was doing for himself, it made him wonder how much more he could have achieved in a warm and loving household.

He put his car in the garage when he got home, noticing as he did so that his two sons' bikes were not in there. They'd no doubt gone off out with mates and were probably enjoying a kickabout in a local park somewhere. They were good kids. Never gave him a moment's concern.

He found his wife in the kitchen, checking something in the slow cooker which was giving off an inviting aroma. He went over to put his arms round her and nuzzle her neck.

'Cupboard love!' she laughed, wriggling in his grasp. 'It won't be ready for ages yet. The boys aren't coming back until half six, and I didn't expect you this early. I'll put the kettle on, though.'

'I had a visit from the police to say young Ian has gone missing. I'm a bit worried about him. I can't get him on the phone. Seems he might have been a witness to a violent crime and is probably scared of the consequences. I'd go out and look for him, if I had any clue where he might go. I don't like to think of him out there by himself, feeling scared.'

She turned to smile at him.

'I like how much you care for that boy. It showed I was right in my judgement, marrying you. I knew you were a nice man who tried to do the right thing.'

Faulkner laughed as he said, 'Stop it, you're making me blush!'

'Oh, before I forget, can you quickly check the garden fence again? I think that dog from next door has been back in. I heard a noise from near the shed and I didn't want to go and look. You know I'm wary of the thing.'

'I don't think it's a nasty dog, love. Just one which doesn't get much fuss and attention at home. I'll go and look now, put your mind at rest.'

It was chilly outside. A persistent drizzle, recently started, making it feel colder than it really was. Faulkner walked the length of the boundary fence, checking for old and new signs of the neighbour's collie dog slithering its way underneath as it seemed to like doing.

Nothing new. All of his recent repairs to keep it out were still intact and there was no sign of any further activity. He stepped onto the large piece of rock he'd put in place to stop up one of its favourite digging sites. The dog was in its own garden, checking something interesting, visible and audible only to itself, in the middle of the lawn. It was lying perfectly still, staring in the fixated way collies often displayed. It did little more than lift its head and pat its tail on the ground at the sight of him.

'All right, Scribble?' he asked it. 'Not you this time, then. Why don't you go in out of the rain, you daft mutt?'

He got down off his rock. The prospect of a hot cuppa was very inviting. Then he thought he'd better go and check the shed. His wife was bound to ask if he had and perhaps there was a cat shut in there somehow, to account for the noise she had heard.

Everything looked in order, all tools in their rightful place. Except not everything. There was a large green hessian sack, which he used mostly for collecting up autumn leaves, which was always kept hanging up on a nail on the back of the door.

It was currently on the floor right in the far back corner, covering up a distinctive shape.

'Ian? Is that you, lad? Why don't you come into the kitchen? Kettle's on, and it's a bloody sight warmer in there than in here.'

* * *

It was probably as well that Oscar Smith wasn't responding to any of the DCI's phone calls. Ted was getting angrier the more times he rang and the more messages he left without any response.

He realised, with a twinge of annoyance, that he didn't know where the man was staying so he couldn't even go round there to confront him over his underhanded trick with the Williams couple and the warrant.

He supposed he ought to find out and at the same time make sure that Smith hadn't overdone it on the schnapps and made himself ill. He realised he owed him that much, after the efforts Oscar had gone to in flying out to recover him. He also knew Trev wouldn't let it rest if Ted hadn't even invited the man out for a meal, as instructed.

He knew there'd be a note somewhere of Smith's current address. Probably in Mike Hallam's office. He tended to keep hard copies of any such useful information as a safety net against a day when the computer systems might be down, for some reason.

He found the address easily enough and decided the only certain way to catch up with the currently slippery Smith would be to go round there, if he wouldn't answer his phone.

The guest house turned out to be a pleasant Victorian semi to the south of town, going out towards Hazel Grove. Ted's ring at the doorbell was answered by a woman who looked to be in her forties.

She greeted him pleasantly enough but added, 'We're full, I'm afraid, if you've come about a room.'

'No, thanks, I live not far away. I'm trying to find a work colleague who's been staying here. I need to talk to him and I can't get an answer from his phone. I wondered if he might be in, or if you might possibly know where he is, please. It's a Mr Smith, from London.'

Ted was too sharp to have missed the fleeting expression on her face which told him that yes, she did know Mr Smith

147

and that such knowledge had not led to respect. Quite the opposite.

Her mouth pursed up as she replied, 'Oh yes, Mr Smith. The policeman. I believe he's still in his room. Would you like me to go and knock on his door for you?'

Ted produced his warrant card and held it up for her.

'I'm a policeman, too. Would it be all right if I go up and knock myself? I'd like to surprise him.'

The woman's face changed. She'd clearly picked up on the hidden message behind Ted's words and approved. Ted wondered what Oscar had been up to whilst staying there.

'Oh, please do,' she told him. 'His room is just at the top of these stairs, on the right.'

Ted wasn't at all surprised that the woman felt a sudden need to tidy up in the already neat and well-ordered hallway as he was making his way soundlessly up the carpeted stairs.

Ted's first knock at the door produced nothing but a low groan from inside. His second, slightly louder, was followed by the sound of movement from within. It took a third knock before the door was opened a crack and Smith peered blearily out at him. Unshaven, half dressed and looking decidedly the worse for wear.

In an instinctive defensive movement, he tried to shut the door, but Ted's foot was already placed to block it, shortly followed by his shoulder.

'Hello, Oscar. Your phone seems to be out of service so I thought I'd come round in person. Aren't you going to invite me in?'

Chapter Fifteen

'Fran, love, this is Ian, my apprentice. You've heard me talk about him. He's in need of a hot cuppa and probably something to eat,' John Faulkner told his wife as he ushered the youth into their kitchen.

Ian Hedges, eyes down, shuffling in discomfort, mumbled an ''ello, Mrs Faulkner, sorry to bother you,' then stood uncertainly in the middle of the warm kitchen, shivering visibly and looking like a lost soul.

'Hello, Ian, it's nice to meet you finally, after hearing John sing your praises. And it's Fran. We're not formal in this family.

'You look frozen through. Sit down. I've not long put the kettle on. What would you like? Tea? Coffee? Hot chocolate?'

She saw how his face lit up at the last suggestion so she smiled at him.

'Good choice. It's what my boys will be looking forward to when they get home soon. Hot chocolate it is then. Coming right up. Go on, sit yourself down and make yourself at home. It won't take me long to make it. Supper won't be ready for a while but there's always plenty of biscuits in this house. Or I could make you some toast, if you'd prefer?'

Ian was looking bewildered at such a welcome from a stranger. John Faulkner pulled out a chair for him at the kitchen table.

'Sit down, lad, don't stand on ceremony.'

Ian hesitated, then said, 'Me clothes is all mucky. I don't want to dirty owt. I slept in 'em last night. I didn't know where else to go.'

'Tell you what, Ian. Take your shoes and your trousers off here – the missus won't look – and I'll take you up to have a nice hot shower. My older lad, Jason, is not that far off your size. I'll lend you some of his clothes for now, and we can put yours in the machine for you. He won't mind, I'm sure.'

Still the young apprentice hesitated.

'I don't want to bother you.'

'Don't be daft, lad, it's no bother at all.'

John Faulkner came back down with the pile of dirty clothes, once Ian was safely installed under the shower, having been told there was plenty of hot water so not to stint. He bundled everything into the washing machine and set it going.

'These don't look as if they see the inside of a washing machine all that often. And the poor lad spent the night in our shed, huddled under that green sack I use for leaves. That was the noise you heard, him trying to move about a bit to get warm. Sorry to dump him on you like this, love. I wished he'd come and knocked on the door, instead of half freezing out there.'

'Don't be daft! It's what any mum would do, if she had an ounce of maternal instinct about her. Just imagine if ever our Jason or Charlie found themselves lost and away from home and came across someone who wouldn't help them. Doesn't bear thinking about.

'I didn't know you'd given him our address, though.'

Faulkner chuckled.

'I haven't, but I've always said the lad is sharp. He must have seen it in the office somewhere at one time and stored it away in his memory, in case he ever needed it. I'm glad he felt he could come round here, at least, even if he was worried about asking me directly for help. He's a good lad, underneath. If he'd had a decent mum, his life might have been a lot different.'

'This violent crime he might have witnessed, though,' his wife went on, her expression worried. 'Does that mean he's in danger? With the wrong sort of people after him, if they know, or even guess, that he might have seen something he shouldn't have? And if he's come here, is that danger likely to follow him here? Because of course I want to help the lad. Any decent person would, looking at the state of him, especially any mum. But I wouldn't want any harm to come to either of our boys as a result.'

'Me neither, of course. Last thing I want. But I feel responsible for Ian, so I want to do right by him, too. As soon as he's had his shower and some scran, I'll phone one of the officers who came to see me, get them to come here and advise us on what's best to do for him. And for all of us.'

* * *

The export schnapps must have been strong stuff, judging by the state of Oscar Smith. He was bare-chested and barefoot, wearing what looked like a pair of tracksuit bottoms. They'd clearly been hauled on hastily in response to Ted's repeated knocking at the door as they were on back to front.

Seeing Smith without a shirt, Ted couldn't fail to notice that the distinctive scar on the man's face continued down his neck and across to his shoulder. It must have been a serious injury, as perilously close to some major blood vessels as it appeared to be.

'Sorry, guv,' Smith told Ted, without a discernible hint of any sincerity. 'I turned the phone off so I could catch up on some sleep after our adventures. What can I do you for?'

If he had any notion that Ted now knew about his dodgy dealings in getting a warrant for the Williams couple from their previous case, he certainly wasn't showing it. Ted decided to play along with the pantomime for the time being.

'I'm here at Trev's insistence. He's very keen to take you out for a meal before you go back down south, which I assume will be Monday, or thereabouts, once you've written everything up. I'll be coming with the two of you, of course, to pay the bill. I'm aware of the debt of gratitude I owe you.

'I doubt we'd get anywhere worth going to at such short notice for this evening, but he can probably pull a few strings where we're well known to book a table for lunch tomorrow. If you're free?'

Smith looked surprised and more than a little touched. He'd clearly imagined the unexpected visit from the DCI was about something else entirely. Probably about him being out of contact. He couldn't believe Darling didn't yet know about his dirty tricks with the arrest warrant, unless he hadn't caught up on everything. He expected there would be fireworks to follow when he did.

Smith didn't much care. His methods on his own patch were often decidedly dodgy and underhand. That was in part why he got the results he did. Darling's softly-softly approach might be fine up here, but it would never do against some of the types Smith and his team had to deal with in the capital.

'That's great, guv, I'd like that. But you honestly owe me nothing. Just doing my job and using what modest skills I have. I liked your Trevor, though. Nice bloke. Very intelligent. His German is excellent, if a bit posh for everyday use. It would be good to meet him again in better circumstances, and Sunday lunch sounds the ideal way to do it.'

Ted got his phone out to call Trev.

'I'm with Oscar now. He says thanks for the invite, and if you can find anywhere, he's up for lunch with us tomorrow, before he goes back down south.'

Smith was still smiling, scratching absent-mindedly at the scar tissue on his shoulder as if he still felt the sensation of whatever sharp object had caused it.

As Ted ended his call he said, 'Right, Trev will sort it and let me know when and where. Keep your phone on so I can pass the details on to you. I'll come and pick you up, if necessary, now I know where you're staying, and I can certainly run you back afterwards, if you need me to.'

'Thanks, guv, I really appreciate that. I'll look forward to it.'

Smith was looking relaxed and pleased at the unexpected turn of events. The DCI seemed to be turning to the door, ready to leave. His verbal attack, as he spun back round, caught the Met officer completely unawares.

'And Oscar, if you think your underhand trick with a dodgy warrant for our couple in custody is going to get you anywhere, you can think again. We nicked them, we're keeping them, and our warrant to do so is very far from dodgy.

'We have excellent working relations with the CPS and your bit of fiction has been passed their way to assess its authenticity. We don't do anything off the books here, which is why, when I raise something like that with them, it will be taken very seriously.

'If it stands up to detailed scrutiny – and that is currently the big question – then you'll get your turn with them, but all in good time. You're behind us in the queue. Am I making myself clear enough on that?'

Smith fell back on one of his stock answers. As usual, without a shred of sincerity about it.

'As crystal, guv. As crystal.'

* * *

Gina planned to follow up on her own the call from John Faulkner, about having found the missing teenager, Ian Hedges, sleeping rough in his garden shed. That was, following protocol, subject to DS Mike Hallam's approval. It seemed low enough risk, but she wanted to cover herself, and he raised no objection, simply giving her the usual reminder about personal safety.

Faulkner himself opened the door to her and had a few quiet words, filling her in on the background, before showing her into the kitchen.

'Ian's scared to death about whatever he might have seen. He spent the night out there shivering in our garden shed. He said he didn't know where else to go.

'He wasn't at all keen on me calling the police, but I said that was the safest thing we could do. I hope I was right about that.

'He's had a shower and we've fed him. I want to help, so does the wife. But we have teenage boys of our own so naturally enough, we're worried about anyone knowing he's here and coming after him, putting any of us in danger.

'He didn't go home because he knows full well that mother of his would be neither use nor ornament in helping him. I'm not about to kick him out on his ear, not from work, nor from my home. But I have my own family to consider as well, of course.'

'I completely understand that. Let me have a word with him and I'll see what I can suggest.'

Following Faulkner into the kitchen to talk to Ian, Gina half wished she had Maurice Brown with her. He was always the one who could get the most reticent of witnesses to talk to him. It was for that reason they'd decided between them that he should go to the hospital and see if he could get any more from Martin Jackson than Gina had managed to do.

There was something solidly reassuring about Maurice. People instinctively trusted him; knew that, although he was a copper, doing his job, he would always do it fairly, without distorting facts or cutting corners. He'd had some outstanding success at talking to young and traumatised witnesses and victims. Now that Martin Jackson was slowly making some improvements, enough to have been taken off the critical list, it was time to see what Daddy Hen could get out of him.

Ian was still sitting at the table in the kitchen of the Faulkners' home, wearing borrowed clothes and looking like someone in a dentist's waiting room anticipating root canal fillings with no hope of anaesthetic.

'Hello, again, Ian. Remember me? I'm DC Gina Shaw. I came with DC Brown to talk to you. You told us that you hadn't seen anything or anyone at the scene of the crash. But I don't think that's quite true, is it? I can't understand why you felt the need to go on the run, nor to spend the night hiding in Mr Faulkner's shed, if you'd really seen nothing.

'If you did see someone you recognised, I can appreciate why you would feel afraid to tell us. But we could arrange protection for you. There are things we can put in place to keep you safe. But only if you agree to talk to us.

'The first thing to do would be for you to come to the station with me to give a statement. You don't need to have your mum or anyone else present for that. You're not under arrest, not being treated as a suspect, purely as a valuable witness. If you're worried about someone finding out about you talking to us, we can talk about ways to keep you safe.'

Ian's expression was looking more worried with everything Gina said to him. He threw an imploring look towards his boss; clearly the person he trusted most.

'But could I come with him to the station, if Ian wants me to?' Faulkner asked, correctly interpreting the look. 'Even if I can't be in the room while you interview him. Could I at least sit and wait for him, then perhaps bring him back here, just for tonight, until we know what you can sort out for him?'

He was looking at his wife as he asked the question of Gina, aware of her concerns for her own family if anyone really was looking for Ian and determined to stop him from talking.

'I don't want to be no bother,' Ian mumbled, but the expression on his face showed how much he wanted the presence of someone he so clearly trusted.

Gina spoke first, anxious not to lose the chance of getting any kind of a witness statement from Ian. He was, to date, their only hope of any first-hand testimony.

'I'm sure we could sort something out. I can take you into the station the back way so there's much less chance of you being seen by anyone, and I'm in an unmarked car, so there's nothing to raise any flags.

'What do you say, Ian? Will you try to help us? Even a description of anyone you might have seen could be very valuable to us. If you don't know their real name, anything else you could tell me might be helpful. We could get you to work with someone to make up an image of what they look like. That could help us enormously.'

Ian's eyes were everywhere round the warm and welcoming family kitchen. In his brief time in the house he'd received more kindness and compassion than he'd previously encountered in his short life. He felt safe. The prospect of leaving the sanctuary he'd found was not tempting.

But the images on constant replay inside his head were so vivid he sensed he would never forget them. The young black lad he knew by sight, but no more, walking along, minding his own business, smiling to himself as he listened to something in his earphones, a sports holdall slung over one shoulder.

The big, black vehicle, the make of which he did know by sight, and knew he had seen it before, purring up behind him like some sort of a black panther, stalking its prey.

Then the roar of an accelerating engine, the squeal of tyres mounting the kerb, the shattering crash as the youth was smashed straight through the shop window, shards of glass flying in all directions.

And, clearly visible to him in the front passenger seat, the twisted, seemingly grinning face of JJ. The mouth opening in what looked like laughter as feral as the snarl of a hyena.

That image was burned into his memory. One he would never forget. Never.

Chapter Sixteen

Maurice Brown had his warrant card in his hand ready, knowing he needed to get past at least one Firearms officer in order to visit Martin Jackson in hospital.

When he got there, he saw that there was, in fact, an armed officer at each end of the corridor where Martin's room was situated. It had been decided that having anyone planted directly outside the right door was simply signalling where he was. He was being treated as a high-risk witness, which meant keeping his exact whereabouts secret.

'DC Brown, to see young Martin,' Maurice told the man, deciding he must be getting older since he thought the lad didn't look old enough to be standing there with a gun.

The officer checked Maurice's ID carefully before nodding to him to continue. It was good to see the young victim's protection was being taken seriously.

'Any signs of anything suspicious?' Maurice asked him before he went on his way, making conversation as much as anything.

'We'd have reported it if we'd seen anything,' the AFO told him, pleasantly enough. 'But no, all quiet so far.'

Maurice tapped softly on the door before going in.

'Mrs Jackson, is it? DC Maurice Brown. I wondered if I could come in and have a word. If that's all right with you, and with Martin. Hello, Martin, I'm Maurice. Is it all right if I talk to you a bit?'

Maurice hadn't seen the victim before, only listened to Gina's account of her visit, so he couldn't tell if he looked any better than before. He still seemed to be in a bad way, but at least his eyes flickered open at the sound of a new voice. He was still linked to a heart monitor.

Thelma Jackson smiled broadly. She took an instant liking to this different detective who began by speaking directly to her son rather than about him, as some people would have done. There was something solid and dependable about him, too. A reassuring presence, she felt instinctively.

'Do come and sit down, officer. There's a spare chair here, look. My husband's just popped out to the shops for a few things we thought Martin might like. To make him feel a bit more at home, and to help him with his memory, and speech.

'Martin's doing quite a bit better now, thankfully. Not as many tubes, which is nice for him. He gets very tired though, don't you, love? And speaking is still a bit hard.'

Maurice pulled the chair closer and sat down. Martin's eyes were open and studying him warily, but so far that was the only sign that he was aware of what was going on around him.

'Do you have any news for us, officer?' Martin's mother asked Maurice. 'Are you any closer to finding who did this terrible thing to Martin?'

Maurice replied to the mother, but all the time his eyes were on the injured boy in the bed, watching for the slightest reaction to what he was saying. Anything at all which might indicate that Martin knew something. Something important, which was going to take a lot of patience and reassurance to get out of him. Qualities Maurice possessed in abundance.

'Please call me Maurice, Mrs Jackson. I'm hoping I might be going to liaise with you both a bit more on this case, so I want you to trust me, and to feel you can talk to me, any time you need to. About anything you want to know, not just the case. I'll always try and answer honestly.

'Here's my card, look, with my phone number, and I mean it, call me any time you want. I'm a dad, as well as a copper, to five children, so I know how worrying it can be. Especially when something like this happens out of the blue.'

He spoke next to the boy in the bed, anxious to include him in everything. Wanting to establish from the start that he was on his side and there to help him, in whatever way he could.

'Martin, I don't know if you've been told, but there are now armed police officers outside your room, one at each end of the corridor. Which means you're completely safe. No one can get anywhere near you in here. The officers are there twenty-four hours a day and will be for as long as you are in here.'

Even as he was saying it, Maurice was hoping that was guaranteed. He didn't want to promise the world, only to find the officers being pulled for an emergency somewhere else. It was important to reassure Martin that he was safe. Safe enough to start helping them with the case, without fearing another attempt on his life.

'The first thing I want to tell you both is that we have a new eyewitness to what happened, who's come forward. Someone who saw the whole thing.'

Martin's eyes flickered unmistakably at that news, while the heart monitor showed a brief blip.

'They've been able to name one of the people in the

vehicle which hit you, Martin. A front seat passenger. A nickname, rather than a name, we think, but it's one we've heard before.'

Martin's mother was about to say something but Maurice gave her a clear indication with a hand gesture not to. Not at that stage. He wanted to watch Martin's reactions carefully, without any interruption.

'Now, I know you're finding it hard to say much at the moment, Martin. I just need you to give me some indication, any way you can, if you saw anyone you knew at all. Even if just by sight. Then, if you can do somehow, to give me the name or nickname that person goes by.

'And please remember, you are safe here. Two armed officers, standing between you and anything you're afraid of, and they won't leave their posts.

'So, did you see someone, when you were hit by the car, that you recognised? That you might have come across before? Perhaps someone actually in the vehicle?'

A violent spasm seemed to shake Martin's whole body for an instant. His mother made to leap to her feet but once again Maurice dissuaded her with a gesture. His eyes were fixed on the monitor. Nothing seemed to have changed.

He was no medic. He didn't know a lot about what was wrong with the victim. But to his eyes, it looked as if he was seeing some sort of internal struggle between fear and wanting to do the right thing rather than anything medical. He hoped he was right and he wasn't putting the lad in any kind of danger. Martin had had enough of that in his short life.

But no doubt the monitors would remotely alert medical staff, if and when needed, so they could come and sort out anything that happened.

'I'll stop any time you want me to, Martin, and get someone to come to see to you if it's all getting a bit much for you. If you can manage to help with this, though, it could really improve our chances of bringing someone to justice for what they did to you.

'Did you see someone? Did you recognise anyone in the vehicle?'

Martin had improved enough to make a small but unmistakable movement of the head. An attempt at a nod. An affirmative answer.

'That's great, Martin. You're doing really well. Now, is there any way you can tell me this person's name? Even their initial would be a big help. Take your time.'

Martin's mouth was trying to move, to form something. A word? A letter? Whatever it was, he was not succeeding. He looked increasingly frustrated with each failed attempt.

'Perhaps we should stop now,' Martin's mother said, her expression anxious.

Martin made a distinct tutting sound of annoyance, trying to make a gesture with his right hand, the one nearest to Maurice, which at first Maurice didn't understand. Then it dawned on him.

'You want to write something?'

He got out his notebook, laid it on the bed next to the gesturing hand, then carefully put his pen in reach of the seeking fingers.

It took Martin several painstaking attempts to get hold of the pen at all. His mother made to help him, provoking another frustrated noise from Martin.

In the end, the only way he could lift the pen at all was in his fist, like a stabbing implement.

Maurice held the notebook steady as Martin tried to make

the pen connect with the paper. Finally he managed to scrawl a big, uneven capital letter. It had taken a Herculean effort, but there was no mistaking what it was.

The letter J.

Martin was looking directly at Maurice, willing him to understand so much more from that single scrawl. Maurice was doing everything he could not to prompt or lead him in any way. To have any evidential value at all, it had to be in Martin's own words, in whatever way he could register them.

Maurice waited, silently willing him to go on. Martin was clearly exhausted but determined to finish what he'd begun. He let the pen slip from his grasp then slowly, painfully, lifted up his thumb.

Once. Twice.

'The letter J. Twice. J. J. Is that what you mean, Martin?' Maurice needed to check for himself to be absolutely certain of what the youth was trying to tell him. 'You saw someone you know by the initials J. J. in the car which ran you down?'

Martin's eyelids were closing, extreme fatigue overtaking him. He made one last supreme effort. A weary but unmissable thumbs up for an affirmative.

He was admitting to having seen the person known as JJ in the vehicle which had mown him down.

* * *

Ted caught up with the members of the team at the end of the day. He was keen to have some hint of progress after juggling figures around to try to show best use of resources. Paperwork was never his favourite part of the job but it went with the rank and responsibility.

Gina Shaw spoke first.

'I had a call from John Faulkner, the electrician who has Ian Hedges as an apprentice. He told me Ian had spent last night sleeping rough in his garden shed because he's scared stiff and didn't know where else to go. Faulkner thinks that Ian was definitely a witness to the incident with Martin Jackson. He almost certainly saw someone he recognised.

'I went round there. Ian certainly knows something, and he's intelligent enough to know that something is enough to put him at serious risk from the gang involved. Especially if they get any inkling that he's been talking to us, or to anyone else. Like the Faulkner family, for instance.

'It took an awful lot of persuasion before he would come to the station to talk to me. But he did, and we were able to work together on producing a composite of the person he clearly recognised at the scene, which is why he first denied any such thing, then went on the run.

'Boss, I didn't want to promise him anything without checking with you first, but his safety has to be the number one priority, surely? John Faulkner said he could stay there for now, but he has a family and he's worried about their safety if Ian carries on living there and if someone is out to get him.

'I don't think he'll do a runner from where he is, so after he'd helped us I left him there for now,, to check what we could do for him.'

'You did the right thing, Gina' Ted told her. 'First off, let's get an unmarked car watching the house round the clock. But please make sure Mr Faulkner is aware. We don't want him or his family getting scared if they think it's someone from the gang watching them.

'Will Ian talk more eventually, d'you think? If he feels

safe enough? And does he actually know anything? Is that the impression you get from him.'

'I think he does, yes. And I don't think he'll talk without assurances. He seems to care about the Faulkners a lot more than his mother. So he's worried about them getting dragged into all of this.'

'Boss, sorry to cut in here but it's relevant,' Maurice began. 'I've been to see Martin. He's apparently better than he was but the poor lad is still in a bad way, still not able to speak. He was determined to help, though. He managed to write the capital letter J then make a gesture to say two.

'I know that in itself would be weak testimony, especially to take to court, but I took it to mean he was trying to tell me that JJ, whoever they are, was at the scene. And he did indicate the person was actually in the vehicle which hit him.'

'Good, that's progress. And at least we know Martin is safe if he's under Firearms protection. So it's only right we do the same for Ian and the Faulkners. An unmarked car, at the very least, until we can sort something long-term for Ian, which should then lift the risk to the Faulkner family.

'Gina, can you arrange that before you finish today, please? As much as anything to show Ian and the Faulkners that we take their welfare seriously.

'What news on the joint meeting with Drugs and SCIU? Rob?'

'Sorted for first thing Monday morning, boss,' Rob told him. 'SCIU will fill everyone in on the technical details but when I visited the site with Evan Thomas, he showed me tyre marks which clearly indicate that the vehicle was actually accelerating hard as it mounted the kerb, so that seems to add weight to an attempted murder charge.

'He also suggested I ask a glazier or a window cleaner about the properties of a window like the one Martin was shoved through, because that might add weight to making it an attempted murder charge rather than an assault with intent.

'I've not yet tracked down a glazier but I'll be talking to a man called Rob Holland this evening, who calls himself "the fastest window cleaner in the west". I've picked him because he does on occasion clean windows in that road, so it's worth a phone call, at least.'

'Good work, everyone,' Ted told them. 'It may seem slow, but we're going in the right direction. Let's hope the joint meeting will turn up a few more leads. Someone, somewhere knows for certain who this JJ person is and where we can find them. We at least have the beginnings of a case against them, so let's build on that. Thank you, everyone.'

* * *

Trev was in the kitchen cooking when Ted got home. He was still in his breeches, having been out riding with his friend Willow that afternoon, and still had the lingering smell of saddle soap and horse sweat about him.

His filthy top boots were lying in a muddy heap in the middle of the hall, next to the boot jack he'd used to haul them off.

Ted walked up behind him and put his arms round his waist.

'You smell a bit rural,' he told him. 'It's as well I like the smell. But it reminds me how long it's been since I came out riding with you. My trusty steed will have forgotten me, and

I'll be right back to basics, remembering how to rise to the trot.'

Trev put down the spoon with which he'd been stirring and sampling something bubbling away on the hob, then turned with a hug of his own.

'I was about to sort out the first problem with a shower, hopefully before you got back, but you're earlier than I expected. Which is all to the good, as now I'm busily thinking up a way to work on the second, even as we speak.'

Chapter Seventeen

'Are you awake enough to be listening?' Ted asked the buried form of his partner, hidden under cats and bedclothes.

Trev's response was muffled by the pillow into which he was speaking. He was never a morning person, especially at the weekends, and although Ted was going in to work slightly later than his usual starting time, it still counted as obscenely early to Trev.

'I need advance warning of police interrogation on a Sunday morning. My jury is still out on the answer to that question.'

Ted smiled to himself. It was not an unexpected reaction, but he wanted to make sure Trev understood a few of the ground rules which Ted was imposing on their lunchtime date with Oscar Smith.

Trev had managed to wangle a table for them at rather a good restaurant, which didn't come cheap. Ted was more than happy to put his hand in his pocket for that as he genuinely felt indebted to Smith. What he really didn't want, though, was Oscar having any hint of where they lived. Ted was always paranoid about his privacy, but even more so where Smith was concerned.

The man would surely be going back south soon. Once he'd written up all his various notes, and accepted that even if his probably dodgy warrant for the Williams couple was taken seriously, which seemed unlikely, there was nothing to

168

keep him in Stockport in person for any longer. Even his own boss seemed in no hurry to call him back, and Ted could imagine why that might be.

'I'll come and pick you up before I go for Oscar, because I don't want him knowing where we live. Same for coming back. I'll drop him off first, if he's going straight back to his B&B, then you. It's just possible he may want to go into work to write up his notes, in which case I'll drop you off at Cherry Tree and you can walk from there. Is that all right with you?'

'Do I have the right to a solicitor before I answer any police questions?' Trev asked, rolling slowly and carefully onto his back, avoiding squashing any cats, and opening bleary blue eyes.

'Seriously, Ted, couldn't you have told me all this last night, rather than waking me up at sparrow's fart to tell me?'

Ted laughed out loud at the question.

'I did, but I should have told you before you opened the wine, it seems. Is all of that okay for you, though?'

Trev was already burrowing back down under the duvet, seeking sleep once more, replying with an ironic, 'Yes, boss.'

* * *

Steve was the only team member in the main office when Ted walked in. He didn't even look up from his keyboard but he did say 'Morning, sir'.

'Morning, Steve, anything new to report?'

Steve paused in what he was doing and looked up.

'I'm working on trying to find anything on record about anyone called or known as J, with just the letter, or Jay, like the garden bird, either as a single or double letter. So far with little real success, although I've found several mentions as a presence.

'I've started widening the search for other letter combinations which would sound phonetically as a J. For instance, there's the Dj sound in Arabic names like Djamal. There's also Djordje, which is Slavic.

'Some of those can be girls' names too, feminised, usually with an A at the end. Like Djamila. I'm doing that because some of the descriptions of the person are ambiguous and I thought it would waste time concentrating on male names until we know JJ's gender for certain.'

'Good thinking, Steve. You're quite right. We tend to assume, with something like this, that it's a male but we know to our cost that some women are capable of acts every bit as horrific as any man.'

Ted was thinking back to an earlier case where the identity of the young killer had shocked all of them. Violent crime knew no boundaries, of gender, class, or anything else.

'Sir, would it be all right for me to ask Océane for her thoughts on tracking the name? She's brilliant at the sort of lateral thinking which might unearth it for us, but I wouldn't do it without asking you. She does still have full clearance.'

Océane was Steve's girlfriend. Steve was outstanding at any type of computer-based research, but Océane was in another league entirely. Ted had never yet heard of her being defeated on any such thing. She'd briefly been a member of Ted's team, before being clawed back by Headquarters, to be based at Central Park. Last Ted had heard, she was in the States on an exchange visit, learning even more useful tricks from the FBI.

'How would that work? Is she still in America?' Ted asked him.

Steve was always polite and respectful to the DCI. Even when he asked such questions. There was no hint of condescension in his reply.

'She is, sir, but we talk most days, and we're still able to work closely together. Any kind of mind games involving words, or names, come to that, is right up her street. I'm not promising, and I'd do it in my own time, but maybe we could come up with some suggestions between us, possibly before tomorrow morning's joint meeting, but that would depend on when she's free.'

'Excellent, Steve, thanks for the suggestion. I'm not going to be in all day today, just on and off, but you have my number. Let me know if anything comes up which might advance us.'

* * *

Ted had given Trev a time half an hour before he planned to pick him up. Knowing his partner's form for poor punctuality, especially on a non-working day, he worked out that he stood an outside chance that way of him being at least out of bed and in the shower by the intended departure time.

He was sure Smith would not be late. Of all his many faults, unpunctuality had never manifested itself as one.

Ted was obsessive about it. He bundled Trev into the back of the car while he was still clutching one sock in his hand, and trying to sort out the buttons of his shirt, which were out of sync.

'Ted, we're only going to lunch with Oscar. It won't matter if we're fashionably late. And I was nearly ready on time – for once.'

'Oscar's ex-military. He won't be late. And I don't want to start the meal with him getting one over on me. Nor do I want to get pulled for speeding, trying to make up time.'

Trev was now half-lying on the back seat, one leg in the air, while he pulled on the missing sock.

'I do hope you two aren't going to be willy-waving for superiority throughout the meal, Ted. This is supposed to be a nice lunch out to say a big thank you to Oscar. Just think, without him flying out to your rescue, you might still be stuck down a badger hole in a German forest. Promise me you'll behave.'

Ted's temper was at least improving as he saw a chance of getting to Oscar's lodgings more or less on time. Smith was waiting outside when they arrived. He'd made an effort for the occasion, wearing a suit Ted hadn't seen him in before, with a clean and well-ironed shirt and, as ever, his Royal Military Police regimental tie.

Smith was politeness itself, offering to sit in the back

instead of Trev, greeting Ted politely and almost deferentially, speaking to Trev in German to begin with.

He looked round the restaurant approvingly when they arrived, and made a point of remaining standing until Ted, the senior officer, had sat down. He was clearly going out of his way to behave.

They'd only just finished the starter when Oscar's phone rang. He glanced quickly at the screen then said apologetically, 'I'm really sorry, guv, I need to take this. It's my Oma, my grandmother. If I don't answer she'll be phoning the police in two countries thinking something's happened to me. Sorry, I'll be as quick as I can.'

He swivelled half round in his seat to take the call. Trev mouthed across the table to Ted, 'You see? Perfectly charming.'

Oscar seemed to be finding it hard to get a word in edgeways. When he did manage to say something, he then listened to a reply, before sighing and holding the phone out to Trevor.

'Would you mind having a few words with Oma? In German, please. She can speak English, but refuses to. I told her I was out to lunch with someone and she wants to know who. She doesn't believe I know anyone who would take me out for a meal.'

There was such a note of sad truth in the way he said it that Ted found himself, for a brief moment, feeling sorry for the man.

Trevor was in his element. He could talk to anyone,

in several languages, and was clearly charming the elderly woman at the other end of the phone.

'I owe a lot to my Oma. What about you, Ted?' Smith risked the informality now. 'Do you have grandparents you have to keep half an eye on? I certainly feel a big debt to my Oma, for all she's done for me. She more or less brought me up after my dad committed suicide.'

Ted's worst nightmare. Talking about himself and his domestic circumstances. Especially to anyone from work. Most of all, to Oscar. But the man was staying civil, seemingly holding out an olive branch, and he had laid bare his own personal tragedy. Once he went back down south, Ted thought it highly unlikely their paths would ever cross again, so he unbent a little.

'Sorry to hear that, Oscar. Not an easy situation, for anyone.

'My dad's parents, and my mam's father, all died when I was too young to remember them. My mam's mam was a murder victim, in a case the team investigated. Clearly, I had to take a back seat on that one.'

Smith's eyebrows shot up at that.

'Blimey. As poker hands go, there is no beating that one. And I think I know you well enough now to know you aren't winding me up.'

Trevor was still chatting away on the phone, seemingly quite happy to be doing so. Ted hated to break the mood, but there was something he was itching to know.

'It's probably not the right time to ask this, over lunch. But what are your plans, Oscar? I'm forever grateful for your help to me personally, but surely you need to be getting back to the Met some time soon?'

'I thought I'd save the Germans a bit of work and submit my reports about your abduction in German so they don't need translation. If it's all right with you, I'll come into the nick tomorrow to get everything typed up and sent off. Then I'll be out from under your feet, guv.'

There was a hint of a wistful tone about the way he said the last sentence which gave Ted a swift pang of guilt for having asked. It was no exaggeration to think the man had possibly saved his life. If the two officers from the car, or the other men in the ambush had come back and found him ...

If nothing else, he would not be sitting here about to enjoy a good meal.

* * *

Monday morning briefing for Ted's team was happening in the incident room to allow space for officers joining them from other units for a pooling of ideas and information about the hit and run.

Uniform officers from Stockport, first responders on site after reports came in, were in attendance, together with Evan Thomas, the sergeant from SCIU, with two of his team, and two officers Ted had not met before from Drugs, a DS and a DC.

'Unless anyone knows different, the only lead or partial ID we have so far is talk of a mysterious character known only as JJ, who's implicated by eyewitnesses to the crash itself, but also, from more anecdotal evidence, as being involved in drugs supply.

'What we don't know for sure at present is whether or not JJ is male or female. Unless anyone here knows differently?'

The Drugs sergeant shook his head as he said, 'Pretty much sums up the intel we have. We keep hearing mention of this JJ character but they always seem to drop off the radar before anyone gets close. They clearly have some clout with the gangs in the sense of having their ear and being able to summon up muscle. All our usual informants seem scared to death by the very mention of the name. But we're still no further forward.

'The only descriptions we've had are probably about the same as you – shaved head, tats, piercings. Pretty much unisex as regards clothing. Slim to the point of skinny, which doesn't help with gender identification. Height around a metre sixty-five, or thereabouts, but reports on that vary.

PC Susan Heap spoke next. She'd been one of the first on site after the crash, and had been talking to any eye witnesses who'd not simply melted away, realising how serious the incident was.

'Sir, it was worse than drawing teeth trying to get

anything from anyone still at the scene when we got there. Pretty much nobody saw or heard anything, apparently, or nothing they would share with us. Just the odd muttered mention of a JJ. We've been trying that name out on anyone we've talked to since. Just mentioning it guarantees instant clamming up, so whoever they are, they're clearly well known and in a powerful position, or with a direct line to those who are.'

'How unusual is this sort of a punishment, warning, whatever it was meant to be, using a vehicle as the weapon? Sergeant Thomas?' Ted asked.

'A new one on us with a pretty much certain drugs connection, sir. Although you might be surprised to hear that a vehicle as a weapon of choice is not as rare as you might think. Not on our patch, but there was a recent case of a woman deliberately mowing down and killing the husband she was divorcing because he wouldn't give her custody of the dog.'

A muted sound of amusement rippled through the room. Ted let it go. Looking for the funny side helped with the tougher parts of the job. As long as it didn't spill over into disrespect, he had no problem with the odd moment of light relief.

Ted looked across at Steve Ellis and asked, 'Steve, how are you getting on with finding any trace of a JJ on record?'

Steve was never at ease with anyone from outside attending a briefing. But he was more sure of his own ground when speaking about his own areas of expertise.

'Sir, with Océane's help, I've been trying every permutation of JJ we can think of, but nothing at all concrete has come up so far. We've still got a few ideas to run with, though.'

'So does anyone have any idea as to what JJ could be? A name, a nickname? If so, what? Let's have some ideas, anything we might have overlooked, which Steve can then run through the system.'

'We had a French connection in the last case,' Mike Hallam put in, 'and they like double-barrelled first names, don't they? So why not something like Jean-Jacques?'

'There was a jockey called Jonjo O'Neill,' Jezza told them. Her general knowledge came mostly from her brother's obsession with making his own set of Trivial Pursuit questions. 'Won the Cheltenham Gold Cup on Dawn Run, and Tommy could tell us the exact date. The Irish also like double first names.'

'It could be a stammer, of course,' Gina put in. 'My sister Jenny developed a stammer in her teens, and she had a lot of difficulty with her own name. She always got stuck on Juh.'

'Right, Steve, that gives you a few more possible angles to work with. And please let's not forget, according to everything SCIU have found out, this was no accident. This was a deliberate attempt to kill or seriously injure a young man who'd told his mother he'd been approached by someone known as JJ to run drugs to the clubs where he coaches and refused to do it.

'So next big push, please – let's start on interviewing anyone who attends those clubs who might give us more on this JJ. Or anyone else who's approached them offering drugs, or wanting runners to distribute them.

'I know,' he went on, hearing another murmur run through those present. 'It's a mammoth task which will need everyone available. So let's make a start.'

Chapter Eighteen

Oscar Smith was in the DI's office early on. Both it and the main office were empty, with the joint briefing happening downstairs. It meant he could crack on with writing up his report to send to the German police, then get on the next south-bound train on which he could get a ticket.

He might even get back early enough to collect his cat, Clive, from the cattery. Smith would never admit it to a living soul but he missed the little bastard when he had to go away. Clive, of course, would probably piss up his master's leg in protest at his absence but would show no signs of having missed him.

Before he did anything, though, Smith wanted to call his DS, Tony Taylor, while there was no one around to hear what he had to say.

Occasions when Oscar Smith climbed down over anything were as rare as rocking horse shit, as he would put it and be the first to admit. He was certainly not going to do it within earshot of anyone.

'Tony, it's me. I should be heading back later today but I need you to do something for me first. Priority. Before you do anything else.'

'Fire away, guv.'

'That warrant for the Williamses. Make it disappear. Officially. Without trace.'

'Disappear, guv?'

'Fuck's sake, Tony, buck up. Disappear. Cancel. Withdraw. Whatever. Say you've since found out the original intel was unsafe. Say anything you need to. But get the bloody thing cancelled. Wipe all mention of it off the system.'

'I don't even know if that can be done, guv, never mind how ...'

'Tony, the whole purpose of having dodgy JPs in our pockets is for moments like this. It was never genuine in the first place, so getting it to vanish into thin air should be even easier than getting it issued. Use your initiative and get it sorted. Asap.'

Taylor was careful to make sure his sigh wasn't audible over the phone.

'Consider it done, guv,' he replied, whilst wondering how the hell he was going to achieve it, and what it was likely to cost him in palm-greasing.

Whatever the price, though, it was always preferable to a bollocking from the DI. It had been like all Taylor's birthdays come at once to have Smith out of the way whilst he and the rest of the team got quietly on with their work. Efficiency always improved the minute the gaffer was off the scene.

'D'you need me to pick you up from the station, guv? Let me know a time, if you do.'

It was the last thing Tony wanted to do, but he thought he'd better offer. You could never tell with Smith when he would go off on one at the slightest excuse. It had been amazing with him away. Everything running smoothly, without the constant fear of him biting everyone's heads off for the least little thing.

'No, you're all right, Tony, thanks.'

The call ended abruptly at that point, almost as if Smith had realised what he'd just said.

Tony sat for a moment, phone still in his hand, staring at the screen in wonder, and not for the first time since the DI had disappeared off to the frozen north.

DC Shane Walker was the only other team member in the office. He noticed the DS's expression and asked him, 'Everything okay, sarge? Something up with the gaffer?'

Taylor shook his head as he replied, 'Well, whoever it was sounded like the gaffer, and swore like the gaffer. But he said thank you, for the first time in living memory, so it can't have been him.'

'Feck me sideways!' Walker replied. 'What do they put in the water up there in the north if it's done that to him?'

* * *

Gina Shaw followed Ted up to his office at the end of the joint briefing, asking for a quiet word.

'I don't want to sound paranoid, boss, but I didn't want to bring up the subject of Ian Hedges in a meeting with officers I've not met before. I know it should be safe to do so, but I also know from experience that sometimes, some of them, especially from Drugs, sail a bit close to the wind, so I thought I'd keep it on a need-to-know basis.'

'Fair enough, Gina. Like you say, there's no need for everyone to know everything about a potential key witness, one who needs maximum protection. The fewer who know, the easier it is to track the source of any leaks which might occur. What's the situation with him currently?'

'His boss, John Faulkner, is a really good man. He's letting him stay with him and his family for the time being, now there's a watch on his house at all times. He's also personally taking him to and from work with him, and there's full surveillance there, too. Clearly he's concerned about his own family, though, so the minute he gets a whiff of us having to pull the obs cover, he'll want new arrangements to be made, for sure, which will mean finding somewhere secure to put Ian.'

'I hate to sound mercenary, because I want Ian kept safe as much as anyone does, but are we getting any return on our investment? In terms of what Ian is prepared to tell us, I mean. Because I need to be able to justify the cost, of course,' Ted told her.

Ted's role was always to walk the slippery tightrope between such things as protecting important witnesses and not making too big a dint in his budget.

'Ian's a bright lad. He's trying to help us, but he's smart enough to know how much danger he's putting himself in by doing so. He clearly knows JJ by sight, enough to put them at the scene, which tends to suggest that JJ, and probably others in the gang, know him, too. Probably enough to notice if he suddenly drops out of sight.'

Ted nodded towards the spare chair for Gina to sit down. She shook her head at his offer of a brew as he went to put the kettle on.

'How useful was he in terms of a description for JJ?'

'Well, he came up with a composite he was happy was as close as he could get. The big problem, of course, is he seems genuinely not to know JJ's gender or age. He wouldn't even make much of a guess.'

'Is that likely?' Ted asked her. 'That he wouldn't have at least some idea about either/or. Or is that him trying to protect himself? Seeming to help us, but then not giving us enough to be of any real use for ID purposes?'

'Jezza and I have been discussing that. She's the expert, of course, in changing appearances, from her drama training. She's shown me some photos of herself from her portfolio from back in the day, and some more recent ones she's had done to keep her hand in. Honestly, boss, in some of them she could easily pass for a teenage boy. Remember when she dressed me up and took me out with her, both of us looking nothing like coppers? I think it's perfectly plausible that people might not know if JJ is male or female, or what age group they are.'

Ted sat back at his desk with his mug of green tea as Gina pulled up the composite on her phone to show to him. There was certainly nothing immediately age or gender-defining about the image which confronted him.

An instant, powerful message. A gaunt face. Dark smudges under the eyes. Prominent cheekbones. A face that looked like its owner was in need of some square meals. Eyes which had clearly known suffering. Ageless, as well as androgynous.

'There's something about this face. Something cleverer than you might first imagine, I think,' he told Gina. 'The tattoos, the piercings, the shaved head. They should be distinctive, but when you look more closely, they're so common they have the opposite effect.

'Look at the tattoo on the side of the neck and face. A cobweb and a spider. How many of those are there? We could get Steve to search on the system, but I'm betting there would be dozens, possibly hundreds.

'The same with the piercings. Nothing original or distinctive about any of them. Quite the opposite. Most people would be hard-pressed to list any of them specifically.'

He looked from the image to Gina as he said, 'I may be completely off the mark here, Gina, but d'you know what this makes me think of? Someone working undercover and trying a bit too hard to blend in. To me, this looks like someone playing a part and not doing very well at the camouflage they're trying to hide behind. A bit like a story I once heard about an inexperienced Drugs officer who blew his own cover trying to score, when his jeans were not only too clean, but ironed, with front creases, too.

'I don't want us to get bogged down on my hunch because I could be completely wrong. But before we set too much store by this supposed likeness, can you please discuss it with Jezza, without telling her my ramblings, and see what she says about it. Also get Steve to do searches on the various things like the tattoo for the statistics of how common they are. Or not, of course. I may be well off the mark.

'The other thing I need you to do is slightly trickier. I know Drugs were represented at the joint briefing this morning. But in the same way that you preferred not to talk about Ian Hedges in front of them, is it possible, even remotely, that they aren't sharing everything fully and frankly with us?'

Gina was staring at him now, disbelief on her face.

'You think JJ might be an officer in deep cover? But JJ was seen and ID'd in the vehicle which nearly killed Martin. Surely, even at the risk of blowing their cover, they wouldn't go to such lengths?'

'Unless they've gone completely rogue. It sadly wouldn't be the first time. See what you can discover, but be careful who you ask and what details you give.

'I hope I'm wrong, but we can't afford not to check out

all possibilities, no matter how seemingly far-fetched. There's something about JJ that doesn't sit quite right with me, but I can't yet pinpoint what that is.'

* * *

Ted was knee deep in admin tasks when his mobile phone interrupted him. Jock McClintock calling. Ted suspected he might be overly optimistic to be hoping for any word of his would-be kidnappers, but he was always optimistic of good news, of a break to take them forward.

'You always were a jammy bastard, Ted,' McClintock began without preamble. 'Always the luck of the devil. Even Mr Green said that.'

'Not sure I would count a night spent down a badger sett in a cold, wet, German forest as all that jammy, Jock. So what I am supposed to be lucky about this time?'

'I don't know about you but I was impressed by *Kommissar* Hoffmann. I got the distinct impression that he hates bent coppers as much as you and I do. He's been all over the matter of your abduction like a man possessed. I know the Germans have a reputation for efficiency, but the speed with which he's come up with some answers is incredible. He must have access to more manpower and resources than you or I are used to having at our disposal, for sure.'

'Sorry to rush you, Jock,' Ted told him, 'but I have the unenviable thrill of going over spreadsheets with my Super quite shortly, so if you could keep it to the edited highlights ...'

McClintock laughed.

'Sorry, I was forgetting you're no longer a humble foot

soldier, like me. In brief, then, it all hinges on one of life's cheesy coincidences, so don't shoot the messenger.

'Hoffmann went straight into this all guns blazing and his first act was to get a look at the financial state of the two suspected officers, Meyer and Becker, your escort-cum-translator, and the driver. There was a small, but not insignificant payment into Meyer's bank account, which he had a great deal of trouble explaining away, very shortly before the incident. Something which could conceivably be a down payment on something, pending completion. He can't or won't explain it satisfactorily.

'A background check on him reveals he has a brother, who is also a police officer, and said brother ...'

'Is somehow connected to the custody arrangements of our suspected murderer and serial rapist, Joel Hammond,' Ted finished for him. 'Am I right?'

'Damn it, Ted, anyone would think you were a copper or something,' McClintock chuckled. 'Yes, spot on. The brother had apparently mentioned to him knowing where Hammond was being held and between them, they saw the beginnings of an idea of how to try to sort his release with a hostage exchange, while lining their pockets as a result.'

It was Ted's turn to laugh.

'Don't ever take up writing crime fiction, Jock. A supposed twist like that in a book would guarantee you a string of bad reviews. But you and I both know that's so often the way cases finally come together.

'So what's the situation now, with them? I'm assuming the brother has also been arrested?'

'All charged, all in custody, all in separate secure locations. And under constant surveillance, because we know that the fate of police officers under arrest is often uncertain.

'Plus this, of course, opens up the way for charges to be laid here against them all of attempting to pervert the course of justice, and so on. But don't worry, Ted, in poker terms, you still have the winning hand with your murder charge.

'And I'm pretty sure that with all of this going on in the background, no country with a claim on your man Joel Hammond is going to be rushing to try to override yours. I'm guessing you're going to get him back a lot sooner than any of us would have thought possible.

'So all of this means I'm going to need full statements from you and DI Smith asap, please, about all aspects of your abduction.'

'Mine's nearly there. I'll give it a tweak and a polish and send it as soon as I can. Oscar's busy with his as we speak. He's doing it in German, to save you translation costs, he said. He's off back down to London as soon as that's done.'

'Do I detect a small note of relief in your voice as you say that, Ted? I mean, I know he rode to your rescue like a knight on a shiny white Airbus, but he's certainly a … how shall I put it diplomatically … a bit of a character.'

Still chuckling to himself, Ted went to find Oscar to chase him up for his statements, and to give him the rest of the news from Jock.

Smith shook his head in disbelief.

'Well, one of us has the luck of the devil, guv, and I'm betting it's you. They always say check family and close friends first, for anything like this, but this is unbelievable, the way it's all slotted together so neatly.

'I've just about finished my report, apart from checking the last *Umlaut* and *Eszett*, so once I send it off, I'll be out of your hair.

'Oh, and guv, that warrant. My DS tells me there was a reliability issue over some of the witness statements. He's getting it withdrawn.'

That was clearly going to be the closest Smith would come to holding up his hands for trying to pull a fast one. Maybe, just maybe, it would make the man think twice in the future about bending the rules to such a blatant degree. Ted doubted it, but he was an eternal optimist.

Ted held out his hand to Oscar across the desk.

'Well, Oscar, it's been an interesting experience working with you. I owe you a debt for coming to my rescue, so feel free to call it in whenever the need arises. I doubt whether our paths will cross again in the future so thanks again and safe journey home.'

Smith shook the outstretched hand warmly enough, with none of his previous Alpha-male nonsense.

'Oh, I think they probably will cross, Ted,' he told him, once again dropping formality now he was leaving. 'I can't imagine those three German coppers pleading guilty, not for a moment, so it's likely you and I will be called as witnesses at some time in the future. Which means we will quite possibly find ourselves, if not on the same flight to Frankfurt, possibly in the same hotel, through one of life's little coincidences. I'll look forward to renewing our acquaintance.'

Chapter Nineteen

Ted went to find Mike Hallam before going to see the Ice Queen. Now it was likely they'd be getting Joel Hammond back sooner than they'd dared hope, on a murder charge as well as the serial rape charges, he wanted to make sure the file on that case was complete, watertight, and ready to go to CPS.

They'd been incredibly lucky to be getting him at all, never mind early. But now he'd become a bit of a hot potato, it seemed Germany couldn't wait to get him off their hands. Ted didn't want any holes in the paperwork stopping them from charging Hammond with everything they could. He also wanted to ensure there was a strong recommendation on the file that he should be remanded to a high security prison, because of the likely risk that there would be other attempts to secure his release.

'Do you want me to put Virgil on that next, boss, while he's on paperwork?'

Ted shook his head.

'At the risk of racial stereotyping, I think Virgil will be better placed on the Martin Jackson case now. There's a chance that any black friends of Martin might possibly be more comfortable with Virgil than talking to someone else.'

'We both know what he's going to say to that. "Is it because I is black?",' Mike said, in a fair imitation of Virgil's stock phrase, always trotted out with tongue firmly in cheek.

'He could be ideal, though, for talking to young people from the clubs where Martin coached. Maurice, too. We know youngsters will usually talk to him. And we need every lead we can get on this one. Who else can relate well to sporty youngsters?'

'Jezza,' Mike said promptly. 'Even though she doesn't follow much sport herself, she's got a head like an encyclopaedia for all the details, thanks to her Tommy. Rob's still liaising with SCIU on the crash itself, and he wants to follow up with this window cleaner he's got hold of, just in case there was anything significant in the place they chose.

'I know probably even less about football and other team sports than you do, boss, so I'll take over the Joel Hammond file myself, to free everyone else up to work on identifying this JJ. Somebody, somewhere, must know something more concrete about them. I can't believe no one could hazard at least a guess at their age and gender.'

Ted was less convinced. He knew he and Mike moved in different social circles, so their experiences would vary. He was thinking in particular about Trev's younger sister, Siobhan, currently going through a few issues with her own sexual identity. Ted hadn't seen her for a while in the flesh, but looking at her on the phone screen over Trev's shoulder to say hello, there were times when, without knowing her, he'd have been hard-pressed to make an accurate guess at her age or gender.

Ever since he'd first met her, she'd presented as far older than her actual years. Being at a boarding school with strict rules on appearance and dress, she hadn't yet gone as far as shaving her head or getting any visible tattoos, but Ted could well imagine how androgynous she would look if ever she did.

'I'll try to get to our junior self-defence club on Wednesday evening if I can, too,' Ted told Mike. 'There's a chance that some of the youngsters who attend might have been approached by this JJ person at some point. Or know of someone who has. Most of them will usually talk to me. If I can't go for any reason, I'll ask Trev to raise it with them.

'Let's show the composite around all the clubs, but I won't put it out on general release just yet, subject to the Super agreeing. There's a chance it would make the person disappear off the scene before we find them if we did, for one thing, and so far they're the only tentative lead we have. It might, potentially, put other lives at risk, too, if the gang decide to issue another strong warning about the dangers of anyone talking to us.

'Can you also see about getting us into local schools to talk to pupils about the risk of drugs, and to see if any of them might have anything to add. Make sure they know they can always speak to us in confidence. That would be a good starting point for Maurice and Jezza. Liaise with sports teachers, see if they've heard anything about anyone they teach being approached about drugs of any sort. Perhaps performance-enhancing ones, or so-called.'

He made to leave the office then turned back.

'Oh, and CCTV, Mike. It's a racing certainty that most of the clubs will have it these days, even the smaller ones. They'll no doubt be storing some expensive kit they need to protect, so let's see if we can pick up JJ on any footage anywhere, if they've been hanging around trying to sell drugs or to recruit new runners. And most of the schools will have it too.'

'That's another thing I'm struggling to understand, boss. Nobody seems to have heard this JJ person speak, so how do they get on selling drugs, or recruiting for the gangs?'

Ted pulled out his mobile, tapped briefly on it, then held the screen out to Mike.

'This is how,' the message said.

* * *

Virgil Tibbs had done some phoning ahead before his first visit to the hospital to see Martin Jackson. He wanted to make sure the Firearms officers on duty knew he was coming and what he looked like. He was used to being judged entirely on his appearance and he was anxious to avoid an incident with an armed police officer who might not know him by sight.

He'd also phoned Martin's parents, to put them in the picture. All of the team members were being careful to keep them informed and on side throughout the enquiry. Virgil was tasked with showing Martin the likeness of JJ which Ian Hedges had helped to construct, and that was likely to be extremely disturbing for him, especially if it was at all accurate.

His first call of all had been to Martin's medical team, for their opinion on whether or not he was yet stable enough to cope with what was likely to be a shock. They couldn't afford to wait much longer for his confirmation of whether or not the picture matched the person Martin knew simply as JJ, but there was no point in risking causing him a relapse by rushing into what was likely to be a distressing ordeal.

Virgil was wearing his ID prominently round his neck, but took the precaution of having his warrant card in his hand as well as he pushed through the swing doors at one end of the corridor. He breathed a sigh of relief at the sight of a

Firearms officer he knew.

'Hello, Roy, mate,' he greeted him, putting away his warrant card. 'I'm glad to see a friendly face. I'm always getting mistaken for a pimp or a dealer.'

'Can't imagine why, Virgil. Big softy like you?' the officer replied. 'You're here to see the young lad, I understand. How's he doing? Can't begin to imagine what his family are going through. Parents are very nice. They always stop to say hello, and to thank us. We're just doing our job, but it's always nice to be thanked.'

'Any sign of any trouble? Anyone dodgy hanging around?'

Roy chuckled at that point, without looking at Virgil as he spoke. His eyes never ceased their endless scanning of the corridor for any sign of anything out of the ordinary.

'You're the dodgiest person to come through those doors on my shift. Good luck with talking to Martin. I hope you get the bastards who did this.'

Virgil went first to the nearby family room where he'd arranged to meet Martin's parents, having phoned ahead to tell them he'd arrived. He was greeted warmly, with handshakes from both of them.

'DC Dennis Tibbs,' he told them. His nickname was fine in the office but he stayed professional when working outside.

'As I explained on the phone, I'm here because I want to show Martin a photofit likeness made up by an eye witness to the collision. It shows the person known only as JJ, at this point. I believe Martin has already indicated to one of my colleagues that he knows of someone who goes by that nickname.'

Virgil was picking his words carefully, trying to be

tactful. He knew Martin's father hadn't been in the room when Maurice had been asking questions about JJ, and he wasn't sure how much the father knew about Martin having been approached by JJ in connection with drugs supply.

Thelma Jackson saw his hesitation and told him, 'It's all right, officer, I've now told my husband everything Martin told me about being approached by this JJ person, talking about drugs.'

Walter Jackson spoke then, clearly still angry at not having been kept in the picture before.

'You should have told me at the time, love. So should Martin. If I'd known back then about this character, I'd have gone straight to the police to see what could be done about him, and then this terrible thing might not have happened to Martin.'

Virgil cut in at that point, anxious to avoid any sort of blame game, which wouldn't be helpful to any of them.

'I honestly don't think there's any guarantee of that, Mr Jackson. From what we know of these drugs gangs in general, they are completely ruthless and go to great lengths to flex their muscles. They tend to come down heavily on anyone who tries to make a stand against them. To make a public example of them, as a warning. Even for a simple refusal to play along.

'If you had come to us about JJ, there's no guarantee we'd have been able to track them down, or to prevent such an incident from happening, unfortunately.

'I notice, Mr Jackson, that you said 'him' in connection to JJ. Do you have some knowledge to show that they are male? Something Martin might have said? Mrs Jackson?'

They both looked confused for a moment, exchanging glances. Mr Jackson spoke first.

'Well, I assumed it was a lad. I think you did, too, love, didn't you? I mean, you don't think of girls being involved in drug running and such like, do you?'

Unfortunately, through experience, Virgil did. He knew that acts of criminality often knew no gender boundaries. A female might even be an asset to the gangs. They might be better at approaching other young people and gaining their confidence. Although from the composite picture of JJ he was there to show to Martin, he couldn't imagine their physical appearance, if it was accurate, would be all that reassuring to anyone.

He got out his phone and pulled up the image. No harm in showing it to the parents before they went in to see Martin, on the off-chance they may have seen the person hanging round, waiting to try to get a word with Martin.

Walter Jackson took hold of the phone first, pushing up his glasses so he could look at it more closely.

'Well, that's not a face you would forget in a hurry,' he said. 'If he's trying to look threatening, he's certainly succeeding. I wouldn't much want to come up against him on a dark night. But I can definitely say I've never seen him before. I guarantee I would remember if I had.

'What about you, love?' he asked, passing the phone to his wife.

She studied it much more closely than he had, eyes scanning the screen, taking in every detail.

'No, it's definitely not someone I've ever seen before. And like Walter says, I'd certainly not forget in a hurry. But I wouldn't be as convinced as you, love, that this is a male. I can't tell you what, but there's something about the face – those eyes, in particular – that makes me think they could possibly be female. Or have been female, at some point.

Perhaps it's someone who's one of those – what d'you call them, now – transgender people. Or possibly what we used to call a tomboy.

'And I know they've almost certainly been involved in this terrible thing which has happened to Martin. But I see sadness behind this face, somehow. And I know it's not a real person, it's just an artist's impression, or whatever you call it when a computer does it. It makes me feel sorrow and suffering. And not just to our boy.'

Walter Jackson made a scoffing sound as his wife handed the phone back. But Virgil filed away what she'd said in the back of his mind. It was most probably fanciful nonsense but it was interesting that whereas the father was adamant the face was male, his wife had floated the idea that it could be female, and Virgil had long since learned to keep an open mind about such things.

'So is it all right if we go and talk to Martin now, please? I promise to do my best to try not to tire him too much, or upset him, but we really do need his help with this. The hospital did say they'd put a nurse with him while I talk to him, just in case.'

'Yes, they told me that, too,' Mrs Jackson told him. 'I just need to press the bell and someone will come. I do hope it's not going to be too much for him, seeing that face again.'

Virgil was apprehensive, looking at the youth in the bed. He only needed to ask him two questions, requiring him only to indicate yes or no. But to do so he needed to show him the composite picture of someone who was potentially one of those who'd tried to kill him, and that risked having a dramatic effect on him.

The nurse who came in to join them was an instantly reassuring presence. She checked all of Martin's vital signs first then told Virgil he could go ahead; she would remain close to all the time.

Martin looked understandably apprehensive as Virgil began to speak, first introducing himself, holding up his warrant card.

'Martin, I know you previously indicated to my colleague that you did see someone in the vehicle which hit you who you recognised. I now have a facial composite, compiled by a witness to the incident.

'I understand it will be difficult and challenging for you to look at it, but I really need you to do that for me, please. Then I'll ask you just two questions. First if you recognise the face as someone you've seen before. Then secondly, if it's that of the person you mentioned to my colleague as being in the vehicle.

'Is that all right with you? And could you please show me how you would like to signal Yes.'

His hand shaking, Martin managed to lift his thumb.

'And for no, please?'

Martin's head moved fractionally from side to side against his pillow.

'That's fine, Martin, thank you. Tell me to stop if ever you feel the need of a break.'

Virgil held up his phone and showed the face, enlarged as much as he could, to Martin.

An instant shudder went through the young man's body but, as Virgil asked him, 'Have you seen this person before?' he managed to lift a thumb from a hand still shaking.

'That's great, thank you. And next, is this the face of the person you know as JJ, please?'

Another convulsion of fear, which made one of the monitors bleep. The nurse nodded reassuringly. Nothing to be unduly worried about.

Another thumbs up, more determined this time.

'Thank you, Martin, that's perfect. I'll leave you to rest now, and thanks again. Thank you everyone.'

Virgil had his phone on silent mode but felt it vibrating in his pocket as he left the corridor and started down the stairs. He took it out to check. Mike Hallam calling him.

'Yes, sarge?'

'I wasn't sure if you were still with Martin, but you're the nearest to an incident that's just been reported. A serious assault. Very serious. Possible attempted murder so we need a Serious Crime presence, if you can take it?'

'Just finished with Martin and got the positive ID we needed, so yes. Where is it, and what are the details?'

Mike gave him an address which was not all that far from the hospital.

'The address is Ian Hedges' home address. From info received so far, it would seem the victim is his mother, and it's not looking good for her. You get round there as soon as you can. In the meantime I'm getting the watch on where Ian is now doubled, in case this was a message to him. And I'm crossing all fingers and toes the mother didn't tell her attackers anything about where the lad works.'

Chapter Twenty

'Miss? Miss!'

The insistent small voice behind Jezza was accompanied by the sound of hurrying feet on the wooden floor leading from the sports hall where she'd just been talking to pupils.

Jezza stopped and turned back, sizing up the young girl trotting towards her eagerly, hoping she was not going to be a time waster, wanting to talk about her pet rabbit rather than the case.

Jezza badly wanted to go back with some sort of a lead, at least. She'd been lucky at the school to encounter a supportive and cooperative headteacher who'd accompanied her to the sports hall where some of the school teams were being put through their paces.

Her audience were mixed ages as they were grouped by teams rather than school years. This girl looked like one of the younger ones, but it was always hard to tell and she wasn't about to pass up on any chance of information on the current case.

She made her face and voice encouraging as she replied, 'Yes? Is there something you want to tell me? What's your name?'

'Cathy, Miss. And yes. My brother and me got stopped going home from sports club.'

Jezza looked round for an empty room nearby. On the off-chance this was actually going to be something of use to her, she didn't want to be standing in a corridor where anyone might walk past and see her talking to the girl.

Cathy was clearly sharp, at least. She correctly interpreted Jezza's look around them and said, 'We can go in here, Miss, there's no one in.'

She held open the door to an empty room, allowing Jezza to go in first. Observant and polite was a promising start, Jezza thought, as the two of them found seats.

'What can you tell me, Cathy, in connection with what I was talking about earlier?'

Jezza got her notebook out to jot down anything useful. Trying to record the girl risked her drying up.

'Me and my brother belong to the same basketball club. He's older than me, and in another school. He's very good. Plays for the town and county.

'We were walking back from practice together one night, a few weeks ago. There was a car parked near the end of the road, with two people standing leaning against it. One of them said hello to Richie, that's my brother. Like he knew him a bit. At least knew his name.'

The girl paused for a moment, watching Jezza make notes. Jezza stayed quiet. Whatever the girl wanted to tell her, she wanted it in her own words, with no prompting. Once she'd had her say, then Jezza could go over it for anything which needed further clarification.

'Richie didn't seem to want to stop and talk. He was, like, hurrying me away from them. It felt like he was a bit worried about what they wanted with him. One of them spoke, but the other didn't say anything. Just stood there, looking a bit creepy.

'I turned to look back but Richie told me just to ignore them. I tried asking him where he knew them from, but he didn't want to talk. We walked home faster than we usually do. I could hardly keep up with him, and he kept looking back over his shoulder to check they weren't following us. He seemed really scared of them.

'He's always refused to tell me anything about them, but then you came and asked if any of us had ever been approached by anyone near where we do sports, so I thought I'd tell you.'

'That's excellent, Cathy, thank you. Now, can I ask you for a few more details, please? A few things which might help us identify who these people were.'

'The car was a fairly new black BMW,' Cathy told her confidently, trotting out the model number with the air of someone who knew their cars.

She smiled as she went on, 'I'm the petrol-head in the family. I love cars. Richie probably wouldn't be able to tell you the make, never mind the model.'

Jezza made a note – definitely not the same vehicle as the one involved in the collision – then said, 'What about the people? What can you tell me about either of them?'

'One was short, very thin, a shaved head, tattoos. He didn't speak at all. Just stared hard at Richie. The other was quite tall. Muscly. Like the sort of person you see outside clubs stopping the wrong people going in. A bouncer, is it? He seemed to know Richie. He called out to him by name.'

'Can you remember what he said?'

'I'm not as good on details like that, but something like "did you think about what we said, Richie? You could make yourself a bit of money". I think that was it.'

'And they were both men?' Jezza checked, trying to sound as casual as she could.

'Well, the thin one was more like a teenager, I think, not

an adult, but I'm not sure, really. Richie was that keen to get away. It was strange, in a way, because I thought the big one, the driver, looked scary, but Richie seemed more worried about the smaller one who never said anything.'

She looked worried, at that point, as she hurried on, 'I don't want to get Richie into any trouble. It seemed like he was doing his best to avoid the men.'

'I will need to talk to him, though,' Jezza told her. 'What I'd like you to do, if that's all right with you, is to give me a phone number for your mum or dad so I can call and make an appointment for a time when I can come and speak to you all together. You and Richie, with your mum and dad.

'Don't worry, though. You're not in any trouble, you've done the right thing in telling me this. But I do need to talk to anyone who's seen anyone like the two people you've described. And thank you for that, and for all the detail. You've been very helpful.'

* * *

There was still an ambulance parked outside the home of Ian Hedges' mother when Virgil drove round there from the hospital. There was also a police car and two officers, already taping off the scene of a potentially serious crime.

Virgil paused to pull on shoe covers and gloves, as a bare minimum, before he entered the property. He found the ambulance crew working to stabilise a woman lying on the floor before they could begin to think of moving her. He hadn't encountered either of them before so he introduced himself, standing well back out of their way, then asked for a sitrep.

The female technician, who'd introduced herself as

Lorna, spoke first.

'We'll need her a lot more stable before we can even think of transferring her and we've got a lot of work to do to get there. You're Serious Crime, did you say? So you know she's a torture victim?'

'I didn't, no. She's connected to one of our protected witnesses, so this address meant the report was flagged up to us. And in the circumstances, that news is worrying. Can you tell me what sort of level of torture? It might help assess the likelihood of her having talked.'

'I can tell you that one of her nipples was ripped off, but I can't tell you what with. And you probably know that's one of the most sensitive parts of the female anatomy, so she would have been in horrendous pain.

'She's also suffered serious head injuries, which is what is concerning us most at the moment. At an unscientific guess, I would say her head was banged up and down hard on something. Possibly the floor, or the hearth. So there's zero chance of you getting to talk to her any time soon, if that's what you're wanting to do.'

'Sorry if that sounded a bit insensitive. But I do need to assess the risk to our potential witness, as a priority, following this attack. I'll call it in but then I'd better stay, on the off-chance she comes round. I promise not to get under your feet.'

* * *

Rob O'Connell was back at the scene of the collision to talk to the window cleaner, Rob Holland, to see if his experience could add anything relevant regarding the location where the incident took place.

Rob wanted to know if it had been an opportunistic attack or planned in advance, which would add weight to the attempted murder theory. He'd found out that it was a route Martin walked regularly from one of the sports clubs, usually at the same time, but he wanted to pinpoint why that exact spot had been chosen.

SCIU were concentrating on trying to trace the vehicle itself, and its apparent use as a weapon with intent. Rob was trying to cover the wider picture, with the now almost certain drugs connection.

He shook hands with the other Rob and explained what he was looking for; the lines along which he was thinking.

'I was hoping you might be able to tell me a bit about why this particular spot, and whether or not there was any reason to choose this window in particular, rather than any of the others on this road. If it helps, I'm told reliably that it was made from float glass.

Holland was nothing if not thorough. He was clearly taking his role as a potential expert witness seriously. He first checked the now boarded up window, carefully examining any tiny remnants of glass fragments which clung to the frame.

Then he strode up and down a bit, measuring out distances, looking at site lines, comparing with other available shopfronts on the same road.

Finally he turned back to Rob O'Connell to sum up.

'Well, if someone wanted to seriously injure, or even kill someone, a big float glass window like that would be ideal. It's a great glass for shop windows because of its good transparency, and it's a good insulator. It's a big clear expanse to aim for, too, so even if the target tried to dodge out of the way the driver could still swerve a bit at the last minute and probably still hit them.

'Float glass is brittle and tends to break into vicious shards which can be lethal. So was that luck or did someone know that and aim for it deliberately? That's a question for you.

'But there's another reason the driver probably chose this particular shopfront to aim for, although I'm sure you'll already have thought of that. It's not my area of expertise, of course, but depending on the size of vehicle, and the amount of momentum they needed to get up the kerb and keep on going until impact, isn't this about the only place along here where they could do that? I mean, between the parked cars, the letter box, the recycling bins and the dog shit bin?'

Rob mentally kicked himself up the backside. The window cleaner was right. He had spotted something so obvious that Rob had overlooked it himself. Luckily Holland seemed like a decent bloke who wasn't making a big thing of it. He was so glad he hadn't asked anyone from SCIU the same question though. They would have taken him for a total idiot, not a DS from Serious Crime.

'Thanks, mate, I really appreciate your help. You've given me a lot to think about.'

* * *

Gina Shaw had arranged a meeting with one of her former colleagues from Drugs. Not one of those who'd attended the joint briefing, but someone she knew from way back. She was meeting him in a quiet coffee shop out of town, knowing he was likely to be working undercover, as he so often was. She'd been home to change, to dress down so as not to draw any attention to herself, nor to the person she was meeting.

She wanted to find out if the boss had been onto anything at all with what he had said about JJ. About there being something overdone about their appearance. She thought it was highly unlikely to be an undercover officer but if anyone would know, and might agree to tell her, it would be Baz, the man she had come to meet.

There was certainly nothing overdone nor suspicious about Baz's appearance, and he definitely looked nothing like a copper. Gina had always got on with him, found him more accepting of a female officer than some of his colleagues. Total equality was still something elusive, in some fields more than others.

'Now then, young Shaw,' he greeted Gina, sitting down opposite her. She'd already got him a black coffee, remembering that was pretty much all he ever drank. 'How's life in Serious Crime, and to what do I owe the honour of a visit? Not that I'm complaining. Always nice to see you.'

'Thanks, Baz. I've come to pick your brains on a case we're currently working on, with a Drugs overlap.'

He frowned at that.

'Yes, I know you had some of the team over to pool ideas. What makes you think I can tell you any more than they did?'

'Because I can usually rely on you to tell me the truth, rather than the version I'm supposed to accept.'

He smiled at that, nodding to her to go on, whilst taking a mouthful of his coffee.

Gina got out her phone, where she had the likeness of JJ, which she pulled up and held out to him.

'Do you know this person?'

'Course I do. That's JJ. Don't tell me you've finally got your hands on the little shit when we've been trying for ages to collar him and not succeeded yet.'

'Him?' Gina queried. 'You think it's definitely a him?'

Baz looked from the screen to her and back again.

'Course it bloody is. Look at him. Can you see anything female in that?'

'I honestly don't know. We have one person who thinks they're female. And you've never caught them? Ever? Not even for questioning, then had to let them go?'

'Never. Little bastard slips through any net we cast. Like bloody Scotch mist.'

'Hence the next question. Could it be an undercover officer? One none of us know about?'

Baz stared at her in disbelief.

'You need to have a word with your dealer, Shaw, if you think that. Whatever they're giving you is bad stuff.

'An undercover officer? It would have to be someone from right outside the area for none of us to know them. Wherever you're getting your daft ideas from, you want to take no notice of whoever's spouting shit like that.'

* * *

'Boss, it's Virgil,' he said into his phone. 'I'm still at Mrs Hedges' house. She's in a bad way. They're trying to get her stable enough to move.

'Thing is though, boss, whoever it was has tortured her. Badly. She must have been in agony, with the things they've done to her. If she was conscious while they were doing all that, I can't imagine how she wouldn't have talked, unless she passed out.

'So what I'm trying to say is that whatever cover you've got on where Ian works and is staying for now, it needs to be the maximum available. If she did talk, they'll be coming for him next, for sure, and they're likely to take extreme measures to stop him from saying anything, if they suspect him of knowing too much.'

Chapter Twenty-one

Ted decided to go in person to sort out adequate protection for Ian Hedges, and also to be the one to break the news to the teenager of the attack on his mother. He could easily have sent one of the team but he wanted a reason to get out from behind his desk and the seemingly endless paperwork, as much as anything else. It would also be good to feel that he was actively involved in the case, at least on some level.

He had the advantage of not looking anything like the typical mental image most people had of a police officer, so he was unlikely to draw attention from anyone who might have been trying to find Ian. Ted had done quite a few pieces to camera about various cases he'd worked on, so there was always an outside chance someone would recognise him that way. But he always kept a walking jacket in the car and if he wore that and ditched his tie, he might look suitably different from his formal police persona. And if he parked his service vehicle some distance away and warned the officers keeping watch that he was on his way so not to react to his presence, his visit shouldn't raise any flags.

He also phoned Ian's boss, John Faulkner, to let him know he was coming. He'd be glad of the man's presence when he had to tell Ian the news about his mother. He'd no idea about the relationship Ian had with her, but hearing of the attack on her would undoubtedly still come as a shock to him and increase his anxiety about his own safety, since he'd started cooperating with the police.

There was a chance that news of the assault on Ian's mother could be the last straw in terms of Faulkner's kindness in giving the lad a temporary home as well as a job. Ted didn't think Ian's mother would have been in a position to tell her attackers where Ian was living. He knew from Gina and Maurice that she didn't seem to have much of a clue where exactly he was working. But those two had been able to find the place from minimal information so there was a strong likelihood that whoever had tortured Mrs Hedges would find it, too, if they wanted to locate Ian badly enough.

That possibility presented a major problem. If Ian was no longer safe where he was staying or working, the big question would be where they could put him so he'd be out of harm's way and wouldn't stop cooperating with them altogether. For the moment, he was pretty much all they had.

Ian Hedges barely looked up as Ted walked into the work premises and headed for the partitioned-off space labelled as the office. Ian was concentrating hard on what looked like a complex electrical circuit board, though it seemed to be presenting the youth with only a slight challenge.

Ted went first to find John Faulkner and introduce himself, then Ian was summoned to the office, making the small confines feel cramped.

Ian listened in silence to everything Ted had to say to him, when Faulkner called him into the office. Ted was studying the youth's face as he spoke to him but it remained a closed book. He would make a formidable poker player. Ted suspected that lack of expression was a coping skill learned from living in a house where things might not always have been easy for young Ian, growing up.

His first words, when Ted had finished speaking, were, 'I

kept telling her summat like this was going to happen to her, letting all them strange men into the house when she were there by herself. And not always one at a time.'

Ted noted that was his first thought, before he even asked about how his mother was. He waited for a moment, expecting that question to come. When it finally did, it wasn't quite as he was expecting.

'Should I go and see her, then? In hospital, like?'

Ted wasn't sure if the seeming indifference was another coping mechanism, or if Ian really hadn't quite grasped how serious his mother's situation was.

'I'm not even sure if that's possible just yet, Ian. She is very seriously injured and I imagine they'll want to stabilise her before even close family can visit. I'll make sure you're kept informed of when you can see her, though. Does your mother have any other family members we should inform?'

'Dunno really. Never met anyone. Don't even know who me dad were. Not sure she does, neither. Can I get back to work now?'

He looked to John Faulkner as he asked.

'Go on then, lad. I'll come and check on how you're doing in a bit. And I'll take you to see your mam when you're allowed to, if you want me to. If you want to have someone with you.'

Once Ian had left the office, Faulkner turned to Ted, shaking his head.

'That lad is a little diamond, considering all he's been through. He could have turned out all wrong, with that background. He could have gone along with the whole drugs gangs thing. Another stereotype. He's clearly brought himself up and he's about the best house guest we could have. He always does the washing up. Volunteers and won't take no for an answer. Sets the table, too. Keeps his bedroom spotless, and the clothes we've been lending him, although the ones he turned up in didn't seem to have had the same care at home.

'I know it sounds heartless of me, but whatever happens to his mother, it strikes me he's a bloody sight better off without her. I wish he could stay with us indefinitely, but I can't take the risk to my own family if there's anyone after him who would attack his mother that seriously.'

'I haven't told you the half of it, either,' Ted told him. 'I promise you I will increase the watching presence on him for now. But what you've just told me about how he looks after himself has given me an idea. Somewhere he might consider going where his safety would be guaranteed. It might not appeal to him at all, of course, but I'm going to make some enquiries from someone I know. It might possibly be the best thing for him, both in the short term, and in the long run.

'I'll keep you posted about his mother's condition, and about this idea, if it's even workable.'

Ted walked back to where he'd left his car, eyes constantly on the lookout for any sign of anyone hanging around.

He took his phone out as he slid into the front passenger seat and called up a saved number.

'Oscar? Ted Darling. I need to pick your brains, please. Could a bright, house-trained sixteen-year-old lad, trainee electrician but also passionately interested in mechanics, and very good at his work, according to his boss, in need of a safe and stable environment, join the army, and how would he go about it, please?'

* * *

Gina was still dressed down from her earlier meeting with Baz, her former colleague from Drugs, when the team got together at the end of the day for a progress report. Ted noticed she was not the only one sporting a changed appearance.

She'd reported quietly to Ted before the team get-together on everything Baz had told her.

'And would he know if there was someone undercover from Drugs? Someone from out of the area, perhaps?' he asked her.

'I suspect he probably would, boss, but I couldn't swear to it. Baz is one of those coppers who somehow always manages to have a finger on every pulse, although nobody ever knows how they manage it.'

Jezza was also dressed in a way which made her unrecognisable; nothing like her usual work persona. Her hair was pulled right back and tied into a severe pony tail at the back. One side of her face and neck sported what looked like an ink line-drawing to Ted, who was standing at the other side of the room. She was wearing an oversized sweatshirt with a hood. The overall effect was boyish.

Ted was well enough used to Jezza and her little ways not to make any comment. She would doubtless reveal what it was all about when she was good and ready.

He started things off by telling the team members who didn't already know about the attack on Ian Hedges' mother. He'd phoned the hospital for an update beforehand.

'She's still critical and the prognosis is still guarded. She hasn't yet regained consciousness and the person I spoke to either couldn't or wouldn't tell me if they think she's likely to. I've been to see Ian to put him in the picture. He didn't show any inclination to go and see her.'

Maurice spoke up at that.

'Not surprised, boss. Trying not to judge the woman, because I don't know what her life's been like to make her how she is, but that was a long way from a warm and loving house to bring up a boy in. She couldn't even tell me and Gina where he worked, for goodness' sake. That lad is so well thought of at work. Imagine what his life might have been like with a better home. And I can't imagine any parent giving up their child to save their own skin, no matter what was done to them.'

Virgil was usually the joker of the team. Self-deprecating, always finding something to make some sort of a quip about. This time he was quieter and more serious than usual.

'Maurice, I couldn't see the half of what they'd done to her, and I really didn't want to. I'd like to believe that I'd die before I ever let any harm come to Daisy. But seeing the state they left her in, I can well imagine she would say anything she thought they wanted to hear to save herself from any more of the same. I suspect they only left her alive as a warning to Ian of what would be coming his way if he doesn't keep his mouth shut.

'The one good thing about the whole sorry scenario is that for once, her lack of interest in him might just be the thing that keeps him safe. I know you found where he works, in the end, but there's just a chance they won't do. Not yet, at least. Hopefully he might be safe for a bit longer.'

'So with the torture element on Mrs Hedges, are we going on the assumption that she might have told her attackers something about where Ian is?' Mike Hallam asked. 'Does that mean he's going to need to be moved? And if it does, will we then lose him as a potential witness? I can't say I'd blame him if he clammed up.'

'It's very early days yet but I have had a thought about a possible solution to that. I've no idea if it's even feasible, nor if Ian would agree to it, but it is the safest option I can think of for him,' Ted replied. 'I'll let you know how it pans out, if it does.'

Then he turned to Jezza to say, 'All right, DC Vine, you have our full attention. I'm sure I'm not the only one eager to know how you're going to use your dramatic skills and training this time to enlighten us about some aspect of the case. The stage is all yours.'

'Sorry if this all seems a bit am drams, boss, but it's sometimes easier to illustrate a theory this way than to try to explain it simply in words. It's about two things. The fact that whoever this JJ is, they always seem to manage to disappear in a puff of smoke before anyone can get a hand on them. And the possibly significant fact that there seems to be a lot of uncertainty about their gender.'

She stood up and moved into the centre of the room where everyone could see her. All eyes were riveted, waiting to see what she was about to come up with. They all knew by now that Jezza's ideas were always worth listening to, if nothing else.

As she stood there, her whole posture, even her physical appearance, seemed to change in front of them. Her head dipped. Her shoulders rounded. She looked shorter. She certainly looked nothing like the attractive young woman they all knew her to be. In fact there was nothing feminine about her. They were suddenly looking at what could easily have been a teenage boy.

She held the pose for a moment longer, then looked up

and asked, 'So, male or female?'

'Well, I know you very well, bonny lass,' Maurice told her, 'but I'd be hard-pressed to tell. But even with not knowing that, there's still that distinctive facial tattoo. Some people have mentioned that, but not all that many. That's impossible to make disappear.'

Jezza smiled fondly at him as she said, 'I was coming to that.'

The hoody she was wearing was several sizes too big for her, with a kangaroo pouch pocket at the front. She reached into that and pulled out a long blonde wig which she slipped on deftly, adjusting it so the hair screened her face and part-covered her cheeks. The distinctive tattoo effectively disappeared. At the same time she totally changed the way she was standing. Another visible metamorphosis in action.

'What about now? Male, or female?'

All of the team members knew Jezza's skills by now. Even so there was a stunned silence for the moment. Ted spoke first.

'Impressive as usual, Jezza, and you've made an important point that we all need to remember. We don't yet know JJ's gender and we need to keep that in mind when we interview any witnesses, without leading them. Gender-neutral pronouns, please, but at the same time, nothing at all to plant an idea in anyone's mind that this is someone who changes their appearance from one to another to suit.

'Good work today, everyone. We're making progress, even if it sometimes doesn't feel like it. We need to find this JJ but let's not forget the rest of the gang, including the driver of the 4x4.'

'And I had news of another vehicle from the school visits,' Jezza put in, now back to her work persona. 'A black

BMW, hanging round sports clubs. Again with mention of someone very like JJ. I've circulated the details and copied in Drugs and SCIU, although again, the plates are likely to be false once more. But it's something else, at least.

* * *

'This is a pleasant surprise,' Trev greeted Ted when he arrived home at an almost civilised time, for once. 'Have you solved the case and caught all the baddies?'

Trev was in the kitchen, cooking. Seemingly for the five thousand, to judge by the amount of food being prepared. Tantalising smells were making Ted realise how hungry he felt, and he could summon up no recollection of what, if anything, he had eaten at lunchtime.

The downside, as ever, was that the entire space looked as if a mob of angry gremlins had made a raid on the cupboards, and the sink was piled with more pans and dishes than Ted realised they actually owned. No doubt the meal would be well worth it, but it was going to take some serious clear-up operations afterwards, and that would be his job. As long as he didn't get called back to the nick for any reason. Preferably a breakthrough, which they were badly in need of.

He made his way through the troupe of cats, stopping to stroke each in turn, as he replied.

'Still a long way off that, sadly, but we've made some progress. As a matter of fact, I had to phone Oscar today, to ask his advice on something. He was surprisingly helpful, too.'

Trevor turned from the cooker, smiling, and took the time to plant a kiss on Ted's cheek.

'You see? He can be positively charming when he wants to be. And his Oma was delightful when I spoke to her. I'd love to meet her one day. She was a champion skier, back in the day. Did you know?'

'I didn't. Not something that's come up in conversations I've had with Oscar. And I can't see us popping over to Germany to meet his granny any time soon, so don't get your hopes up.'

'You can be extremely boring sometimes, Mr Policeman. Did you know that? You should also know by now that I usually get my way in the end. Now go and phone your mother while I finish cooking, before she forgets the sound of your voice.'

Chapter Twenty-two

Ted was in early the following morning. He wanted to check up on the state of Ian Hedges' mother before he did anything else, as that would partly inform how the day went for the team.

The news was still much the same as the day before but Ted did manage to discover she had not yet regained consciousness. The hospital had at least arranged to have her on the same corridor as Martin Jackson so that she, too, could benefit from the Firearms officers still in place to protect him. If she hadn't told her attackers everything they wanted to know, there was a strong chance they might try to get at her again.

Ted also wanted to talk to the Ice Queen first thing about releasing the likeness they now had of JJ. He found her in her office, another early bird, so sat down with her to explain his thinking, beginning with an account of Jezza's portrayal.

'I don't want to plant ideas over gender in anyone's head, or we could be going off on false trails all the time, but I wondered whether to mention that there's a chance the person may sometimes wear a long wig. I'd appreciate your thoughts, ma'am.'

As ever, the Super had set her coffee machine going as soon as she'd walked through the door, and now put a cup in front of each of them before she sat down to consider what Ted was saying.

'I would worry that, if we showed different likenesses, one shaved head, the other with long hair, that might be too confusing. Especially as we have no way of knowing hair colour, presumably. I don't see the harm in mentioning that the person may change their appearance, to include long hair, on some occasions. Otherwise we risk people discounting a facial similarity simply because of no shaven head.

'Any news on any other suspects yet? And, I'm sure you will have considered the possibility, but as this JJ appears not to speak, could they perhaps be deaf and if so will you need a signer when you finally catch up with them?'

'Good point, ma'am, I hadn't considered deafness and I should have. I was rather getting hung up on a speech impediment as the possible reason for being seemingly non-verbal. DC Ellis has been working on collating all details he's found from anywhere which mention JJ. Still no ID yet, though.'

'We need a result soon, chief inspector. We're currently getting a battering in the press, as I'm sure you're aware. Catching this person JJ would be something, at least, even if not much in the greater scheme of things.'

'Ma'am, Drugs are concentrating on the rest of the gang for now and we're sharing intel constantly,' Ted was doing his best not to sound defensive, although he was feeling it. 'At the same time SCIU are concentrating on the driver and vehicle, so far with nothing new thrown up.'

'And the young witness, Ian Hedges? Is he still cooperating fully? Because he's currently accounting for quite a chunk of your budget in terms of protection and we need value for our investment in him.'

'I'm working on a possible solution to those costs,

ma'am. He has cooperated to date but clearly the attack on his mother is a worrying factor. We don't know what, if anything, she told the gang about Ian's whereabouts. Because I think we can take it as read that the attack on her was related to the case and not just a result of her seemingly seeing men for money. The timing would certainly indicate that.'

'Release the likeness immediately, with a mention of the possibility of a wig. Let's see what that brings up. But then let's start seeing some results, please. Solid ones.'

* * *

After a sharp tug on the lead like that, some senior officers would respond by jumping all over their team for better results. Not Ted. He took his responsibilities seriously and the buck always stopped with him. If the team members weren't getting the results, it was up to him to improve his direction of them, as far as he was concerned.

'Steve, can you start us off with what you've found out about JJ, please? I still think, rightly or wrongly, that they might be the key to all of this. And after your demonstration, Jezza, I've agreed with the Super to circulate the likeness and mention the possibility of the use of a long wig to change appearance.'

'Sir, with Océane's help, I've run every permutation of JJ we could come up with through the system and ended up with zero of any real use. Plenty of hints and mentions in various cases but all anecdotal. Nothing concrete enough anywhere to result in an arrest, let alone a conviction.'

'Can you collate, summarise and circulate what you have, please? We need to find JJ, as a priority. We do at least have witness reports putting them in the front passenger seat of the 4x4 at the time of the attack on Martin. Whether those witnesses would stand up to cross-examination in court is another matter. If they'd even agree to go that far.

'Is there any way you may be able to pinpoint where JJ might be operating from? Are the reports just within our area, or further afield? That might help us narrow down where they might be living.'

'Mike, in similar vein, can we please have a list of schools and clubs where JJ has been sighted? Can we somehow get ahead of them by trying to keep more of a watch on those where they've not yet popped up, as far as we know?

'I'll talk to Inspector Turner about some more help from Uniform and PCSOs on that, although I'm not optimistic. Oh, and do we have a sitrep on Martin? How is he doing today?'

'Boss, I phoned the parents first thing. He was understandably a bit tired and unsettled after naming JJ but they report he's caught up with himself a bit today and is doing better,' Virgil told him. 'I'm not sure there's much more he can help us with at the moment, not until he improves a bit and hopefully gets more speech back.'

'Right, everyone, let's try and make this the day we get our hands on JJ.'

* * *

Ted had barely got through the door, after a courtesy knock, before Inspector Kevin Turner said an emphatic 'No' without even looking up from his paperwork.

Ted chuckled then replied, undeterred, 'Firstly how did

you know it was me? And secondly, you don't know what, if anything, I was about to ask you for.'

Ted pulled out the spare chair and sat down as Kevin looked up at him with a theatrical sigh.

'Firstly, you're the only person I know who can come into a room without making any sound at all, apart from the door opening. And secondly, I recognise your aftershave. With detection powers like mine, can I join your team? I might have less paperwork and admin that way.

'But seriously, Ted, you've got about every spare officer I can give you at the moment to help on this one. We'd be running on empty for everything else if I let you have more. Yes, I know it's a nasty one, but I can't give you bodies I haven't got.'

'I'm not here to beg for bodies, for once,' Ted told him. 'But I've now got a composite of a main suspect. We're releasing it to the media so I wanted to ask if you could circulate it to all your officers immediately and get them asking around for sightings. With an arrest on sight instruction for suspected attempted murder, if it can be done without putting themselves or anyone else at risk. A nasty character, for sure. Probably the front seat passenger in the vehicle which mowed young Martin Jackson straight through a float glass window.'

Ted forwarded him the picture as he was speaking and Kevin studied it carefully.

'Well, he's a nasty looking little sod and no mistake. I wouldn't fancy meeting him on a dark night.'

'Definitely male, you would say?'

Kevin looked at him in surprise, then looked back at the face staring at him from the screen.

'You're not going to tell me that this is a lass? Well, I

suppose it takes all sorts and you'd think I couldn't be surprised by anything after so many years in the job, but I'd certainly think this was a lad. Unless you know better, of course.'

'Something Jezza said, and we both know she's sharp, especially on changing appearance. She's fooled us a couple of times in the past to make that point.

'We've been wondering how JJ can somehow just melt away from the scene every time they've been spotted. She showed us how, complete with a drawn-on facial tattoo, then a long wig which covered the side of her face and changed her appearance completely. And it really did alter all perception of gender and appearance.'

He pinged off another couple of pictures from his phone in Kevin's direction as he said, 'We're getting a second likeness done, with the long hair, but not yet circulating that one to avoid confusion. In the meantime I took a couple of Jezza doing her demonstration, to give you an idea.'

Kevin's eyes widened as he looked at the latest shots.

'Bloody hell, Ted, that's barmy. If I shoved on a long blonde wig, I'd look like a bloke in drag. Nothing more. Everything about Jezza changes. She doesn't just look like a lad in the first one, she IS a lad. And if your JJ really can change their appearance in the same way, it's no wonder they can melt away unnoticed.'

He looked back at Ted as he said, 'The screen or the stage missed out big time when Jezza decided to join up instead.'

'And I'm eternally grateful that she made that choice. It's not the first time her drama training has been a pivotal point in a case, and I really think she has something with this suggestion of hers. So if you can please circulate both pictures to your officers but with a strong warning that this is potentially a dangerous character, who might well be in the company of others as bad if not worse.'

* * *

Ted decided to go and see Ian Hedges himself once more. The boy's mother was at least now stable, although not yet in a fit state to be interviewed. The hospital informed Ted when he phoned that the woman had received no visitors to date. Clearly Ian was in no hurry to go and see the woman who had given birth to him but had seemingly not done much else by way of being a mother to him.

Ted was anxious to run his idea for the ultimate safe place past both Ian and John Faulkner, and also wanted the opportunity to try himself to see if he could get any more useful information from Ian about where they may be able to find JJ.

'I'm sorry to take up more of your time Ian, and Mr Faulkner …'

'John, please.'

'Thank you. John. But we are anxious to find JJ. With your help, Ian, and what we've had from other people by way of description,' Ted kept that part deliberately vague, hoping it would encourage Ian to keep talking, 'we're now able to release a likeness, but I wondered if there was anything else at all you could tell us which might help us find JJ.'

Ted was trying to keep things gender neutral without drawing attention to the fact that he was doing so. If Ian was convinced the person was male, Ted didn't want to risk planting even the grain of an idea in his head that that might not be the case. It would risk corrupting his witness testimony and could leave a hole in any evidence he might be asked to present to court at a future date. If ever they got that far.

'Do you know where JJ lives, for a start? Any indication of where it might be? Even if only a rough guess, that could help as a starting point.'

Ian shook his head.

'Dunno for sure. I don't think he drives, though. Never seen him driving, only being driven or walking. He walks a lot, too. I often see 'im walking. So I figured he might be somewhere local, like. In Stockport, at least.'

'Thank you, that's potentially useful information.'

'Am I in danger, talking to you?' Ian asked him. 'After what they done to me mam? If that weren't one of her blokes, it could of been someone trying to find me, I reckon. I don't know what she might of told them if they hurt her bad enough. So will they come for me next? I know you said we're being watched for now, but that won't last forever, will it? So what then? What happens to me if I help you?'

John Faulkner was smiling to himself, listening. He said to Ted, 'I told you that this lad was sharp, didn't I? And he does have a point. What guarantee does he have of a realistic level of protection for as long as he might need it? And what would any witness protection programme offer a lad of his age, with the mother he has, even if she survives?'

'One thing I will promise you is that I will never lie to you. Either of you,' Ted told them both. 'I can't guarantee your one hundred percent safety, Ian, and it would be wrong of me to claim I could. But that would be my target, certainly.

'Your witness testimony could be vital to us, but not at the price of putting your life at risk. If you agree to help us, it might well be in your best interest to go into some form of witness protection programme, and that would involve a new identity, somewhere else, and no contact at all with anyone from your previous life.'

He saw the youth's face fall at his words and went on, 'But there might be another way, if you would consider it, at least.

'John, you put an idea in my head, telling me how tidily Ian keeps his personal space. Ian, this might not appeal to you at all, but it would certainly offer you far better security than I could guarantee you. Have you ever thought of joining the Forces? You can do that at sixteen. You need the signature of a parent or guardian, but I've been talking to someone who says that in your circumstances, there may be a way round that, if necessary. With your interest in electronics and mechanics, there could well be an opening for you.'

Ian was frowning, looking more puzzled than disapproving.

'I never thought about that. Don't you need a load of certificates or summat to get in? I'm crap at exams.'

'Not necessarily, if you have aptitude to learn, and you would certainly seem to have that. The man I spoke to is Detective Inspector Smith of the Metropolitan Police. He's a former army officer. I'll give you his number. He said he's more than happy to talk to you, if you want to know more.

'He's a bit …' Ted hesitated over the right word, 'a bit different. But he'll tell you everything you want to know, and he'll tell it like it is. He doesn't mince his words, for sure. Here's his number. He said you could call him at any time.'

Ted scribbled it down quickly as his phone was ringing

and the screen showed it was Rob O'Connell calling him. He needed to take it.

'Boss,' Rob was sounding breathless as he spoke. 'I'm out with Uniform and we've spotted JJ. He's legging it fast but we're after him and I've called reinforcements. We might well get him, boss.'

He'd dropped the gender neutrality at the prospect of arresting their prime suspect to date.

'Be careful, Rob. Give me the location and I'll be right there.'

Ted was already halfway to the door, nodding a farewell to Ian and John.

'Full risk assessment before you do anything, or let anyone else go near. Watch out for anyone else with JJ, coming to their rescue. And do not take any unnecessary risks.'

Chapter Twenty-three

Ted jumped into his service vehicle, switched the blues on, cut out into the passing traffic with inches to spare and put his foot down.

On a good day he could get to Rob's last known location in a little over five minutes. If he hit any heavy traffic, he dreaded to think how long it might take him.

He kept his phone on hands-free so he was in constant contact with his DS, at the same time as being in communication with the station to summon up any available units to go to Rob's assistance. He had no idea if JJ would be armed so what the risk level was likely to be. As a precaution he advised extreme caution to anyone attending.

Ted knew he could usually rely on Rob to be level-headed and not take unnecessary risks. At the same time he also knew how badly the whole team wanted to get their hands on JJ, their only solid lead to date on the case. A strong desire like that could well cloud normally sound judgement.

The blues could take Ted through red lights, where safe, and give him priority in most situations. What it couldn't do was help him with the plague of bad drivers who seemed to choose the precise moment when he needed clear passage to perform the most ridiculous of manoeuvres, then to stall their vehicle in panic as they saw the flashing blue lights on their tail. If he could have spared the time, he would have stopped to book at least two of them.

But time was something he didn't have. At the moment one of his officers was running headlong into potential danger, intent on collaring their prime suspect at any cost, including his own safety.

One area car was already in attendance, with PCs Ashton and Ray, now on foot, in pursuit of both Rob and JJ, but they were still some distance away. Another unit was on its way, less than two minutes from the scene. Even so, not knowing what JJ might be capable of, and especially whether or not they were armed, nor with what, Ted didn't like those odds.

'Do not engage, Rob,' he ordered him. 'Try to keep JJ in sight, but don't try any daft heroics on your own. You've now got four Uniform officers not far behind you and I'm not far away, so just try to keep eyes on JJ until they catch up. And keep all of us posted on your location if it changes.'

JJ's headlong flight was taking them and their pursuers away from the town, across waste ground on the edge of industrial sites. Ted was steadily closing the distance between him and where the action was. He could already see the area car, now stopped a short distance away, its two occupants running fast in the direction Rob had taken in pursuit of JJ.

'There's a fence in front of us now. High security fence,' Rob panted into his phone. 'He can't get over that, he's going to have to turn left or right ...'

Then a loud expletive before Rob shouted, 'He's going up it, like a bloody little monkey. I'll have to grab him.'

Ted's shout of, 'Do not engage without back-up,' was drowned out by Rob's next words.

'Come 'ere, you ...'

Ted was out of his car now, head down and sprinting as fast as his legs could take him, trying to get to his officer before anything serious happened.

He heard a thud which must have been Rob's mobile phone hitting the ground, then a sharp cry of pain and more swearing. Muffled but still audible over the phone, he heard PC Ashton's warning shout.

'Taser! Stand still and drop the weapon. Police officer armed with Taser!'

Ted was within sight now. He could see Rob O'Connell on the ground at the bottom of a high security fence. As he closed the distance, he could also see a shaven-headed figure standing over Rob, knife in hand, head swivelling from side to side to assess for danger and to find an escape route at all costs.

The arm with the weapon went up, ready to strike again, just as PC Ashton repeated her warning, a split second before discharging her Conducted Energy Device.

It found its target, knocking JJ clean off their feet to fall, twitching, close to where the DS was still on the ground.

With JJ now safely disabled, Ted went straight to Rob O'Connell who was bleeding from the left shoulder and wincing in pain.

PCs Ashton and Ray were dealing with JJ, first checking vital signs, then handcuffing them as PC Ashton explained they were being arrested for assault on a police officer. The second car had just arrived, two more officers hurrying over to see what action was needed from them. Ted called out for a first aid kit as he crouched down over Rob to assess his injury.

'Just a flesh wound, boss, I think. I grabbed him by the ankle but he pulled a flick knife on me.

'Which was precisely why I told you to keep your distance, Rob. If he'd had a gun, we might not be having this conversation. You need to go to A&E to get this properly seen to.'

He could hear PC Ashton trying to question her prisoner about their identity so he called across to explain the situation.

'PC Ashton, we have reason to believe this suspect may be non-verbal, so we need to be careful in how we try to communicate.'

JJ was shakily back on their feet now, being supported by PC Ray. Close to, they looked even thinner than Ted had imagined, and completely androgynous. They kept their shaved head down, making their face impossible to read.

'I'm Detective Chief Inspector Darling, from Serious Crime. Are you able to understand what is being said to you?'

No reply.

'Do you speak English? Do you need an interpreter?'

No reply.

'Can you hear what's being said to you? Do you need a sign language interpreter?'

PC Ashton had clearly done basic training in alternative communication. She put her hands where JJ couldn't fail to see them and made several gestures with her fingers.

No reaction.

'Well, we've tried. PC Ashton, PC Ray, can you please take this suspect, who we believe to be JJ, to the station and get them booked in and processed ready for interview. Please note the gender-neutral pronoun. We don't, at this stage, know this suspect's gender so please ensure everyone is aware of that and understands that it's an issue which requires sensitive handling.'

He turned to the occupants of the second vehicle to say,

'PS Maxwell, PC Smith, can you please take DS O'Connell to A&E.

'Rob, leave me your car keys and I'll arrange for someone to collect your vehicle from here and come to the hospital to get you once you've been seen and treated.

'Thank you, everyone.'

'It's just a flesh wound, boss, it doesn't need A&E.'

Rob O'Connell, now with a dressing in place thanks to PC Smith, was still playing the stoic.

Ted turned to look at him.

'A&E, DS O'Connell. That was not a suggestion.'

* * *

Sergeant Brian Clark had seen many strange sights in his suite during his long service as a custody sergeant. His instincts told him the person PCs Ashton and Ray had just delivered to him might possibly turn out to be one of his most challenging to date.

'Sarge, all we know about this suspect is that they are known by the name JJ and we've just arrested them for assault on a police officer. DS O'Connell. He's on his way to hospital.'

PS Clark picked up straight away on the pronoun. He was hoping one or other of the PCs was going to tell him the person's gender because he was blowed if he could tell from looking at them whether they were male or female.

'Oh, and DCI Darling, who was at the scene, did say there's a chance this person may be non-verbal.'

PS Clark stifled a sigh and tried not to do a visible eye roll. He was wondering why the difficult ones always seemed to be brought in when he was on duty. Before he could even start to process the arrestee he needed to find some way of communicating with them.

He looked at the figure standing in front of him. Hunched shoulders, head down, no eye contact. It was impossible to tell anything about them, except that they looked in need of a few square meals.

'Right, JJ, is it? I'm Sergeant Clark. You've been arrested for assault on a police officer. You're at Stockport Police Station. Do you understand?'

He waited enough time for some sort of response.

There was none.

He reached next for a printed card which he held out to the prisoner as he asked, 'Do you understand and speak English?'

The card repeated the question in several different languages.

Still no reaction. This could be a long session. As custody sergeant, he was responsible for ensuring the person standing in front of him was fully aware of their rights, including access to free legal advice, and having someone notified of their whereabouts. He couldn't do that until he knew if the prisoner could hear and understand him.

And he was really starting to wonder if the person in front of the desk could hear. They certainly showed no reaction at all, to anything he was saying, or to anything else going on round them.

He decided he didn't want anything about this case to be able to come back and bite him. He was going to play this one by the book, right from the start. As long as he couldn't find a way to communicate with the person, he wasn't happy to proceed. And that started with not wanting the person put in a cell when he had no way of assessing their suicide risk,

235

for one thing.

'Right, I'm not satisfied that you understand enough of what you're being told. You are under arrest, and remain so, but before you're processed and put into a cell, I'm going to get a doctor to check you to see if you are fit to be questioned.

'For that reason, you'll be put in an interview room, with someone watching you at all times, pending medical examination. You'll be given refreshments in the meantime, but you are not free to leave. Do you understand?'

Still no reaction.

He checked something on his desk then told PCs Ashton and Ray, 'Take them to interview room three. That's free at the moment. Stay with them until I can arrange someone to relieve you.'

'Sarge,' they responded in unison, shepherding their prisoner away.

'And that, Brian, is an object lesson in passing the buck,' Clark told himself with a satisfied smile.

* * *

Ted went to get a sitrep about JJ as soon as he arrived back at the station.

'I wasn't happy they understood enough of what was going on around them to put them straight into a cell, sir, so I've called the duty doctor and JJ is in an interview room under constant watch until the doc gets here,' PS Clark told him.

At least he knew the DCI wouldn't jump all over him and insist procedure was bent out of recognition to give them the chance to interview someone who'd apparently knifed one of their own.

'Speaking of that, is there any news yet on Rob O'Connell, sir?'

'Early yet to expect any, realistically, as he wasn't blue-lighted in. He kept insisting it wasn't serious but it still looked like quite a nasty slash.

'Speaking of which, have you at least managed to search JJ for any other weapons they might have concealed about their person?'

'Again a tricky issue, sir,' Clark told him. 'Without knowing if they understand it was hard to explain, but yes, we did a body search, though not an intimate one. That presented another problem, not being sure of their gender, so not knowing who should carry it out.

'I've been trying from the start to make sure there's nothing to come back to bite us about procedure on this one.'

'I appreciate it, Brian,' Ted told him, less formal now in his gratitude. 'I think we'd do best to wait for the medical verdict and then, depending on what that reveals, proceed with an interview under caution.

'We don't even know JJ's age, for a start, so we've no idea if we could be dealing with a juvenile. Did you form any opinion on that? An educated guess?'

'Don't ask me to guess young people's age, sir. My grandkids are only littlies but some of the stuff they come out with is so grown up. I honestly struggled to pick up anything about JJ. Certainly not gender. Could easily be male, female or whatever you'd call someone in between.

'As for age, that's really difficult because I never got to see their eyes. Won't make eye contact at all, and it's often the eyes that give it away. My best guess, if forced, would be between late teens and mid to late twenties.

'I did notice some scars on their hands and fingers which could possibly be signs of self-harm, which was one of the reasons I thought it best to stop and see what the doctor has to say. To assess for more self-harm or even suicide risk, before we even think of putting them in a cell. I hope that was all right, sir?'

'Essential, I would say. To cover ourselves, if nothing else. Thank you. I'd better go and see who's in who I could put on interviewing them, if and when we get the green light. Can you let me know when the doctor comes and what the verdict is, please?'

Only Mike Hallam and Gina Shaw were in the main office when Ted went upstairs to head for his own. Both looked up eagerly, waiting for an update on Rob. Word had quickly spread through the station that he had been injured and taken to hospital.

Ted shook his head.

'No news yet, but it's a bit early. Right, update. We have JJ downstairs. Refusing to say anything at all. We don't really know if they can speak, or what language they use. Nothing, really, and still no clear indicator of gender. Custody sergeant has called the doctor in to check that we're all right to go ahead with questioning them. So Gina, how do you feel about making a start on that, when we can?'

'Fine by me, boss. Concentrating first on the attack on the DS, presumably, since we've got our witnesses to that?'

'Begin there, then see where you can go, assuming you get anything at all. I'll be in my office until we hear if the doctor gives the all clear, then I'll come and watch how it goes, to get a feel for where we go next.'

It was quicker than Ted had feared when he got a call from downstairs to say the doctor had been and was happy there was no obvious medical indicator that JJ was unfit to be questioned. He too had not heard a word from the suspect but on a preliminary examination, had detected no obvious medical reason for the refusal to answer questions.

'Right, Gina, see what you can do. No pressure, no high expectations. Just see if you can establish any kind of a rapport which might at least give us something. Remember I'm right next door so if you're not comfortable with how it's going, just give me a sign at any time.

'Keep the Uniform officer in the room with you for now, just in case of any trouble.'

JJ was sitting at the table. Head down, shoulders hunched, looking thin, cold and miserable, rather than an immediate threat. But Gina was experienced enough not to be lulled into a false sense of false security.

Gina sat down and started the recording, identifying herself then asking, 'Can you please begin by giving me your full name?'

'J-J-J...'

JJ's throat was working convulsively with the effort of trying to form a word. They finally lifted their head and Gina found herself looking into grey-green eyes showing immense sadness and suffering.

'Juh-Jenny Sh-Sh-Shaw.'

Gina leapt up from her seat in shock, before her legs buckled completely. The quick-thinking PC in the room caught her moments before she hit the floor.

Chapter Twenty-four

Ted took Gina into the next room, where they could still see the person who'd identified themselves as being her sister, Jenny, who had disappeared from her home when she was just fifteen.

'First question I have to ask you, Gina, is are you positive that's your sister? It's a long time since you've seen her and she must look very different now. I'm assuming she looked nothing like this when you last saw her. So are you certain?'

'I didn't recognise her until she looked at me and I could see her eyes clearly. They're a very distinctive colour. Grey-green. She used to make a joke about it. She said they were like dirty sea water.'

There was a slight break in her voice as she was speaking, no doubt remembering the sister she had known in her childhood. Trying to balance that against the broken person sitting not far away from her now, on the other side of the two-way glass.

Even as they watched, Jenny Shaw bent her legs up so her feet were on the seat, then folded her arms protectively around her shins and began a slow rocking movement. They could both clearly hear her start to sing as she swayed.

'Rock-a-bye baby on the tree top,
'When the wind blows the cradle will rock.
'When the bough breaks the cradle will fall,
'Down will come baby, cradle and all.'

A sob escaped Gina's throat as she heard the clear, sweet voice, child-like and without a hint of its former stammer. Her hand moved towards the glass, as if she could somehow feel the contact with her sister through it.

'She used to sing that to me when I was very little. There was less than two years between us but she was always my big sister. My protector. Always there for me. I think she knows I'm watching. She's signalling to me.

'Boss, you have to let me talk to her. She'll talk to me. I know she will.'

Ted was shaking his head before she'd even stopped speaking.

'You know that's not possible, Gina. She can't be interviewed by a relative, it would blow any case against her out of the water. I know she's your sister, and I can imagine how hard this is for you. Probably for her too. But please don't forget she knifed a colleague, and we haven't yet heard how Rob is doing. I can't let you anywhere near her. You know that.

'But if she can sing like that, does that mean she could talk to us, if she wanted to?'

Gina shook her head.

'I don't think so, boss. I know some singers have bad stammers which can disappear completely when they sing, so it's not a sign she's putting it on, I don't think, if that's what you were thinking. Jenny never stammered when she was young, as far as I can remember. It only started as she got older and I was a bit too young to understand why. It wasn't all that bad then, though. You could still understand what she was trying to say.

'Boss, I understand I can't interview her, but would you at least let me talk to her? Please?'

'You know the rules, Gina. We can't be seen to be treating her any differently to any other suspect, just because she's your sister. But before we try to proceed any further with her, I'm going to get a psych evaluation. I know she's been passed as medically fit to be questioned but I'm seriously concerned about her current state of mental health. I'm assuming you saw nothing like this before she disappeared.'

'Not remotely, boss. She was quieter as a teenager, withdrawn and sometimes moody, but that's not all that unusual. She was very bright academically. Always studying hard, so a bit introverted because of that.

'So what can I do to feel I'm of some use on the case? Shall I go and see how DS O'Connell's doing and take him home, if he's fit to be discharged?'

'I'm not sure that would be appropriate in the circumstances …'

'Boss, Rob's going to find out sooner or later that it was my sister who stabbed him. I'd far sooner he heard it from me first.'

'Are you fit to drive? You've had a bad shock. Are you sure you don't want to take a bit of time to get over it?'

'I'm fine, boss. Really. Time isn't going to change anything. And I should go and tell my parents, in person, what's happened, if you're all right with that? It's going to be a terrible shock for them, so it might be better coming from me.'

'As a precaution, I want you to be well out of the way whilst Jenny is here, but you can do a few useful things, so you don't feel totally sidelined. Start by phoning Stepping Hill to see how Rob's getting on and when he's likely to be fit to be discharged, and keep us posted.

'Whilst you're phoning the hospital about Rob, check up

on Ian Hedges' mother to see how she's doing, then let me know. Call the Jacksons, too, and inform them that we have the person we believe to be JJ in custody now, which should be reassuring for all of them.'

'Then go round to your parents, to at least tell them Jenny has been found alive, although clearly not too many of the other details at this stage. That's something you really do need to do in person, not over the phone. Then take the rest of the day off.

'I'll need to get someone to dig out the misper files on Jenny, assuming she was reported missing at the time. I'd be interested in the likeness of her which was released then, for one thing.'

'Yes, she was reported as soon as my parents knew she'd gone missing. That was not long after she'd come home one day from her extra coaching sessions for exams.

'I remember how strange it was at the time. The posters all over the place, with my sister's face looking at me. It was on the TV and in all the papers, too. There were no sightings which led anywhere, but that's not surprising if she maybe changed her appearance as soon as she left home.'

He saw her hesitation to leave and said gently, 'Gina, you know I won't let anything happen to Jenny in our custody, despite her having wounded one of our own. And when you let your parents know she's turned up, it might be best if you don't give them too many details yet about her emotional state, either. It's going to be a lot for them to assimilate.'

Gina still hovered, clearly wanting to be with her sister now she had reappeared, but knowing and accepting that wouldn't be possible. Finally, she went back to her desk to collect up her things, then left the building.

Ted sat for a moment, staring through the glass at the

image of a broken human being, still singing and rocking, occasionally smiling to herself. He found it difficult to remind himself that that might be exactly what he was looking at. An image. A clever ploy. A device to convince anyone observing Jenny Shaw that she was as much a victim in all of this as anyone else.

He sighed as he got to his feet. There was so much potential with this case for things to go badly wrong that he was determined to cover every eventuality from the outset.

* * *

Gina decided to go in person to the hospital to follow up on Martin Jackson, and on Ian Hedges' mother. Encouraging but slow progress for the former, little change to the latter.

She wasn't about to go against the boss's orders and visit Rob in person. It was only making trouble for herself and things were already difficult enough. She could, however, phone him from the car park. She knew he would have wangled a way to keep his phone with him and switched on. Then she could go and see her parents to tell them the news about Jenny, both good and bad. They lived on the south side of Manchester, so not too far to drive.

She was not looking forward to either. First to telling a valued colleague that it had been her own sister who had stabbed him. Then to telling her parents that although the wait for news was over, in that they would now know their missing older daughter was at least alive, they would have to deal with the knowledge that she was in custody awaiting serious charges. And if the potential attempted murder charge in the case of Martin Jackson was successfully brought against her, she could potentially face life in prison.

If Jenny was not broken now, she would doubtless be by such a sentence.

Unsurprisingly, Gina found Rob was still waiting for treatment. He told her he was screened off in a side bay. Staff were aware he was a police officer and what had happened to him, so were keeping him away from other patients. He had at least been through triage and had some pain relief.

He sounded slightly drowsy but pleased to get a call from one of the team.

'Gina! Where are you? Have you come to rescue me?' he asked hopefully.

'Sitting in the car park because the boss has forbidden me to see you. I'll explain why in a minute. I phoned first for a sitrep on your condition, and I don't think you're going anywhere until they've practised their embroidery on your shoulder. As long as they don't throw you out before then for bad behaviour.'

She was doing her best to keep it light. At some point, she was going to have to tell him, and she was dreading it.

'At least we got the little shit, though, eh? Tasering was too good for him, although I did enjoy watching him squirm, getting what he deserved.'

Gina went quiet. Even in his part-doped state and at the other end of the phone, Rob noticed the change.

'What's wrong? Don't tell me he got away again?'

'He's not a he, he's a she. And she's my sister. Jenny. The one who disappeared when she was fifteen.'

Rob went so quiet that Gina was seriously worried the shock might have been too much in his fragile state.

'Rob? Rob? Are you all right? Speak to me.'

'Your sister? She's JJ? But how …?'

Rob had so many questions in his mind he couldn't begin

to formulate a single one.

Then he said, 'God, Gina, I'm so sorry. I'd no idea. It must have been a hell of a shock for you. I shouldn't have said what I did.'

'I don't blame you at all. I expect I'd be feeling the same if she'd stabbed me. You weren't to know that's who it was. I didn't know myself. I didn't recognise her at all when I first saw her in the interview room. And then only when I looked at her eyes.'

'I can't get my head round it. Your sister? So can she speak? Or is that just another way of disguising who she really is?'

'She did start to stammer, not long before she disappeared. It seems to be much worse now. She can barely say her own name. She can still sing, though, fluently. She keeps singing the song she always used to sing to me when I was little. That's what convinced me it really is her. But she looks like someone highly disturbed.'

Gina was losing it, rapidly. Tears were starting to slide down her face, despite her best efforts to hold her emotion in check. Rob could clearly sense her pain through her voice.

'Hey, don't worry, Gina,' Rob told her. 'You're not responsible, for any of this. Whatever happened to JJ to make her what she is now, it was nothing to do with you.'

'Now I have to go and tell our parents about her, and I've no idea how I'm going to do that.'

Gina clearly heard the sound of a curtain behind pulled back and a brisk voice addressing Rob.

'Right, Mr O'Connell, we can take you for treatment now. You need to switch off your phone, too. But we shouldn't keep you much longer before you can go home.'

Gina was busily drying her eyes with the back of her hand

as she said, 'Call me when you're ready to leave and I'll make sure someone comes to pick you up. I'd better go and tell my parents now. Wish me luck.'

* * *

'Gina! Darling! What a lovely surprise. Why didn't you let me know you were coming? I'd have made your favourite cake. Your father's in his hothouse, pampering his orchids, as usual. I'll give him a call.'

The woman at the front door held it wide open in welcome, proffering a cheek for her younger daughter to kiss, before leading the way through to the kitchen and conservatory at the back. She put her head out of the back door and called, 'Gray? Gina's here to see us. Come inside, dear, I'm putting the kettle on.'

She bustled about the kitchen, getting out mugs, putting them back again in favour of bone china cups and saucers. Chattering away all the while so Gina had no chance to get a word in edgeways. Not that she wanted to. She was dreading what she had to say as it was. She didn't want to have to say everything twice if her father didn't appear soon.

'I've got a nice new brand of Earl Grey, if you want to try that? Or do you prefer coffee? It seems so long since you were here, although I'm sure it isn't really. Oh, here's Dad now. Are you having tea or coffee, darling?'

With a guilty pang, Gina suddenly realised what all the nervous prattling was about. This wasn't just a visit from a daughter. It was a police officer in their kitchen. Someone who might possibly be about to shatter all the hope a mother had been nurturing through long, anguished years of waiting for news of a missing child.

'Gina, darling,' her father crossed the kitchen in a few strides and wrapped her in a warm hug that took her breath away, physically and emotionally.

She'd almost forgotten the constant and spontaneous affection from both parents, shared equally between their two cherished daughters. Hugs and kisses and fondness, always in ready supply.

What happened? What went wrong? How could Jenny have gone from this warm and loving home where she lacked nothing, not food, nor clothes, nor love and affection, to what Gina knew her to be now?

Why did she leave? Gina was only thirteen at the time, and young for her age. She couldn't make sense of it all. Not then, still not, now. She tried to reconcile the image of a happy, smiling Jenny in the setting which now surrounded her, with the broken, thin, gaunt and silent person with the tortured eyes whom she'd seen in the interview room.

Only her parents might be able to shed some light on what had happened. But first she needed to find a way to tell them.

'Mum, Dad, I'm here to tell you that Jenny has been found.'

She heard the gasp of relief from her mother. Knew her next words were going to shatter every last vestige of hope for both her parents.

'I'm sorry, but Jenny's in police custody accused of stabbing a police officer, one of my colleagues, and also on suspicion of being an accessory to the attempted murder of a teenage boy.'

Chapter Twenty-five

Gina's reactions were swift. She was across the kitchen fast enough to stop the freshly-boiled kettle falling from her mother's hand as Angela Shaw staggered, legs buckling at the impact of the words.

Gray Shaw was only seconds behind in his movements, strong arms folding around his wife and helping her gently into the nearest chair. He was looking at his second daughter in total disbelief.

'Jenny? Jenny did that? Our little Jenny? Are you absolutely sure, darling?'

'I'm really sorry. I wish it could be a mistake, but it isn't. There were several police witnesses, including my boss, DCI Darling. Jenny's in custody, pending a psychiatric report.'

'She's nothing like the sister I remember. Nothing at all. She can barely speak, for one thing, her stammer is so bad. Much worse than I ever remember.'

'Look, sit down, darling, let's all talk about it. Have a cup of tea. I imagine it's been a shock to you, too. Tell us everything you can. Anything you're allowed to about what's happened. Is your colleague seriously hurt? Will we be able to go and see Jenny?'

Gina sat down at the table. The years seemed to fall away. No matter how bad a day she'd had as a child, everything always seemed better for sitting down with the parents she adored, drinking tea and putting the world to rights.

Why could that not have been enough for Jenny? What could have gone so catastrophically wrong in her young life that it couldn't have been sorted by sitting and talking about it, round this table, which had been the focal point of so many deep and meaningful discussions?

'You won't be able to see her yet, no. She'll be questioned once she's had a psychiatric evaluation to see if that's appropriate. She's been passed as physically fit, but her mental state is causing concern. She genuinely seems unable to speak with any degree of fluency. She struggled to give me her name. I don't remember her stammering anything like that much.'

Gina was observant. Trained to look for body language. Even after the traumas of the day, she didn't miss the loaded look which passed between her parents at her last comment.

She looked searchingly from one to the other as she asked, 'Did she? When did it get that bad? Something must have caused it. What?'

Angela Shaw reached out both hands across the table to grip her husband's, ignoring her cup of tea. Her hands were visibly trembling, and all colour had drained from her face.

'We should have listened, Gray. We should have believed her.'

'Listened to what? Believed what?' Gina demanded.

Her voice had a hard edge to it now. A police officer questioning them, not their daughter asking about family matters.

'We thought she was exaggerating. And Ming denied any such thing. He was always a bit overly demonstrative in showing affection. It was so kind of him to take an interest in Jenny and to give her extra tuition. He wouldn't hear of us paying for his time, either. He was her godfather, after all.

Devoted to her, and to you too, darling.'

Gina's mind was racing, dredging up memories long forgotten. Professor Menzies Thomson. Uncle Ming, as they always called him. A renowned expert in human anatomy and physiology. A lifelong friend of her father's, a frequent visitor to their home, always bearing lavish gifts for his god-daughter, and never forgetting a little something for her younger sibling.

Gina's tone was pure ice as she asked them, 'What did Jenny say? Did she make allegations about Ming?'

'Darling, we really did think it was all a bit exaggerated,' her father blustered. 'Teenage fantasy sort of stuff. I've known Ming since we first started prep school together. He's always been very affectionate. You must remember that yourself. Always cuddles and kisses and tickles for both of you when you were little. There was nothing wrong about it. He did it in front of us, for goodness' sake. We'd have soon put a stop to anything not right.

'He used to babysit the two of you, as well, when you were little. He was always volunteering when your mother and I wanted to go out. Surely you can remember that, sweetie? You must remember how kind and affectionate he was to you both. We would never have put either of you at any risk. You must know that, don't you?'

And suddenly Gina did remember. Things long buried deep in her mind. Waking to hear Jenny screaming in the bedroom they shared. Ming sitting on Jenny's bed soothing her and reassuring little Gina with, 'It's all right Gee-gee, darling. Your sister was having a nightmare so I came in to reassure her.

She'd totally forgotten the childhood nicknames

Ming used for the two sisters. Gee-gee and Jay-jay. Georgina Gayle and Jennifer Jayne. Two little girls, close in age, inseparably close emotionally. Sharing everything. Toys, bedroom, clothes. More like twins than ordinary siblings. Jay-jay always singing her little sister to sleep with that lullaby.

'Rock-a-bye baby, in the tree top.'

'Hush, Jay-jay, my little love, everything's fine. The night monsters have gone and I'm here now. Uncle Ming is here.'

Then the soothing sounds of his voice singing a traditional Scottish song, until both little girls found sleep again.

'Ally, bally, ally bally bee, sittin' on yer mammy's knee'.

Gina's voice was glacial as she demanded, 'What did Jenny say about him? What was she accusing him of? Specifically?'

Her parents exchanged a helpless glance. Her father's voice was defensive as he said, 'Well, you know what it's like for young girls. When their bodies start to grow up. So quickly. Going from child to woman almost overnight, it can seem like. And Jenny in particular seemed suddenly to blossom very quickly.

'Once that happened, of course we stopped him babysitting for you. It would have been wrong on so many levels and he was the first to point that out.

'But then when Jenny started to get serious about her studies and he was offering to tutor her, we thought that was too good an opportunity for her to miss. And she seemed happy enough to start with. She was learning so much from him, and you remember she was always a sponge for knowledge. And so serious in her plans for her future.'

He dried up, abruptly, looking uncomfortable now.

'But?' Gina prompted, her tone still hard. 'There's obviously a but, so what was it?'

Her father paused for a swallow of his tea. Stalling for time, anxious to delay the moment when he would have to accept that he was in no small measure responsible for what had happened to his older daughter, through his inaction. And worse, through accepting the word of an old friend over that of his own child.

'It was honestly nothing very specific,' he went on, his tone defensive. 'He always used to kiss her on the cheek – he did to both of you, whenever he came here – but she said it was getting too close to her mouth and she didn't like that.'

'And that was all?' Gina pressed him when he seemed to have dried up.

'Darling, it was all very vague and suggestive, rather than anything else. Jenny was going through the usual self-conscious thing with her figure changing. She was never busty, but she was starting to show boobs. Small, but discernible. She accused Ming of looking at them too much, and sometimes letting his hand brush a bit too close to them if he was leaning over her to show her something in a book.'

'We have a word for behaviour like that at work, dad. We call it grooming.'

Her parents were clasping each other's hands now across the table, each looking as stricken as the other.

'We didn't know, Gina, darling,' her mother told her. 'We honestly didn't know. Neither of us suspected anything like that from Ming, of all people. It was something we read about in the papers or saw on the television. Not something which happened to people like us.

'And do you really think it might be connected in some way to what's happened to Jenny? Can she really have gone from a few inappropriate fumbles to trying to kill a policeman?'

Gina got up abruptly from her chair. Walked three times up and down the hall whilst she tried to contain her rising anger. She knew how different her working life was to the cocooned middle-class security of her parents. The famous PLU – people like us – attitude. She still found it difficult to accept how much it had clouded their judgement. Still did, it would seem.

She knew she needed to calm down. To stay detached and professional. There was clearly more she could get from her parents about what really happened, to help her to understand, but only if she could control her anger about their naivety.

Both her parents were scanning her face anxiously when she came back into the kitchen to join them and to sit down once more at the table. Gina felt a sudden tilt, a role reversal, as she realised they were actively seeking her reassurance and approval, after years of her and her sister doing the same with them.

'How long was it after Jenny told you all this that she disappeared? How long did you keep sending her to Ming's after she first raised her concerns? And when did the stammering start exactly? About the same time? Can you pinpoint any specific point when it began?'

'We didn't send her by herself, darling, daddy always drove her there then went to collect her afterwards. We wouldn't have let her travel that far on her own on the buses. Not a young girl like that, in the evening. Anything could have happened to her.'

Gina nearly choked at the irony of what her mother was saying but tried hard to stay calm. It was just possible that people like her parents really didn't know that statistically their daughter was at greater risk from a family member or close family friend than from a random member of the public.

'And you never noticed anything out of the ordinary when you went to pick her up after the sessions?' Gina asked her father. 'She never seemed upset? Ill at ease? Anything at all which should have raised your concerns?'

'Well, she was always a bit quiet. As if she was tired, really, and Ming always said how hard she had worked. He was very pleased with the progress she was making with her studies. He always walked her out to the car to tell me that.'

'And you never saw him do anything inappropriate around her when he was doing that? Or saying anything with a bit of a double meaning?'

'Darling, it was just Ming, and you know what he was like. A bit of a sense of humour. He'd often say she'd been such a good pupil he would never need to spank her, giving her a little pat on the bottom as she got into the car. But that was just his way. It meant nothing.'

'And is he still alive? Menzies Thomson? Still living in the area?' she asked them.

A definite police officer's question, not that of a daughter asking about an old family friend.

Her father looked concerned at her tone. Uncomfortable about the definite latent menace behind what she was asking.

'Yes, still alive, though not in very good health at present. He had a slight stroke a couple of months ago and it knocked him sideways rather, although he's back home now, at least. Still living in that same big house out towards Bramhall. Still alone, and it always was too big for one person. He has help with it, of course. More so, since he's been ill.

'Darling, you can't seriously be thinking of going to question an old family friend on the basis of some hearsay from years ago, surely? Would you even have the right to do that, considering how well you know him on a personal level?'

'Dad, I've seen the shattered remains of my sister. You still have that dubious honour to come, if and when you are able to visit her. Always assuming she would agree to seeing you.

'If how she is now is in any way connected to her experience at his hands, he needs to be brought to account. There may be other victims. There usually are, with such cases.

'And when it comes to child sexual abuse, there is no time limit on bringing a prosecution.'

* * *

Gina drove away from her parents' house, her eyes blurred by tears, one hand thumping against the steering wheel in frustration at the mess which was unfolding all around her.

She didn't want to go home. Didn't want to go and sit alone in her flat where she knew she would probably open a bottle and then regret it all when she finally woke up afterwards. She could drive round to The Grapes in the hope that some of the team would come and join her. But then she'd struggle to get back home, unless she called a taxi.

Her mobile phone was ringing so she pulled over to answer it. Jezza.

'Right, you, the boss told me what happened. Do not go home on your own. I don't want you getting pissed unless I'm with you, doing the same. Not to mention the drunk dancing. Wait for me outside the nick end of play. Then you're coming back to mine. Nat's cooking supper – it's all arranged – then you'll have to put up with Tommy thrashing you at his own version of Trivial Pursuit.'

Gina had never been more thankful to hear Jezza's voice.

'I might beat him,' she said with a laugh.

'Don't count on it! Bring clean undies and such like because you are definitely staying the night. Once Tom's safely in bed, you and I are going to get seriously bladdered together. I am talking Olympic level piss-up. Nat won't mind. He's tolerant like that. That's why he's a keeper.'

'Thanks, Jezza. I can't tell you how much it means to me, all of your support through this.'

'Oh shut up, you silly tart, that's what team members do. We look out for one another. So don't be late, and don't forget your toothbrush.'

Gina found herself feeling even more tearful when Jezza rang off. For all her brash exterior, Jezza could be incredibly kind and empathetic. Her prescription for the night ahead sounded like the perfect tonic after the day Gina had had.

What she should be doing, of course, was going back to her flat to sort out her overnight bag, picking up a decent bottle of plonk on the way, as her contribution to the evening, then running a long, hot bath, with an obscene amount of bubbles in it.

So why was her car obstinately pointing itself in the

direction of Bramhall as it left her parents' house. A route she'd been driven on many times by her father, with her mother and sister Jenny in the car. All going off to see Uncle Ming.

Good old Uncle Ming. Always a wonderful spread on his table when he invited the Shaw family round. Always catered, never home-cooked, and always lavish.

'Nothing but the best for my two favourite girls and their charming parents,' he always told them, beaming broadly at their arrival, as the two little girls ran into his open arms, to be swung up off the ground in a warm hug of welcome.

How could her parents have been so naive? How could they not have seen what was going on?

Of course she was not going to approach him. Not to speak to him. The boss had a reputation for being quiet and calm, not prone to going off on one as some senior officers she had encountered in her career to date were wont to do. She knew without a doubt that if she stepped out of line on this one, she would be off the case and quite likely off the team, with no hope of ever making it back.

But she'd been told to take the rest of the day off. So sitting here quietly in the car, silently contemplating, looking at the familiar large garden she knew so well – still beautifully tended, she noticed, though probably not now by Ming himself after his stroke – well, that didn't break any rules.

And what if he did happen to look out and spot her there? He would recognise her, she knew. Her parents would have shown him all the photos of her joining the police, her passing out parade, every stage of her career laid out proudly before him.

So let him sit and stew and wonder what a Detective Constable, the sister of his abuse victim – possibly one of many, who knew? – was doing sitting in a car outside his house, staring in.

Chapter Twenty-six

It was taking longer than Ted would have liked to get the psychiatric evaluation of Jenny Shaw done. He could go no further with the case until that had been completed and she was pronounced fit for interview. He was always a stickler for procedure and, with this one more than ever, he couldn't afford to allow anything which would give the defence the get out of jail free card they would be angling for.

He still had no real idea how they were going to be able to proceed with an in-depth interview with someone who was seemingly practically non-verbal. Perhaps he'd get some clue from the contents of the psychiatric report.

All he could do for the time being was to make sure Jenny was properly taken care of. Offered refreshment as appropriate, escorted to use the facilities, but kept constantly under close watch.

Now he knew she was biologically female, at least, he'd asked for, and got, PC Susan Heap to stay with her. She was one of the most experienced officers for such a tricky situation. She'd helped him out on more than one occasion, including probably saving his life once. If anyone might be able to establish something of a rapport with Jenny Shaw, it might well be Susan.

Whilst he was waiting for the report, he thought he'd better go and update the Ice Queen. This was one of the trickiest custody situations they'd had in a long while. She was in charge overall of anything and everything which happened in the station so always preferred to be kept in the picture.

'What news of DS O'Connell?' was her first question as she nodded to Ted to sit down.

'He's being discharged once they've finished treating him, ma'am. Clearly he's going to be off for some time, although he'll doubtless push to come back. We're going to be left slightly short-handed, with him off and with DC Shaw unable to go anywhere near this case, as the sister of our suspect.'

'Time once again to call on the good offices of DI Rodriguez, perhaps? To see if he has any officers to lend you on a temporary basis. Please give him a call and keep me posted.

'Speaking of DC Shaw, was she really unable to recognise the suspect as her own sister? That seems extraordinary, on the face of it.'

'Ma'am, I don't think any of us present took the suspect for a woman, at first sight. DC Shaw said it was only her sister's eyes she recognised. Jenny's clearly been through some trauma herself, which is why I called for psych evaluation before proceeding any further. She's been pronounced medically fit, but I'm worried about her mental state.'

He described the rocking movements and singing, the seeming inability to stammer out more than her own name, and that with difficulty.

'And she hasn't asked for a solicitor? Could she even do that? Can she communicate her needs sufficiently so we can be seen to provide for them? You can imagine what a gift we'd present to a sharp defence counsel if we don't bend over backwards to ensure her rights.

'I have to confess I'm not up to date with the guidelines for interviewing someone non-verbal in this way. I know I can rely on you to follow correct procedure, but do please make sure anyone who has any contact with her doesn't put one foot out of line.

'And how is DC Shaw? It's hard to imagine how much of a shock all this will have been to her. Do please also ensure her welfare needs are taken care of. And on no account must she go anywhere near her sister whilst she's in our custody here.'

'She's gone to break the news to her parents,' Ted told her. 'I thought it might be better coming from her than an officer they didn't know. It's going to be a devastating shock to them either way. It has been to Gina, too. I've told her to take the rest of the day off, and to stay well away from the case.

'As soon as Jenny is pronounced fit for interview, if she is, I thought I'd start the process myself. There's so much potential for things to go badly wrong with this one, I'd sooner it was on my head than any of the team members. I was thinking of having DC Vine with me. A female presence might possibly help, and she can be surprisingly empathetic when necessary.'

'Thank you, chief inspector, as you think fit. Please keep me posted at every stage on this one. And I imagine we might be better to wait for the psychiatric report, at least, before we trumpet news of our arrest to the eager public. We risk making ourselves look extremely foolish if our suspect is later deemed unfit to plead.'

Which was exactly what Ted was thinking himself as he left her office to go back upstairs. A result in the shape of someone in custody, finally. Still in limbo as to whether or not it was going to be a case they could successfully bring to trial.

* * *

Ted went first to find Jezza to tell her he wanted her presence in the interview room if and when they got the green light to talk to Jenny Shaw. Knowing how much Jezza enjoyed challenging situations, he was surprised at her somewhat lukewarm response.

'I thought you'd be pleased to be in on this one, Jezza? I thought it might be right up your street.'

'I am, boss, I am really ...'

'But?' he prompted.

'I know this isn't a nine to five job, but tonight I've told Gina to come round to my flat to eat, and to stay the night. I didn't want her to be on her own at the moment, after the shock she's had. Nat and Tommy would look after her if I'm late back, but I would like to spend some time with her if I can. Sorry to throw up difficulties, boss.'

'Noted. Depending on when we get the report on her state of fitness for interview, there's no telling when we can even start. And I certainly wouldn't want to drag it out into the night because, again, I have to be seen to be avoiding putting someone possibly fragile under too much psychological stress.'

'Couldn't Maurice do it, boss? You know how good he is with anyone broken or damaged.'

'Rightly or wrongly, I wanted a female presence. Let's see how the timing pans out. And thanks for looking out for Gina. It sounds like exactly what she's in need of, after a day like today.'

There was still enough of the shift left to at least begin questioning Jenny Shaw by the time the psych report hit Ted's desk. He scan read it for the salient details. All he wanted to know was whether or not he could proceed to interview. It was wordy and guarded but said, in a nutshell, that there was nothing on initial examination to suggest an interview at this stage would be inappropriate.

He went to find Jezza to discuss how they would proceed. The interview would be visually recorded as well as on audio, but he asked Jezza to give a commentary any time Jenny relied on gestures, nodding or head shakes. He didn't want any ambiguity, any hint of uncertainty which would taint her testimony. Assuming always that she would even try to answer questions, or make some kind of a statement.

Ted stood Susan Heap down when he and Jezza went to start questioning Jenny. No point in tying her up unnecessarily when she would no doubt be needed elsewhere.

The two of them went into the interview room where Jenny Shaw was sitting, not hunched up this time but still gently rocking with her arms wrapped round her body, and singing quietly to herself. The same tune, over and again.

Ted gave a time and date check as the recording started, then identified those present.

'Jenny, just to remind you, I'm Detective Chief Inspector Darling. I was present when you were arrested for a serious assault on Detective Sergeant O'Connell.

'First of all I need to ask you if you require the presence of a solicitor? You were told when arrested that you have the right to free legal advice which can be a duty solicitor, available twenty-four hours a day, and independent of the police, or you can nominate one of your own. Would you like to have a solicitor present?'

'N-n-no.'

'I understand that verbal communication is difficult for you and I want to do everything I can to help you to communicate with us. I know you've used the pen and pencil provided earlier to request drinks and toilet breaks. Is that the easiest way for you to communicate? If so we can do it that way. DC Vine will read your answers aloud for the recording, then we'll ask you to indicate if what she reads is correct. Are you happy with that arrangement?'

'Y-y-yes.'

Ted produced more paper and a blunt pencil, which he slid across the table to her. Jenny pounced on them immediately and wrote something, which she passed to Jezza.

'Where is Gina? I'll talk to Gina.' Jezza read aloud.

'I'm afraid that's not possible. You can't be interviewed by a member of your family.'

Jenny made a sound of annoyance, pulled the pad back towards her and scribbled some more.

'Is the copper all right? The one I stabbed? He scared me. I don't like to be grabbed by anyone, especially not men. I hit out in self-defence.'

Again, Jezza read the words aloud as Jenny scanned Ted's face, trying to read his expression.

'The officer is in hospital, undergoing treatment. That's all I'm able to tell you for the moment.'

The frustration on Jenny's face was clear to read. She picked up the pencil again. Even writing as swiftly as she was, every word was clear to read, the spelling perfect, no grammatical errors. Ted imagined Jezza was thinking exactly the same as he was. How could someone as intelligent as Jenny Shaw clearly was, with a bright academic future in front of her, have ended up here, looking as she now did?

'I'll tell you everything. All of it. I can give you names for all sorts of crimes you probably don't even know about yet. But it will take me ages to write it all down, and I'd find it difficult to do with you sitting staring at me. Can I sit by myself to write?'

Jezza shot a sideways glance at Ted, knowing he would be worrying about the same possibility that she was. Even though Jenny had been pronounced fit to interview, she must know she was facing a likely long prison sentence on the basis of the various crimes she was suspected of. Did she want to be alone to write, as she said? Or possibly to attempt to take her own life?

The more time they spent in her company, the more obvious it was becoming that Jenny Shaw was both highly intelligent, and articulate when she had the right means through which to express herself. They needed her testimony, but not at the risk of losing her.

Seeing their indecision she made a sound of annoyance.

'Here's some names, to show you I'm serious. Jim Mitchell was driving the vehicle which put Martin Jackson through the shop window. I know because I was sitting next to him. David Higginson was the one who ordered it because Jackson wouldn't cooperate over drug supply.'

Both names were known to Ted. Both were people several forces had been trying to get their hands on, so far without success. Whatever else Jenny might be able to tell them, any evidence against those two was of great value.

There was still the risk that leaving her alone might see her trying to kill herself, which would leave anything she had said next to useless in court. And he'd known desperate prisoners go to great lengths to commit suicide. On one occasion a person had simply run full tilt at a wall and smashed their skull before anyone could get near enough to prevent them.

'Leave me alone to write, or I stop there!!' Jenny wrote next, shoving it in front of Ted forcefully.

This was precisely why Ted had wanted to be in on the interview himself. This was a decision for a senior officer. He wouldn't have wanted any of his team to have been put into the position of risk assessing this scenario.

'All right, we'll go out. But there will be an officer outside the door at all times, and another watching over the monitor. You won't be able to see either of them, so hopefully they shouldn't put you off what you want to write, but they will react, straight away, to any sign that you're about to do something other than write. Are we clear on that?'

Jenny Shaw looked at him with something which might have passed for a smile flitting briefly across her thin, anguished face. She nodded, gave him a thumbs up sign, and immediately started to write again.

Ted and Jezza left the room and went straight into the next one from where they could watch Jenny. She had her head down and was writing feverishly, like an exam candidate trying to produce their best work, knowing they were up against a time limit which was creeping towards its close.

'What did you make of her, Jezza?' Ted asked her.

'So difficult, boss. That's the first time I've been in an interview with someone non-verbal, and that makes them so much harder to read. If she is stringing us along, then I wish

269

I could act as well as she does because she's very convincing.'

'I agree. I was inclined to believe her. Even her reason for stabbing Rob had a ring of truth about it. There could be all sorts of reasons behind someone like her having such a fear of being arrested. Or, as she said, of simply being grabbed by a man, although producing a knife like she did is a bit of an extreme reaction.'

'Except we can't know what's happened to her before at the hands of a man, boss,' Jezza told him, with the slightest hint of reproach in her voice.

'Sorry, Jezza, sorry. That was stupidly tactless of me,' he told her hastily, vividly reliving for a moment the time Jezza had been raped at knifepoint, by the man responsible for the impressive scar Ted still had on his arm.

'Right, I'll try to get Susan back to stand outside the door, then you know you'll have someone you can really rely on in any kind of a difficult situation while you keep an eye on her for now, over the monitors. Oh, and Jezza, I shouldn't need to say it, but I will, to cover myself. When you meet up with Gina this evening, you tell her nothing at all of what has taken place in interview to date. Nothing, except to reassure her that Jenny is being treated well and taken proper care of. Is that clear?'

'Oh, don't worry, boss. The only thing Gina and I plan on doing tonight is drinking outrageous amounts, doing drunk dancing and generally having a good time to help her forget all her current problems. So I apologise in advance for the state in which we're both likely to roll in tomorrow morning.'

Chapter Twenty-seven

Ted made a couple of phone calls before he got the team together for an update at the end of the day. He wanted to put both Drugs and SCIU in the picture on the possible progress, and to pass on the names Jenny had given him so far.

He spoke to the same Drugs sergeant who'd attended the joint meeting.

'Well, we certainly know Mitchell and Higginson, sir. Both as slippery as eels, hence they're still out and peddling their stuff. Both have form but we've never managed to bang them up for as long as we'd like to because any witnesses who've tried to talk to us have always ended up suffering a sudden and inexplicable attack of amnesia. Not to mention a few broken bones and lost teeth. One bloke even carelessly mislaid one of his fingers.

'But how reliable is this witness testimony likely to be? I've never had experience of a non-verbal witness before. Not this way, at least.'

'Nor have I,' Ted told him, 'but there must be a precedent. I'm going to talk to CPS to get advice on how we need to proceed with her, so her evidence is accepted in court. She's writing reams, so there's a chance we may get some more valuable leads.

'There's another complicating factor, too, but this is on a strictly need-to-know basis, please, not for general gossip. Our suspect turned witness, JJ, is directly related to one of the team here, so we're having to be extra careful. Suspect's name is Jenny Shaw. I'll leave you to join up the dots for yourself.'

The sergeant swore, then excused himself.

'Can't imagine how hard that must be for Gina. Give her my best, won't you? She's a bloody good officer. Some of my lot probably didn't realise just how good until she left us.

'How solid is this info, on Mitchell and Higginson? Yet more hearsay? We've had plenty of that in the past and never got anywhere with any of it, like I said.'

'Jenny Shaw says she was sitting in the passenger seat of the 4x4 which hit Martin Jackson, with Mitchell driving it. And we have an eyewitness to confirm her presence there. Martin himself also confirmed that. So it's solid enough. Well past the threshold, certainly.'

'Right you are then, sir, we'll go and pay them both a visit to see what they have to say for themselves. I'll keep you posted.'

Ted made a similar call to Evan Thomas, the SCIU sergeant, to give him the name of the driver of the vehicle. The more different strings they could pull together, the better were their chances of getting some nasty individuals wrapped up and out of the way of innocent members of the public for as long as possible.

There were a few things he wanted sorted before the team could stand down for the day so he called them together earlier than usual. Jezza had been replaced by a Uniform officer to keep an eye on Jenny over the monitors. Ted wanted to make sure she was under observation the whole time. It was good that she was communicating so freely and giving them names. He didn't want anything to happen to risk her drying up. Or worse.

'What's the news on Rob now?' he began by asking.

'Finally ready for discharge, boss,' Mike Hallam told him. 'I've sent Virgil off to collect his car then pick him up and see him safely home. He's stitched up and in a fair bit of pain, so likely to be off a few days, which means we'll need reinforcements.'

'Already in hand, Mike, I spoke to Jo earlier.

'Maurice, you've had contact with Ian Hedges. Can you go round to where he works, straight away. See if you can catch him before he knocks off. Let him know we have JJ in custody, but clearly no mention of who they are. And can you also find out, please, if he's decided anything about the idea I put to him as an alternative to witness protection, if he will definitely agree to testify in court, if we get it that far.'

'Will do, boss.'

'Another update, boss,' Mike told him. 'Ian's mother has regained consciousness and is now out of danger. She's talking and apparently lucid, so when d'you want her interviewed?'

'Soon as. Let's see if she can tell us anything at all about her attackers. Descriptions, accents, appearance, anything at all. Also, if possible, what she might have told them about Ian so we can update the risk assessment on him. Jezza, can you speak to her, please? Go now. The sooner we know what she might have said, the better we can deal with the situation. Keep me updated, please. Give Martin and his parents an update at the same time.

'And Maurice, let Ian know his mother's now conscious, in case he wants to go and see her.'

'Wouldn't blame him if he doesn't though, boss,' Maurice replied. 'She doesn't seem to have done much for that lad. Is he still under obs, boss? And if Jezza finds out his mother told her attackers anything about where to find him, is there a plan in place to increase the protection level on him?'

'He's safe enough for now, so let's just hope his mother's lack of interest in him might work to his advantage on this occasion. She might not have told them all that much.

'Jenny has given us the names of Jim Mitchell and David Higginson to start with. Both known to us, certainly to Drugs, so Steve, can you pull up everything on record on those two, although Drugs might well beat us to an arrest there.'

'On it, sir.'

Before Ted could think of finishing for the day he wanted to make sure that Jenny was being well taken care of and was happy to continue giving them names and details. There was still a nagging thought at the back of his mind. The old saying that if something seemed to be too good to be true, it probably was, and he certainly hadn't expected anything like the level of cooperation she was showing so far.

The names Jenny had given them already were high value. Giving them that of Jim Mitchell as the vehicle driver carried extra weight as she was implicating herself by doing so. She was admitting being in the passenger seat, so very much at the scene. It still left the potential for her to be jointly charged on the attempted murder.

Ted had the vertiginous feeling of walking a tightrope. Jenny's testimony was pretty much all they had to identify Mitchell and Higginson and they would doubtless have plenty of cronies who would alibi them as having been somewhere else entirely at the time of the crash. As well as at the time of any other offence they might subsequently be charged with. Plus there was still the big question of how

Jenny could testify in court, and how well she would stand up to doubtless rigorous cross-examination by the defence. With their money and contacts, Mitchell and Higginson were bound to be defended by the best available silks in the business.

'All quiet, sir,' the Uniform officer at the door informed Ted when he went back down to the interview room. 'She's not stopped scribbling all the time I've been standing here. Never looked up once.'

'At some point she'll need transferring to a custody cell so she can rest if she needs to. I'll go in and see how she's getting on.'

Jenny Shaw barely looked up as Ted entered the room, moving quietly as he always did.

'I just called in to see how you're doing, Jenny, and to ask if there's anything at all that you need. At some point soon, you'll be moved to a cell for the night, so you can have something to eat.'

There was already an impressive number of pages filled with her neat, precise writing, starting to form a small stack, and she was showing no signs of stopping yet. The pencil had already worn down so much as to be nearly unusable. Ted would need to arrange for another one for her. He didn't want her to stop until she'd told them all she wanted to.

She took a blank sheet from the pad at his comment, scribbled something on it and pushed it across to him.

'I don't eat.'

Ted could well believe that was true, most of the time, looking at her. He was starting to have doubts about the initial medical assessment of her. How long could she keep going at her current fevered pace without eating something?

There was another issue he needed to check with her

before he could think of going home. He knew the custody sergeant would have checked everything, by the book, but he wanted belt and braces on this one.

'I know you will have been asked already but can I just double check, please? Are you taking anything, medication or drugs, prescribed or not, which you need to keep taking to avoid a withdrawal reaction?'

She shook her head as she wrote, *'Been trying to come off drugs and get clean. Didn't like what they were turning me into. May need something to help me, though.'*

Stopping taking them herself but happy still to push them to other young people, Ted thought to himself, but he let nothing show on his face. He needed to keep Jenny on side. She was currently their trump card and he didn't want anything to spoil that.

'D'you want me to start reading this now …?'

He got no further before she shook her head vehemently, pulling the filled pages possessively closer towards her.

He took a step further back, making a gesture of appeasement with both hands.

'I'll leave you to it, in that case. I'll catch up with you in the morning. Anything at all which you need, you only have to signal and an officer will come straight away. That includes asking to see me. You can do that any time you want to.

'I know our holding cells aren't exactly five-star luxury, but try to get some rest, at least.'

He wasn't surprised that she scribbled again and pushed the paper back towards him.

'Don't sleep much either.'

* * *

Ian Hedges was head down at a workbench, concentrating hard on something his boss, John Faulkner, was showing him, when Maurice Brown walked into the building.

There was a general air of winding down at the end of the day from the other employees there. Vans were being checked and restocked as necessary, then securely locked up for the night.

Faulkner spotted Maurice first. Young Ian was seemingly too absorbed in his work.

'Hello, officer, have you got some news for us? D'you want to come into the office?'

That registered with Ian, finally, and he looked up. There was a fleeting expression of concern on the youth's face. Maurice couldn't help but wonder if it was concern for his mother, or if he was more worried that his own protection was being pulled for some reason. He wouldn't have blamed him at all if it had been more the latter than the former.

'Ian, I've come round to tell you your mam's regained consciousness,' Maurice said when the three of them with in the office and could not be overheard. 'She's woken up, she's talking and there doesn't seem to be any sign of lasting serious damage.'

Ian Hedges' poker face remained unchanged. Maurice might as well have been telling him the weather forecast for some obscure part of the country he hadn't heard of, for all the interest he showed.

'It's good news, lad. It means she's going to be all right, and you can go and see her when you want to. I'll take you there now, if you like,' Maurice told him.

'Or if you'd sooner get showered and out of your work

clothes, I can take you there later,' John Faulkner suggested.

Neither offer seemed to be registering with the youth, let alone tempting him. He stood looking from one to the other of the two men then looked directly at his boss as he asked, 'Do I have to go?'

The two men exchanged loaded looks which spoke volumes. Maurice was thinking of his own children, two sets of twins plus his partner's young son, to whom he was unquestionably always a proper dad. He couldn't think of any occasion when any of his brood wouldn't want Daddy Hen to be there for them. He could tell Faulkner was thinking the same thing.

Maurice answered the boy, his tone kind and caring.

'You don't have to, Ian, no. It's up to you. But if you'd like to see her, to see for yourself that she's doing all right, then one of us will take you, whenever you want to go. You just have to ask.'

'Has she asked about me?'

There was an edge to his voice as he asked the question.

'I can't answer that because I don't know. I could try to find out for you, if you like?'

Ian's tone was bitter as he said, 'Don't bother. She won't have. When she gets out and goes back home, I expect I'll see her then sometime.'

'Ian, you know you're welcome to stay with us for as long as you like. For as long as it's safe to do so,' Faulkner reassured him.

'Talking of that, lad, my boss asked me to ask you if you'd thought any more about an idea he'd put to you. Somewhere safe for you to go. What shall I tell him?'

The transformation in Hedges' expression was startling. He was suddenly animated, full of purpose. He looked to his boss first as he spoke.

'I hadn't made my mind up before, but now I have. Your boss told me about maybe joining up. The army, like. I wasn't sure. Wasn't keen on the idea. I spoke to some copper he told me about. From London. Weird bloke, but helpful. He was in the army before he was a copper.

'Anyway, he told me there was a way I could go and do a sort of army taster thing. A couple of weeks or so. To see what it was all about. To see if I liked it enough to think about joining, but no strings attached. It sounded all right.

'I know if I go to court to say what I know about JJ and all that, I'd be in danger. But not if I was surrounded by soldiers. They couldn't get me there.

'My mam never bothers wi' me. She couldn't protect me. When she got beat up, she probably told them anything they wanted to know about me. So I'm going to give the army a try. As soon as I can get on a course. So tell your boss thanks from me. I'd never have thought of that meself.'

* * *

It wasn't as late as Ted feared before he could get away but he stopped to buy a bottle of decent wine for Trev on the way home, conscious that he'd been rather neglecting him, with the pressures of the case.

He found his partner in the kitchen, setting the table. He had his phone clamped between shoulder and ear and was speaking what sounded like German, although Ted still didn't know much of it. He switched back to English as soon as Ted walked into the kitchen, pausing to greet the cats.

'Ted's home now, so I'd better go. He has the air of someone who's had a hard day and is in need of some food and some special TLC. Looking forward to meeting up again soon. *Tchüss*.'

'Who was that you were talking to?' Ted asked him suspiciously, planting a kiss on his cheek and handing him the bottle.

'Ooh, this is nice. What have I done to deserve this?'

Trev put the bottle on the table, together with his phone and turned back to stirring various pans on the cooker.

'I thought I'd been a bit preoccupied with the current case so it's a little peace offering if you were feeling neglected,' Ted told him. 'And why are you avoiding the question about who was on the phone?'

Trev laughed.

'A bottle of wine, then a police interrogation! It was actually Oscar. He and I have been making plans. As soon as this case is over, you're going to take a few days off and take me out to Germany to see his Oma, and he'll meet up with us there. It will be such fun, she sounds such a character.'

Ted sighed and rolled his eyes theatrically.

'I can hardly wait.'

Chapter Twenty-eight

Ted was in early the following day, long before any of the team. He wanted to read what Jenny Shaw had written before feeding back to the others. Above all, he wanted to check on Jenny's welfare.

He knew there were stations where the fate of anyone who had stabbed a police officer, a colleague, could well be rough. With Superintendent Debra Caldwell to answer to for custody welfare, he knew nothing untoward was going to happen to Jenny where she was.

He particularly wanted to go through everything she had written before letting the team see or hear it, because of Gina. Officer numbers were already down with Rob signed off, until Jo could send them someone, so he really couldn't afford to have to keep excluding Gina from briefings.

He went first to check with the duty custody sergeant, once again Brian Clark.

'Good as gold, sir. No trouble at all, and we have been keeping a very close eye on her. She's refused all food but pretty much drunk her own bodyweight of black coffee. Not that that amounts to very much, the size of her.'

'Is she still writing?' Ted asked him.

'Stopped about four in the morning, sir, according to the notes from the night shift. Been curled up in a ball on her bed ever since. Not sleeping, as such, it seems, just lying there, eyes wide open. She is fine and responsive, though, she's been thoroughly checked on.'

'Thanks, Brian, we definitely need kid gloves on this one. Apart from anything else, the two names she's given us already are high value, so I'm hoping there's more to come.'

'What's she hoping for in return, though? She must know there's not much chance of amnesty for anyone who stabs one of our own. She's bound to be looking for a pay-off, so what is it?'

'I don't know yet, and for the moment I'm not about to check the teeth of any gift horse that comes my way.

'I'll go and see what else her writing has given us, if anything.'

An officer went with him to unlock the cell. Brian Clark was right. Jenny Shaw was folded up in a tight ball. Knees bent up to her chest, arms wrapped around them. She looked rather like a sleeping dormouse, although Ted could clearly see that her eyes were open and staring at the wall in front of her.

There was now an impressive collection of handwritten pages, tidily stacked with all edges aligned, sitting on the floor next to the bed, together with two pencils, both worn right down from all the work they'd been put to.

'Good morning, Jenny. I hope you've had some rest, if not sleep. Would I be able to have a look at what you've written now, please?'

Ted's voice was quiet and polite as usual. The only sign Jenny gave that she was even aware of his presence in the small space was the briefest nod of her head.

'Sorry to insist but was that a yes to taking and reading what you've written? I don't want to remove the pages without your consent.'

Another barely discernible nod, to which Ted responded

with a thank you.

As he moved close enough to pick up the papers, he thought fleetingly that he could potentially be putting himself in danger. Jenny would have been thoroughly searched for any sign of a weapon when she was detained. She'd even been made to remove all piercings so they couldn't be used to harm herself or anyone else.

But how many pencils had she been given? Even a pencil, rubbed hard enough and long enough on paper could produce a sharp point of sorts. It had been a calculated risk letting her have any. There might be one Ted wasn't yet aware of which could be brought into action and heading for one of his eyes the minute he was in range.

With his martial arts training, Ted would make a swiftly moving target, but he was still on high alert as he bent to gather up her writings.

The figure on the bed made no move, no sound. Clearly drained and exhausted, perhaps she might now find sleep, in spite of herself.

Ted withdrew from the cell and went back up to his office to put the kettle on. This time he ignored his customary green tea and made a strong brew. Builders' tea. He sensed he might be in need of some fortification to read through what Jenny had written.

He sat down at his desk and began to read.

* * *

'It all came to a head one evening, not long after my fifteenth birthday,' Ted read. 'I was always young for my age, so not a typical fifteen-year-old girl of the time, although starting to look more like a maturing teenage girl, with boobs

developing.'

He'd already read several pages of background. Details of Jenny Shaw's comfortable and somewhat cocooned safe, middle-class upbringing, together with the younger sister, Gina, to whom she was clearly very close.

There were mentions from early on about Jenny's godfather, Professor Menzies Thomson – Uncle Ming – a frequent visitor to the family home, and happy volunteer babysitter whenever needed for the sisters when they were younger.

Then the seemingly kind offer of Uncle Ming to tutor Jenny and help her to get the exam results she would need to follow her dream of going into medical research. Jenny herself was so thrilled by the prospect early on.

She wrote of the first few niggling doubts about her godfather's behaviour. Of the kisses getting too close to her mouth for her comfort. The seemingly innocent pats on the bottom which became more frequent. She'd spoken to her mother about it. Awkwardly, because she'd felt it was a sensitive subject. Taboo, probably.

Of her mother's laughing response. Her dismissive, *'Oh, darling, that's just Uncle Ming. He's always very affectionate, and he sometimes gets a bit handsy, even with me, until I give him a little slap and tell him he's being naughty.'*

Ted was glad of the stronger than usual tea. From early on in his reading, it was clear to him he was seeing a classic tale of grooming unfolding before his eyes on the pages. That the parents seemed incapable of seeing that for themselves didn't altogether surprise him – it was too common in his experience. But it did make him angry. Very angry.

'One evening when my dad drove me to Uncle Ming's house, he came to the front door when he heard the car pull into the drive, wearing just his dressing gown. He apologised and said something about running late and having only just got out of the shower. My dad opened his window and made sort of a joke about it. Something like "Hide your legs, man, for goodness' sake, you'll frighten the horses," and the two of them laughed like idiots at that.

'Then my dad let me get out of the car and go into the house. Told me to hurry up and do so. Not to keep Uncle Ming waiting to give me my tutoring. He sent a fifteen-year-old girl into a house with a grown man in his dressing gown, without knowing what he might have had on underneath.

'And the answer was nothing. He was totally naked under it, and he was quick to let me know that, the moment my dad drove away.

'This time, when he kissed me in welcome, it was very close to my lips. He'd been drinking and I could taste the whisky on his breath.'

There was a brief tap on Ted's door and it opened, to reveal Gina Shaw about to step into the office.

'Out!' Ted bellowed. 'And shut the door behind you. Next time wait to be told to come in.'

It was so rare to hear the boss raise his voice that Gina shot out backwards so rapidly she almost fell over. But the last thing Ted wanted was for her to catch sight of what her sister had been writing.

It was essential he kept her away from anything to do with Jenny. What they knew already was going to be tricky enough to bring to court successfully. What was written on those pages was dynamite. But Ted was going to need a lot of legal guidance about what, if anything, they could do with it, taking all of the circumstances into account.

He carefully marked the place he was up to in his reading of it, then shut all of Jenny's testimony away in his drawer, put the kettle on and went to find Gina. It was still too early for any of the rest of the team to be in.

She'd gone to sit at her desk but shot to her feet when she saw him approaching, which made him feel more guilty than he did already.

She began, 'So sorry, sir, I didn't mean to barge in …'

'No worries, Gina. I had some documents out which I was keeping as my eyes only, for now. I've put them away, and put the kettle on. Come and tell me what it was you wanted to say.'

She followed him in and sat down, still looking slightly wary, while Ted brewed up for her. Once he'd resumed his place she started to speak, carefully gauging his reaction.

'Boss, I'm not here to try to make excuses for what my sister has done, because there aren't any, in my book. But there are always reasons, behind any extreme change of character. And something my parents were saying when I went to tell them about Jenny shook up some memories I didn't know I had.

'Things about an old friend of the family. Jenny's godfather, who used to babysit us both when we were little …'

Ted cut in, back to his usual quiet tone.

'Gina, I'm going to stop you there, if I may. The document I was reading when you first came in is what Jenny has been writing whilst she's in custody, and there's a lot of it. Some of it very distressing.'

'Does it mention Uncle Ming, boss? Professor Menzies Thomson? Because that's what I've started to remember about. And he's still alive, boss. He's been quite ill recently, but he's still alive, still living in the same house.'

'Gina, please tell me you haven't been anywhere near a potential suspect? Especially one with a direct link to your own family, and with you as a possible witness? Are you deliberately trying to make it even harder for us to bring a delicate case to court?'

'I didn't go near him, boss,' she told him evasively. She was justifying it to herself on the basis of having not got out of the car.

'Well don't. And consider that a direct order. I don't want you in morning briefing either, because I'm going to tell the team some of what I've been reading of Jenny's testimony. You're out of this because of the possibility of you being a witness in any future case we may be able to bring against this Professor Thomson.

'Amongst what Jenny has been writing was another list of names, in connection with the drugs gang. I've made a copy, so I want you to go and liaise with your former Drugs colleagues on that and see what use it is to either them or us. And stay away from anything else at all to do with any possible future case. Clear?'

'Clear, sir,' she assured him, then went out of the office, leaving Ted to get back to his reading, with a feeling of déjà-vu for what was to come.

* * *

He was completely different to how I'd ever known him before. And he clearly hadn't just got out of the shower. He stank as if he needed to have one. Not just the smell of the drink, although that was very strong. But he smelt sweaty and of something else. Something I was too young and innocent to know about.

'It sounds improbable but it's true. I was so nerdy and into studying I hadn't been with anyone, even by fifteen. I didn't even have a boyfriend. Only my books.

'I just wanted to get our study session over and get out of there. I kept telling myself it was only an hour until my dad came back for me, and I could surely manage an hour. All I had to do was keep pushing him away and getting him to concentrate on the tutoring. My mother said it was just his way. Not above patting her on the bottom a time or two, even in front of my dad, who always seemed to think it was funny.

'I didn't. I wasn't liking anything about the way he was behaving. He'd stopped all pretence of covering himself up. He'd undone the belt of his dressing gown so that everything was on display.

'I told him I didn't like the way he was behaving. I tried to push him away. That seemed to excite him even more. He kept trying to lean over and kiss me on the mouth. I jumped up from my seat at the table. I'd gone to sit down because I kept thinking he'd come to his senses and stop it. Stop all of what he was doing and we could get on with studying.

'That was the worst thing I could have done because as soon as I got up, he pushed me over backwards onto the sofa then practically fell on top of me.

'I was terrified. Trying to scream, and to push him off. He put his hand over my mouth, then he forced it open and put most of his hand inside it, shoving his fingers right to the back of my throat. I started gagging. I felt I couldn't breathe. That seemed to excite him even more.

'That wasn't all he put in my mouth. I thought I was going to be sick. Then he raped me. And all the time he was doing *that, he kept shoving his hand into my mouth, still trying to choke me.*

'When he'd finished, he got up calmly and told me to sit down and get on with my work while he went and had a shower.

'I was petrified. I didn't know what to do. I wanted to run but it hurt too much to move. So I sat there, crying and still dry retching.

He came back downstairs with a bowl of water, a wet flannel and a hairbrush. He was clean and dressed and behaving as if nothing at all had happened. He cleaned my face, so very gently, and between my legs, then brushed my hair and straightened my clothes.

'By the time my father came back for me, it was as if nothing had happened. I didn't say a word on the drive home. My father noticed but made a comment that Uncle Ming must be working me too hard and tiring me out. He said it as if he thought it was a good thing.

'When I got home I got straight into the bath and used all the hot water cleaning myself up. I put the clothes I'd been wearing in a bag and slipped outside to shove them to the bottom of the bin. I didn't say a word to anyone. Any time I tried to speak, I could only stammer.

'I waited until the middle of the night, when everyone was asleep. I took a few things and all the pocket money I'd been saving up for books to study. Then I crept out of the house and walked into town.

'I had nowhere to go and no idea what to do. The first person I met was an older teenager selling drugs. I bought some. I'd never done any before. I told him I had nowhere to go so he took me back to his squat. But he was kind to me. He didn't try to do anything to me and when I struggled to

speak to him, he said it didn't matter. He hugged me to sleep that first night and every other night after that until he died of an overdose a few months later.'

Ted took a swallow of his tea, long since gone cold. He could hear the team filing into the main office, ready for morning briefing.

Time to go out there and tell them everything he'd discovered about Jenny Shaw so far.

Chapter Twenty-nine

Jezza Vine was the last team member to arrive, only just on time for the start of the day. She'd been amazed, when she'd woken up, to find that Gina had already stripped the bed, showered and gone, leaving a note on the kitchen table, thanking her hostess for a great night.

They'd been a bit late getting started the evening before, with the working day having run on. But as promised, Jezza's partner Nathan had a hot meal organised for when they got back, ready to eat but not in danger of spoiling if they chose to shower and change first.

Gina had been forced to eat her words after losing to Tommy at his own quiz, four games to one, in short order, and she only took the one victory because Jezza came to her rescue.

It had been the perfect evening for both of them to unwind. Once Tommy had been persuaded to go to his room and stay there, with Nat keeping him company, it left Jezza and Gina to forget all about the case by drinking slightly too much and having the best sort of a girls' night in.

There was a lot of laughter, a fair bit of falling over the furniture during the promised drunken dancing, but only one wine bottle knocked over and spilt, and only one glass broken, which they both voted a triumph.

Gina was clearly up to something, having been awake and out at such an ungodly hour. She hadn't been matching

Jezza shot for shot from the start. That had been noticed, but Jezza had no idea when she'd started seriously applying the brakes. She would have needed to in order to be functioning so early.

It was all too much for Jezza to think about in her current drink-addled state. She'd have put on dark glasses before starting work except that would have drawn too much attention to herself. The last thing she wanted. She needed to keep her head down until her brain decided to join her, in a working state, and hope the boss wasn't going to ask her any specific questions.

There was no sign of Gina in the main office, which gave Jezza some concern. She'd clearly left in plenty of time to get to work punctually, so she hoped she wasn't off somewhere doing something daft. She could well imagine that the boss would not let her sit in on briefings which involved anything about her sister, but she'd expected her to be in the office at the start of the day, at least.

The boss answered her unasked questions for her as he began.

'You'll all have seen that DCs Burgess and Sharp have joined us from Ashton to make up numbers. For their benefit, being new to the current case, and as a reminder to the rest of you, there is a complication on our cases in that the person we've arrested for stabbing DS O'Connell, someone linked to both drugs supply and the attempted murder of Martin Jackson, who we now know to be Jenny Shaw, is the sister of our own DC Shaw.'

He saw the looks on the faces of Burgess and Sharp and gave them a moment to digest the news.

'Jenny Shaw is being remanded in custody and as we now know her biological gender, she'll be remanded to a women's prison. In light of the amount of information she's already supplied, in writing, I've taken the decision not to apply to extend her police custody. She has many complex needs so a police cell is not the best place for her any longer than twenty-four hours at the most, and she has already told us plenty to be going on with. Possibly even everything she knows.

'It should go without saying that what I'm about to tell you about Jenny's written testimony goes no further than this room. It definitely does not get fed back to DC Shaw, in any part. I will decide what to tell her, and at what part of the investigation. Is everyone clear on that?'

He waited until he'd seen a sign of agreement from all those present before he continued.

'I've read through what Jenny Shaw wrote. It's harrowing, and it's always hard to judge simply from the written word. But my inclination is to believe what she's put down. It has a ring of authenticity about it.

'She accuses her godfather, Professor Menzies Thomson, of having raped her when she was fifteen. Jenny, as we now know, is virtually non-verbal. Not from birth but from a time which seems to coincide with the grooming leading up to the alleged sexual assault.

'DC Shaw, whilst knowing nothing of what her sister has written, mentioned having a memory of some slightly disturbing incident involving Professor Thomson. He apparently used to babysit for both girls when they were small.

'What Jenny has written is very graphic in its detail. She mentions that she tried to speak to her parents, to her mother in particular, about her growing concerns regarding her godfather and his actions towards her. This at a time when she was able to speak. Apparently her mother pretty much laughed it off as eccentric behaviour on his part.'

Jezza was not about to talk in public of her own experience of sexual abuse from someone close. Not in an open briefing, with officers from another division there. And certainly not in her current drink-befuddled state. But she could well believe what she was hearing. It matched identically with her own experience.

She'd tried talking to her mother about her concerns when her father started to pay her more attention than she was comfortable with, as she was growing up. Her mother too had brushed off what she'd said.

'Steve, are you at a point where you can break off looking into Mitchell and Higginson to start digging into the professor? Anything at all, even rumour and speculation, at this point. I don't want this in any way to detract from the assaults on Rob O'Connell, Martin Jackson or Mrs Hedges. They remain top priority. But this man, Professor Menzies Thomson, is still alive and living on our patch. He's recently had a stroke but is still living at home, out towards Bramhall. And if even part of what Jenny wrote is true, it needs investigating and dealing with.'

'I've been sharing intel with Drugs, sir, for Mitchell and Higginson, and they've been doing the same. I can circulate what I have, then start on the professor,' Steve told him.

'Excellent. We need to get those two, plus all the other names Jenny came up with, off the streets and being interviewed, at the very least. Our main focus should be to go after any of them on our patch, for now, and leave the rest to Drugs. And they all need to know they're being questioned because of eyewitness testimony. That should rattle a few of them, hopefully even enough to persuade them to say something of some use to us. Mike, can you liaise with Uniform on that, please, thinking of sufficient numbers to round them all up?

'I've sent Gina to liaise with Drugs, to keep her well away from everything to do with her sister. At some point, inevitably, she is going to learn of the allegations about their godfather. But I don't want that to come from anyone here. I hope no one is in any doubt about that.

'Jezza, what's the latest on Martin?'

Jezza wished she could have had warning of that question. Of any question, come to that. Her head was still woolly, her mouth seemingly still filled with cotton wool. She'd taken the precaution of bringing her water bottle in with her and took a quick swallow from that before she even attempted to speak.

She saw the boss's eyes on her and knew she needed to call on all of her performing arts skills to sound as if she was in control of her tongue, at least.

'Boss, there's good news on the Martin front. He's doing really well now. Not yet quite ready for moving to a ward, especially with the added complication of the security level, but they're starting physio for him, and he'll be able to begin speech therapy fairly soon.

'They have warned him and his parents, though, that there's still a very long way to go before they even know how much speech or mobility he may regain. It's a help that he was always very fit and is clearly highly motivated to make the best recovery he can.

'Mrs Hedges is conscious now, too, but saying virtually nothing. They've said there's no immediately discernible medical cause for that, but she did look scared, despite me telling her she was under armed guard. Even if she knows anything at all, my guess is that she won't tell us.

'Oh, and she didn't ask about Ian. Not once. Not how he is, or where he is. Nothing at all. Never even mentioned him.'

'Thank you, Jezza. I'm glad you and Gina had a good time last night,' was Ted's only comment.

Maurice Brown was discernibly rumbling with anger at Jezza's words.

'I know she's been badly injured, but what sort of a mam doesn't ask after their bairn first thing, before even thinking about herself? Boss, you asked me to ask young Ian about your idea. Well, he's going for it. He's looking into joining the army and he's going off on a course somewhere as soon as he can get on one, to find out more about what's involved. He said DI Smith had been very helpful and given him a lot of details.

'At least he might be part of something a bit more like a family than he's ever known before. And if he's not safe surrounded by a bunch of soldiers, he's not safe anywhere.'

'That's something, at least,' Ted responded. 'If he does go down that route, his security is less of a concern for us, in the long term. Because if we do succeed in bringing at least some of the drugs gang members to court, any potential witnesses are going to be a target for intimidation, probably of the extreme kind.

'I'm likely to have to spend quite some time talking to CPS today about the viability, or otherwise, of Jenny's written testimony, given her circumstances. I'll be around if you need me, though, but Mike, you're at the helm for now.'

Mike nodded then asked, 'Boss, now Jenny seems to be cooperating and giving us names, will we still be going ahead with a prosecution for her stabbing Rob? Or will there be some sort of an amnesty deal done by the defence to leave that as a secondary charge in return for her testimony?'

'Final decision isn't mine, of course, but my preference would be to press ahead with it as one of the main charges. I'm never keen on an assault on any officer, certainly not one of our own, being swept aside as an also ran. We're talking wounding here, after all. Grievous bodily harm, at the least, possibly attempted murder. I'm not about to roll over and concede on that, unless I have no other choice.

'And while I'm on to CPS, I need to check with them on our Joel Hammond case, now we know the extradition is at least going ahead in record-breaking time. Although I've been warned that still means months, but rather than the years it can sometimes take.

'I also need to find out who's getting him first, us or Leeds. It's a tricky poker game between our rape case and their murder one, but our files are further ahead, I imagine, so we may yet get first dibs.'

* * *

'Right, Shaw, you're in here. Heath, this is your new cell mate, Shaw.'

The prison officer was showing Jenny Shaw into what seemed like an incredibly small space to house two adult human beings for any length of time, even when one of them was as small and slight as she was.

The female occupant already in there was lying on the top bunk with a book. She was the polar opposite of Jenny Shaw. Taller, considerably heavier, arms and shoulders like a weight-lifter. Despite initial appearances, her appraising glance at Jenny showed no open hostility, only a mild curiosity towards the newcomer.

'Shaw is non-verbal, but I'm sure you'll find a way of communicating. Shaw, Heath is anything but non-verbal. Five minutes in here with her and I guarantee you'll be wishing she was.

'You've a while to go before your evening meal, Shaw, so I'll leave you to settle yourself in. Heath, play nicely.'

The woman on the top bunk lowered her book as the officer left the cell, peering down at her new cellmate.

'You don't speak at all, then? Can't, or won't? And do you understand what I'm saying?'

Jenny Shaw lifted her head slowly, for the first time since she'd set foot into the confined space, locking her strange greenish-grey eyes onto those of the other woman. She nodded her head, once, twice, in the affirmative.

'Well, aren't you a strange looking one, and no mistake. You look like a lad. You're not one of them trans types, are you? They did check if you had a todger, before shoving you in here wi'me?'

Then she laughed loudly at her own comment as she said, 'Just don't fucking think of getting up close and personal wi'me, whichever way you swing. You wouldn't get very far.'

At which point she appeared to lose all interest in the newcomer and went back to her book.

Jenny stood for a moment, looking round her. This was the first time she'd ever found herself in custody and she felt as lost as she looked. She had no idea what to do, where she was allowed to go. Things had been explained to her on admission but most had gone over her head. She was still in a daze with everything which had happened in the last few hours.

She slid awkwardly onto the bottom bunk, shuffling as far back into the corner, against the wall, as she could manage to get. Then she pulled her knees right up to her chest, dropped her chin to them, and folded her arms around them.

The slow steady rocking began as she started to sing, quietly, almost under her breath.

'Rock-a-bye baby on the tree top,

'When the wind blows the cradle will rock.

'When the bough breaks the cradle will fall,

'Down will come baby, cradle and all.'

'Fuck sake!' came an angry bellow from the bunk above her head.

'I thought they said you couldn't talk? You can stop that fucking keening for a start. I'm trying to study up here, believe it or not. So shut the fuck up, and stop rocking. It's making me feel seasick.'

* * *

'C'mon Heath, wakey-wakey, you know the routine by now. Time you were up out of there. I'll make an exception for you, Shaw, you don't know the system yet, but you need to be up, so shake a leg.'

'I thought they said that one doesn't talk. She can certainly fucking sing. Kept me awake half the bloody night with her racket. Swear down, I nearly got out of bed and fucking strangled her.'

The top bunk was creaking now as Heath emerged from her crumpled bedclothes and started to swing herself down to the floor.

The prison officer, a different one this time, bent

cautiously over the bottom bunk where the new prisoner, Shaw, was sitting upright, completely still, knees drawn up to her chest, head down, making no sign of movement, bedclothes draped round her.

'Shaw? Come on, look lively.'

Still no response.

She reached out a cautious hand. There was nothing flagged up as potentially dangerous for this new detainee, but long experience had made her wary of any possible trap.

Her hand encountered only cold flesh. Stiff limbs. There was no way Shaw posed a threat to her now, nor ever would again.

Close to, she could see the torn strip of bedsheet wound tightly round the scrawny neck, biting into the flesh, securely tied to the bedhead, half hidden by the rest of the bedclothes, with which Shaw had literally rocked herself to death.

Self-strangulation. Ironically, the officer had been on a recent course, with several of her colleagues, about the phenomenon and how to look out for and possibly prevent it.

'Oh, for fuck's sake, no, not on my bloody watch,' she grumbled under her breath as she went for the alarm button, shouting over her shoulder, 'Heath, get up and stand perfectly still. Don't even breathe until I tell you you can. And don't go anywhere near Shaw. There's no point now.'

Chapter Thirty

Another late arrival home the evening before, then yet another early start once again. Ted was starting to think that a trip to Germany to meet Oscar's grandmother – even if Oscar himself was intent on joining them – was going to be a small price to pay to keep Trev happy.

Ted let Gina join the briefing for the first part, before any discussion of her sister. He wanted to know what joint progress had been made with Drugs on pulling in any of the names supplied by Jenny. They would need to build solid cases against them without having to rely on any of Jenny's testimony, in case CPS ruled it inadmissible, unless Jenny were to appear in court herself and a way could be found for her to testify, and to answer cross-examination.

He didn't dare think of what she might be like as a witness, and the defence team would be bound to go at her as hard as they dared. He'd prefer to keep her as a wild card, only to be brought out in case of desperate need. Especially as she would certainly be charged with stabbing Rob O'Connell, at the very least.

He let Gina begin, with news of her visit to her old team in Drugs.

'Good news is that they picked up Jim Mitchell, the driver of the vehicle which hit Martin Jackson, very swiftly, boss, and now have him in custody. He's been on their radar a long time but this is the first time they've had anything solid on which to arrest him.

'With luck, there'll be enough of his DNA in the vehicle, if and when it's found, to put him squarely in the frame for that.'

'And Higginson, who apparently ordered the attack on Martin? Any news of him?'

'He's a bigger fish, boss, and therefore better protected,' Gina told him. 'But his every move is currently being watched, so at the very least, it's severely restricting him from carrying out his usual trade. And as Mitchell is seemingly his right-hand man, he's seriously limited for now. JJ was only ever a foot soldier, it would seem.'

Ted wasn't sure if Gina was actually trying to reassure herself about the degree of her own sister's involvement in the case, or if JJ had really been simply a pawn in the gang.

The desk phone in Ted's office was ringing but he ignored it. If it was urgent, someone would take a message. If it wasn't, the caller could try again.

'Good, we're getting there, slowly. Can everyone please make sure you write everything up as you go along and let me have it as soon as possible. CPS are going to be all over this one from the start because of the obvious problems so …'

Ted stopped at the sound of a light knock at the door. An officer from Uniform opened it and put his head round, looking at Ted.

'Sir, sorry to interrupt you during briefing, but we've been trying to put a call through to you and the caller did say it was important. I wondered if you'd be free to take it, sir?'

Ted was about to ask who the caller was but picked up from the officer's body language that it might be better not to say so in front of the whole team.

'I'll go back into my office, then. Please put it through.'

When the phone rang again he answered it with, 'DCI Darling.'

'Good morning, chief inspector, and thank you for taking the call. I'm the liaison officer at the facility holding your remand prisoner, Jennifer Shaw.'

Ted felt a premonition of dread. Any such call, rare as it was, was unlikely to be bringing good news.

'I'm afraid that Shaw was found dead in her cell this morning. There will, of course, have to be an inquest and a full internal inquiry, but at this stage it looks very much as if she took her own life.

'Her cell mate, who, despite appearances to the contrary, and talking the talk, has no history of violence, says that although Shaw didn't speak, she did spend a long time rocking herself and singing a lullaby when she was put into the cell.

'On initial examination, it appears that she used a method known as rocking yourself to death. I don't know if you're familiar with the term?'

'I know about self-strangulation as an erotic thing,' Ted replied, then hurried on, 'Not personally, you understand. It came up on a case file once.'

'It's in fact quite a good way to commit suicide, if you can have such a thing. There's no height or drop required, for one thing. Nothing to cause immediate alarm if a prison officer glances through a door at a busy time. All they would see would be a prisoner sitting on their bed, wrapped in their bedclothes. Even the rocking motion wouldn't necessarily be a red flag. I suspect we've all had days when we've felt like sitting rocking in a corner.

'The biggest danger of self-strangulation as a means of

suicide is that there simply is no turning back, as there at least is with some other methods. By the time the person decides they've changed their mind, the damage is already too severe and it's beyond their control to stop the process. They use a very specific knot for that precise purpose, which is indicative of a serious intention, not just a cry for help.

'I don't want to sound as if I'm making excuses. I'm not. I'm just pointing out that, anyone sitting like that, especially on the lower bunk, could be easily overlooked as a potential suicide.'

'You'll no doubt have had the paperwork from here when she was remanded. I asked for a medical examination and a psych report before we questioned her here. I was concerned, with her being non-verbal, that there might be some psychological reason for that.'

'And nothing showed up?'

'Nothing to contraindicate either interview or remand in custody. There were some scars on her hands which could possibly suggest self-harm, but they were old, and we have since discovered she may possibly have been raped, by a family friend, at the age of fifteen.'

His caller sighed at that and said, 'So often sexual abuse is the starting point for people going seriously off the rails. And we probably both know all too well how the perpetrator of that crime is usually the one who gets away with it.'

'Not if I can help it, this time. Not on my watch,' Ted assured her.

'One thing I'm hoping you can help me with is Shaw's next of kin. As I said, we don't have anything on record and clearly they're going to need to be informed as soon as possible.'

'I can do better than that,' Ted told her. 'One of my team

is her sister. Jenny was a missing person for many years. My officer only just found out that JJ, as she was always known in the drugs gang she hung out with, was in fact her sister.'

'Good grief! I can't imagine how difficult that must be for her. So I can leave it to you for now, then, can I? If you give her my details, tell her if she contacts me I'll make time to see her as soon as possible. I'm assuming she'll also tell any other family members who need to be informed.'

'Thank you for your help and cooperation.'

As soon as she rang off, Ted put the kettle on. He felt in need of a brew and suspected Gina might, too, after she had heard what he had to tell her.

No point in putting it off. The news wasn't going to get any better for the wait.

He went back into the main office, told Mike Hallam to take over for the time being, then asked Gina to join him in his own office.

'Sit down, please, Gina. Would you like coffee?'

She was nothing if not shrewd.

'Am I going to need it, boss?'

'Probably. I won't insult you by going all round the houses. I'm sorry to have to tell you that Jenny was found dead in her cell this morning. It seems probable that she took her own life.'

Gina's face drained of colour, but that was her only visible reaction as she took a seat. She gratefully accepted the coffee the boss put in front of her, picking it up with a hand which shook slightly.

'You'll need to tell your parents, of course, and I would suggest you do that as soon as possible. I'm really sorry for your loss, Gina. Take some time off. You'll need it. There's always a lot to sort out, and I'm presuming you'll want to help your parents.

'There really were no indicators that this was her intention. Nothing on the psych report. I didn't pick up on anything in my interaction with her. She seemed, if anything, relieved to be having her say, finally.

'Finish your coffee, then go and see your parents. I'll inform the rest of the team for you. It's probably easier coming from me.

'Take as much time as you need and let me know at any time if I can do anything to help.'

Gina had her head down as she retrieved her things from her desk then went out, ignoring enquiring looks from Jezza.

Ted broke the news to the rest of the team, received by a few sharp intakes of breath.

'I'm not saying we can blame everything which turned Jenny into JJ on anything which might have happened at the hands of the professor. Including her getting in with the wrong crowd,' Ted told them. 'But if her allegation is true, it would quite likely have had a profound effect on what she became.

'That's why I'm very keen to see what, if anything, there is on record, officially or unofficially, about Professor Thomson. Steve?'

'Sir, nothing official, by way of getting even as far as police interview. But I did find a lot of hints and whispers on the internet. There's even a closed group on social media, which I did manage to take a look at, where several younger female students of his over the years have made allegations about his behaviour.'

'I'm only interested in anything we can use evidentially. But if you could perhaps find some way of contacting anyone who's made allegations, that would be good. I feel if nothing else, we owe it to Jenny. And to Gina too, of course.

'So goals for today are to wrap up as much as we possibly can against all of the names which Jenny gave us. Thank you, everyone.'

* * *

Yet again Gina found herself heading her car determinedly out towards Bramhall, rather than north in the direction of where her parents lived, where she'd been fully intending to go when she left the station.

She knew she shouldn't delay too long in going to tell them the news. They weren't likely to hear about Jenny from anyone else, but it was not going to be any easier to tell them by not doing it as soon as possible.

Gina wanted to be the one to tell Uncle Ming, to his face. To confront him with the consequences of his actions from years ago.

The drugs would have had a lot to do with how Jenny finished up, no doubt. Had she stayed at home to finish her school exams, then gone on to university as she wanted to, she might well have discovered recreational drugs and perhaps started using them.

But had she not run away from the safety of her home after what happened to her, it was less likely that she would have come into contact with the sort of stuff she'd been using and selling to others.

Now she was gone. Dead by her own hand, it seemed. And Gina wanted someone to pay. She had no clear plan in mind of what she intended to do or say to Jenny's godfather. She just knew that the pressing urge to confront him in person wasn't going to go away. In spite of what the boss

307

would say if he found out.

It seemed to take a long time for the professor to come to the door when Gina rang the bell, but she remembered her parents saying he'd had a stroke. He certainly looked a lot older and much less mobile then she remembered him as he opened the door to her.

He looked confused for a moment, then his face lit up with a smile, although not all of his face seemed to be able to move easily now.

'Gee-gee, darling! Well, this is an absolutely wonderful surprise. Come in, come in, please. I haven't seen you for what seems like ages, although, of course, Gray and Angela have always kept me up to date with all your wonderful progress through your career. They're so proud of you, and rightly so.'

There was a definite shuffle to his movements, she noticed, as he turned and led the way into the sitting room she'd been in so many times with her family.

'Would you like some tea, or coffee? If so, I'd better make it now. Once I sit down it takes me forever to get up again these days, I'm afraid.'

'Nothing. It's not a social call.'

Gina could see straight away that her tone had rattled him. If she'd had any lingering doubt at all at what might have happened to her sister at the hands of this man, perhaps even in this room, his expression dispelled them in an instant.

She took a step towards him and had the satisfaction of seeing him shuffle backwards, fear spreading across his face.

'I'm here to tell you that Jenny is back. She's been found, and she's talking to the police.'

She wasn't about to tell him her sister was dead. Not yet.

She wanted to see him squirm first, at the news of her return. He staggered backwards at her words, half falling into the armchair behind him.

Gina bent over him, a hand on each arm of the chair, her face menacingly close to his.

'It won't be me investigating her allegations about you, of course,' she told him.

She didn't even yet know herself what they were. But the way the boss had been behaving about the whole thing, she could take an educated guess. And the way Thomson was reacting now, she knew she was spot on with her deductions.

'But I want you to know, they're coming for you. The police. And I, for one, will be popping the champagne corks. I hope you get sent down for a long time. I hope that word gets out in whatever prison you get sent to of what you've done to a young girl. Because people like you aren't highly thought of inside. There'll be a special reception waiting for you.

'You'll be labelled as a Nonce. D'you know what that stands for? It's said to be Not On Normal Communal Exercise. And do you know why such sex offenders were traditionally at danger of reprisals from other prisoners? Because despite the serious crimes the others will have committed, raping children is considered the worst of the worst.

'So I hope your fellow prisoners find out all about you. About what you've done. And I hope you rot in hell for what you did to my sister.'

Then she stormed out of the house, bracing herself for the ordeal of going to tell her parents the news.

* * *

Yet another early morning start in order to try to catch up with himself. Ted was definitely beginning to think that it might, after all, take more than a flying visit to Germany to appease Trev. Perhaps Ted should also try to find the time to take his partner down to Wales to see Ted's mother, Annie. That always went down well.

He was leafing through accumulated reports awaiting his attention. Anything at all which might have a link to Serious Crime, however tenuous, went across his desk, if only for information.

One such report, in particular, caught his eye, from the evening before. A home carer, letting herself into one of her regular houses after getting no reply to her ring on the doorbell, had found the owner upstairs, dead, hanging from the banister.

The deceased person's name was Professor Menzies Thomson.

Mixed emotions hit Ted in a wave. He would have dearly liked to see the man in court, although it would doubtless have been a long, hard slog to get him there.

What concerned him, though, was wondering if Thomson had got wind of the storm which was about to hit him. Because if he had, the most likely explanation was that Gina Shaw had told him. And that would have to be a disciplinary matter. Not something Ted relished, and certainly not with Gina, given all that she'd been through.

There was a knock at his door and in response to his invitation, it was Gina who came in. She looked perfectly calm and composed, which was going to make handling the situation even more delicate.

Before Ted could say anything, she said, 'Boss, I've come to tell you that I'm handing in my notice.'

'You're leaving the team?' Ted queried, surprised.

'No, boss, I'm leaving policing altogether. I enjoyed my time with Drugs and I've loved being with Serious Crime. You've been a great boss. But all of this, with Jenny, especially having to tell my parents yesterday ... ,' her voice trailed off and Ted could see there were tears in her eyes. 'It's been too much, boss. Too personal. I can't do it any more.'

'But what will you do instead? You're an excellent officer, Gina. You'll be a loss.'

'Oh, I'll go back to graphic design and marketing, I expect. Like I did before. How we first met, if you remember, Eddie, darling,' she told him, harking back to an earlier case when design had been her cover and she'd called him that. She'd been good at it, too, he remembered.

'Well, I sincerely wish you all the best in whatever you choose to do with your future, and I'm always happy to give you a reference, should you need one.'

'Thanks, boss, that's very kind. If it's all right with you, I'd like to slip away now. Take some compassionate leave or something to take me to the end of my notice period. I've never been one for goodbyes, and even more so this time.'

She turned to go, as Ted said, 'Oh, Gina, I thought you should know, before you leave. Professor Thomson was found dead at his home yesterday. He appears to have hanged himself. I don't suppose, by any chance, you would know anything about that, would you?'

She looked him straight in the eye as she said, 'Not a thing, boss, but I can't say I'm sorry. I would have liked to see him in court, but maybe it's better this way. My parents told me he'd had a stroke recently, so perhaps he was finding that hard to cope with.'

Ted's mobile was ringing as Gina left, closing the door quietly behind her. He looked at the screen, sighed, then answered with, 'Mr Green.'

'You and McClintock. That refresher course the pair of you clearly desperately need.'

Green mentioned a date and a location. There was no question as to whether or not it was possible or convenient for either of them. It was an order, more than an invitation, Ted knew to his cost.

It might be possible – just – now they were getting some results. And at least the Ice Queen would be likely to sanction the time off if she knew what it was for. She knew Mr Green well enough to understand that it was a summons, not a choice.

'Oh, and bring that arsehole Smith with you. I didn't care for his attitude. Clearly needs knocking into shape.'

Ted had no idea as to whether or not he could get Jock, let alone Oscar Smith, to answer the three line whip at such short notice. In the circumstances, there was only one reply he could give which would be acceptable.

'Yes, Mr Green.'

THE END

About the author

L M Krier is the pen-name of former journalist (court reporter) and freelance copywriter, Lesley Tither, who also writes travel memoirs under the name Tottie Limejuice. Lesley also worked as a case tracker for the Crown Prosecution Service. Now retired, she lives in Central France and enjoys walking her dogs and going camping.

Contact details

If you would like to get in touch, please do so at:

https://www.teddarlingcrimeseries.uk/

tottielimejuice@gmail.com

facebook.com/LMKrier

facebook.com/groups/1450797141836111/

twitter.com/tottielimejuice

For a lighter look at Ted and Trev, why not join the fun in the We Love Ted Darling group? on Facebook. FREE 'Ted Darling is billirant' badge for each member.

Acknowledgements

I would just like to thank the people who have helped me bring Ted Darling to life.

Alpha and Beta readers: Jill Pennington, Kate Pill, Karen Corcoran, Bren Kübler, Alan Wood, Paul Kemp, Eileen Payne, Valérie Goutte, Margaret Johnson, Jill Evans.

Police consultants – The Three Karens.

Finally a very special thanks to all Ted's loyal friends in the We Love Ted Darling Facebook group. Always so supportive and full of great ideas to be incorporated into the next Ted book. FREE 'Ted Darling is billirant' badge for all members.

Discover the Ted Darling

Crime Series

If you've enjoyed meeting Ted Darling you may like to discover the other books in the series. All books are available as e-books and in paperback format. The First Time Ever is also now available as an audiobook, brilliantly read by Christopher Corcoran. Watch out for audiobook versions of other books in the series, coming soon, as well as further books in the series:

The First Time Ever
Baby's Got Blue Eyes
Two Little Boys
When I'm Old and Grey
Shut Up and Drive
Only the Lonely
Wild Thing
Walk On By
Preacher Man
Cry for the Bad Man
Every Game You Play
Where the Girls Are
Down Down Down
The Cuckoo is a Pretty Bird
Dirty Old Town
The End of the Line
It's Oh So Quiet
A Woman's Heart
No Way to Say Goodbye
Everybody Hurts Sometime

The First Time Ever is also available translated into French by Jean Sauvanet, under the title of 'Darling.'

Made in the USA
Coppell, TX
17 March 2023

14352122R00184